Guns Across the Rio

Copyright © 2007 Dac Crossley
All rights reserved.
ISBN: 1-4196-6913-3
ISBN-13: 978-1419669132

Visit www.booksurge.com to order additional copies.

DAC CROSSLEY

GUNS ACROSS THE RIO

THE RIO

A TEXAS RANGER
IN OLD MEXICO

2007

Guns Across the Rio

ACKNOWLEDGEMENTS

For his last decade, I brought my father here to Georgia, away from his beloved Texas. Every morning, over coffee, we talked of old times on the Texas-Mexico border. Bandit raiders and the sheriffs and Texas Rangers who pursued them, Mexican guitars and cantinas, forgotten trails and train tracks, old cars and fast horses, getaways and gunfights, and strong women who held Texas together. Thanks, Dad, for the stories.

To my fellow students in Harriette Austin's writing classes—thanks for the long, happy hours of discussion. I'm grateful to the White Car Gang for their thoughtful critiques, my Texas readers, Bob Gafford and Tometta Hentz, for their encouragement, and Lizz Bernstein for diligent editing.

The BookSurge Production Team, Richard Ridley, John Mark Schuster and Helen Smith, brought it all together. Good on yer!

CHAPTER ONE

Nacho Ybarra had always admired that urinal! It dominated the *baño*, the room for *hombres*, in the American Bar, a *taberna* in the little Mexican village of Reynosa. Nacho smiled as he walked in and stopped in front of it. A dozen *hombres* could stand side by side in comfort at this marvel, this most magnificent of urinals. It seemed to speak to Nacho of the creative spirit, the artistic soul, of the *peón* of rural Mexico. The life of the *peón* was focused on the daily struggle just to exist, to find enough *tortillas* and *frijoles* to feed his family and an adequate *jacal* to house them. But sometimes the deep-seated urge to create, to surpass the ordinary, emerged and found unusual ways of expression. Thus, some unknown artisan had constructed this enormous urinal, laboriously sculpting by hand the long, curving concrete trough, molding and shaping it against the adobe wall of the *baño*, following the contours of the irregular wall to end abruptly at the back of the building. What kind of heritage, what Spanish or Indian pathos, had burst forward from the breast of that unknown *peón* sculptor, finding a manifestation, at last, in a monumental urinal?

It was beginning to crack. The faded blue paint covering the structure contrasted with the dirty white walls. All was illuminated by a single yellow electric light bulb, the light of rural Mexico. Occasionally, a *mozo* would enter the *baño* and empty a bucket of water into the end of the urinal trough, flushing the stagnant contents away. The urinal simply drained into a hole in the back wall, through which the contents flowed out into the dry dirt of the alley behind it. Like the *Revolución*, Nacho thought, sweeping the *políticos* into the dust, to be replaced by others no different from themselves. And all the while the peasants, the *peónes*, struggled to survive, not knowing whether to resist their masters or to acquiesce in silence. Or in what way the *Revolución* might change their lives. If at all.

As he completed his business, Nacho heard the rattle of spurs and the clumping of boots entering the *baño*. It was early evening, only an hour after dark. Business in the American Bar must be picking up early, he thought. Nacho shook his head, smiling at himself as he forced himself out of his pleasant reverie. It was time to be moving on, to turn his old horse Fogata back towards the river crossing and retrace his steps to Texas.

A man stopped directly beside him and began unbuttoning his fly. Nacho concentrated on fastening his own buttons, head down, not looking to the side. He waved a persistent flying insect away from his face and prepared to leave. Suddenly, he sensed that a second man had stopped directly in back of him. Moving carefully, slowly, to finish buttoning his fly, Nacho wiped his hands on his trousers. He was acutely aware of the lack of his *pistola*, which he had foolishly left outside in his saddlebags.

"Buenas tardes, señor."

The man standing beside him had spoken. Nacho grunted but offered no other reply. Conversation at the urinal was not acceptable behavior.

"Nacho, *amigo mío*, you should remember my young brother Paco. But he has grown some, no?"

Nacho turned to face the second voice that had come from behind him. His uneasiness grew. He did not want to be recognized on the Mexican side of the border. He squinted and stared at the speaker, whose face seemed strangely colored by the light coming from the yellow bulb. The face was vaguely familiar. Nacho glanced towards the man on his left and found another smiling face. Suddenly a feeling of relief surged through him when he recognized the two men. He smiled himself, raising his right hand in greeting.

"Tomás, good evening to you," Nacho exclaimed. "It has been…"

"*Sí*, Nacho, *hay muchos años*. Paco and I, we saw your old horse outside, and we looked for you in the bar. But here you are, in the *baño*."

"Tomás and Paco. The Aguilar brothers. The last time I saw you, you were little urchins in the streets of El Paso. And look at you now. Grown *hombres*."

"And you, Nacho," said Paco with a smirk. "With your little gray beard and gray hair. You have become a *viejo*."

"I am not so old." Nacho started to push away from the urinal, but the two men blocked his way. Each stood with his thumbs hooked in his pistol belt. Big sombreros hung behind their heads. Each man sported a large, drooping mustachio. Two pistols swung low on their hips, over fine *pantalones* with silver conchos down the sides. Silver spurs with large rowels were attached to their boots. Bandoleers containing rows of bullets crossed each chest. They were the very picture of revolutionaries. Or bandits, for that matter. Nacho's own costume suffered in comparison. He wore his trail clothes, wrinkled chino trousers and a cotton shirt, both dusty and worn. On his head sat a stained Stetson with a crushed crown. I must look like a *vagabundo*, he thought.

He took a deep breath and smiled at the two men. "Tomás, fortune has favored you."

"We are revolutionaries," interjected Paco.

"I can see that, Paco. But what brings you to Reynosa?"

"Well, you see," said Tomás, "our old friend Don Francisco would enjoy a visit from you."

Nacho caught his breath, shifting his gaze back and forth between the brothers.

"It is true," continued Tomás. "He has told us many times, *'Muchachos*, I miss my friend Nacho and would like to see him again'. He has asked that you be brought to him. So, all along this lower border, all along the *río*, Don Francisco's *hombres* have been seeking you. And now, Paco and I are the lucky ones who have found you. Please, Señor Nacho, Don Francisco is not far away. You must accompany us. He will be very grateful."

Nacho felt the hair prickle on the back of his neck. A fine bead of sweat trickled down his cheek, and he raised a hand to wipe it away. He tried to suppress a sudden surge of panic. This courteous invitation was not a request, but a command, and one that could not be ignored.

Don Francisco! He was Francisco Villa, known throughout Mexico, the southwestern United States, and indeed much of North America, by the name of Pancho Villa. A dangerous, violent bandit and revolutionary leader.

Nacho continued to stare at the brothers, who quietly waited for his response. He had become acquainted with Pancho Villa a decade earlier, in 1905, when a business venture had carried him upriver to El Paso, Texas. In those years, Pancho Villa and his brother Hipólito were favorites of El Paso society, young bandits trying to assemble a revolutionary army. Unofficially, the United States assisted them in procuring weapons during their attempts to overthrow *El presidente* Díaz. Nacho found himself propelled into the arms business, acting as an intermediary between several El Paso businessmen and the revolutionary army of Pancho Villa. It was enormously profitable, and Nacho still had a sizeable bank account in El

Paso. However, when German nationals began to intrude into the arms trade, Nacho decided that the business was too risky to continue. He extricated himself and returned to the lower Valley.

Why did Villa remember him? Nacho had dealt mainly with the brother Hipólito. But Pancho Villa was known for his prodigious memory. Nacho shuffled his feet, looking for a way out of the *baño*, but the men continued to block his way.

"*Señores*, I have business. Another time——."

The bandits stood firm, their feet rooted in the dirt floor of the *baño*. Neither spoke, but Paco, the younger, slipped his right hand along his belt towards his *pistola*.

Well, so be it, thought Nacho. He had been invited to pay homage to the most famous man in the country. He could hardly refuse. Besides, he was unarmed.

He reached up slowly and settled his hat firmly on his head. "Come then, *señores*, let us visit Don Francisco." Nacho pushed his way between the two brothers and led the way into the street.

The Texas-Mexico border was a dangerous place to be in this, the spring of 1915, as Nacho knew very well. A chaotic revolution gripped Mexico, a confused situation that seemed interminable. Important issues such as patronage and land ownership continued to plague a succession of ineffective governments. Members of the Mexican elite warred among themselves, pulling the *peónes* into their conflicts. Revolutionary leaders and minor bandits ranged across the country, pitting themselves against each other and the federal troops of Mexico City.

Nacho had become alarmed when bandits started launching forays across the border, robbing travelers and raiding Texas ranches. Recent settlers in south Texas, who had been attracted to the area by the productive, inexpensive land, began to board up their houses and flee back to the north. Citizens in the lower Rio Grande valley had petitioned Washington for relief from the bandit raids. Washington's response was to send little notes of protest to the Mexican government in Mexico City. Diplomacy had accomplished nothing.

Texas Rangers patrolled the lower Rio Grande valley, attempting to stem the tide of banditry, but with little success. Their numbers were simply too few. Nacho Ybarra himself carried a badge of those Texas Rangers.

For Mexicans such as Nacho, life had become increasingly difficult on both sides of the *río*. As the bandit raids intensified, tempers ran hot. Armed conflicts occurred frequently, often with Mexicans as unwilling targets. It was difficult to distinguish friend from foe in the borderlands.

There was no guarantee of safety south of the *río* either, as Nacho knew very well. The Mexican revolution had devolved into a clash of bandit armies, and the country suffered and bled. *Peónes* and *haciendeos* alike became displaced from their homes by invading armies. Nacho knew that men could be drafted abruptly into one of the armies or into the *federales*, the official army of Mexico City. After a battle, the survivors might be given a chance to join the army of the victors. Since refusal meant immediate execution, the invitation was usually accepted.

Nacho had not intended to cross into Mexico again until times became more settled. But his daughter had sent word that her husband was riding with Chulo Valdez, a minor bandit. Nacho decided to visit his daughter, Rachel, at her little house near the village of Reynosa, and to take her some money. *Dinero* has a way of easing pains, he knew. So, he forded the Rio Grande, riding his horse across a gravel bar upstream from the old town of Hidalgo. He made his way slowly downstream along the trail by the river, his path lighted by a last quarter moon. Nacho had ridden old Fogata, who was anything but the firebrand her name suggested. She moved slowly and quietly, ears erect, attuned to the sounds of the night. Nacho watched for the hint of a campfire, or even the red point of a cigarette. He listened carefully, but heard only night birds, the occasional voice of a coyote, or a chorus of frogs near the river. By first light, he found himself skirting the edge of little Reynosa. Awakened from her night's sleep, his daughter welcomed him tearfully. Nacho reassured her: her husband was a good man, he would be back soon, Chulo Valdez was an *idiota* who could not find the *Revolución* when it was all around him. A nice little bag of gold coins improved Rachel's disposition immediately and inspired her to prepare a fine meal of enchiladas and frijoles.

In the dark of the evening, before moonrise, Nacho had set out to retrace his steps and return to Texas. But at the last minute, he turned Fogata towards the American Bar in Reynosa. He wanted to look at that marvelous urinal again. Now he realized that this whim could prove to be a costly indulgence.

The Aguilar brothers escorted Nacho south from Reynosa along a narrow, winding dirt road. His companions rode silently, one in front and the other behind him. The moon had not yet risen. The thick, thorny chaparral lining both sides of the road loomed as shadows in the darkness. It was so dark that Nacho could barely see his escort.

Shifting slightly backwards in his saddle, Nacho found that he could slip his hand into his saddlebag, where he could feel the cool grip of his forty-five-caliber revolver. Could he manage to draw his *pistola* from the saddlebag and make an escape in the darkness? It was an action to consider. He would not have to go very far to disappear into this moonless night. But then again, it would be foolish to crash through the dense chaparral in the dark.

Perhaps he could distract his escort with conversation and catch them unawares. "My friends," he said, "how long have you been riding with Pancho Villa? It seems only yesterday that we fought together, after the murder of *El presidente* Madero."

This was only a little lie. Nacho had not actually joined in the fighting. He had supplied weapons to the *villistas* and offered what little intelligence he could gather.

"And did we not help to free Don Francisco from the clutches of the evil *general* Huerta?"

This was not really a lie, only an exaggeration. Victoriano Huerta had plotted to assassinate President Madera. When Pancho Villa was sent to confer with him, Huerta arrested Villa and placed him in front of a firing squad. Only pressure from Villa's friends saved his life, but Huerta had humiliated him and Villa never forgot it.

"And you two—did you not accompany the army? You helped with the campfires and the horses. And now, you are grown soldiers yourselves."

The night swallowed Nacho's attempts at conversation. His escorts, so vocal earlier, remained silent. How had he come to this misfortune? Nacho scratched his short gray beard. His clothes did not match the elegant ones of his escorts. Nacho was a long way from being a soldier in appearance or in dedication. Especially not a soldier in the army of Pancho Villa. Since he had joined the Texas Rangers, only danger awaited him here. He really did not want to encounter Pancho Villa. Never again.

Carefully, he slipped his *pistola* from the saddlebag and held it down by his side. The feel of the pistol grip in his hand lifted Nacho's spirits. He straightened his posture and held the weapon against his stomach. It would be easy, even in this dim light, to dispatch these two youngsters. And make his break back to the border.

Youngsters. They were still children, in his memory. No, he did not want to get into a shooting match with the Aguilar brothers. Could he simply elude them in the darkness? No, it would be unwise to enter into a horseback chase while he was riding old Fogata. He decided to wait and see what opportunities might develop. He returned his *pistola* to its holster in the saddlebag. Gathering the reins more closely, he made note of his surroundings as best he could in the darkness. An opportunity might yet arise.

Suddenly his companions stopped. Paco reached for Fogata's reins and brought her to a halt. Men materialized on both sides of the dirt road, rifles at the ready.

"*Quién es? Ah, Tomás. Y Paco.*"

"*Claro, muchachos. Pasemos.*"

"*Y quién tenemos aquí?*" A figure emerged from the darkness, hands on his hips, waiting for a response. Who did they bring?

Time to take charge, thought Nacho. He shook free of Paco and urged Fogata forward a step or two, then reined her to a halt.

"*Yo soy señor Nacho. Voy a ver* Don Francisco."

Chuckles greeted Nacho's announcement. From behind him came a loud guffaw. One of the guards stepped forward and took hold of Fogata's bridle. "*Espere, viejo!* You will see Don Francisco at his pleasure. If at all."

"*Bastante!*" cried Nacho, gesturing broadly with his left arm. "I have seen children more impressive than you! *Desista!*"

As the guard stumbled back, Nacho gently dug his heels into Fogata's ribs and urged her forward into the camp of Pancho Villa. He was committed. This hand would have to be played out.

CHAPTER TWO

P ancho Villa had appropriated a large hacienda for his use, as was his custom when he was in the field. Villa doubtless had avoided any bloodshed, but he usually prevailed in these matters. The unfortunate *haciendero*, forced from his homestead, feeling lucky to be alive, would have removed his family and some servants and whatever belongings he could carry. Perhaps they were now in Monterrey or Saltillo, in a comfortable hotel, telling their story to anyone who would listen to it.

Fogata carried Nacho to the gate of the courtyard, her head shaking in vigorous protest at being spurred into action. He reined in the horse and stood in the stirrups, looking left and right. A sprinkling of small campfires dotted the prairie beside the hacienda. Could this be the most famous army of revolutionaries in Mexico? Judging by the number of campfires, Nacho surmised that the army had become considerably smaller than it once was. Rumors of Pancho Villa's declining fortunes must be true.

He dismounted and affixed Fogata's reins to a convenient post. Large torches arranged along the sides of the courtyard provided a dim, smoky illumination of the scene inside. Nacho could see a number of soldiers standing or sitting quietly against the walls. In the middle of the courtyard, groups of men and women gathered around small cooking fires. Children milled about, two of them chasing a small dog. A little mariachi band in a far corner was softly playing "La Cucaracha," a favorite song of the *Revolución*. Pancho Villa enjoyed the tune because it was used to mock *general* Carranza, the current strongman in Mexico and Villa's chief rival. Nacho grinned to himself. Only in Mexico could a song about a cockroach become an unofficial national anthem.

The general atmosphere suggested a fiesta rather than an armed camp. Nacho felt some of his tension slip away. He took the opportunity to retrieve his *pistola* from his saddlebag and strap on his holster. He watched his escort as he holstered the revolver, but no objection was raised. Nacho squared his shoulders and stepped slowly into the courtyard.

He found Villa himself seated in a ladder-back chair, tilted backwards and leaning against the rear wall of the patio, holding court with his attendants. His chair was situated on a small dais, elevating him to the level of his companions, who were standing in front of him. He wore his town clothes, a neat three-piece woolen suit. His white Stetson was pushed back to reveal his dark curly hair. His dark bearded face held a serious expression. Villa was in an animated conversation with a small group of men in smart khaki uniforms, who were listening to him closely. Nacho recognized them, members of Villa's private honor guard, his *dorados*, the "golden ones." Nominally a force of one hundred men, intensely loyal to Villa, the *dorados* formed the core of his military organization. Nacho examined them carefully, looking for familiar faces. He exhaled a small sigh of relief when he did not find Rodolfo Fierro among them. Fierro, Villa's designated executioner, was a man without scruples who followed Villa's instructions to the letter and carried them out immediately. Fierro had been known to interrupt his lunch in order to execute a prisoner, then resume eating as if nothing had happened. Nacho had no desire to become reacquainted with him.

He considered the possibility of turning around and simply melting quietly into the darkness. Evidently he was not a prisoner. He had been allowed to retrieve his revolver. Nacho had no intention of joining Pancho Villa's ragtag army if he could avoid it, and for good reason.

After all, Nacho Ybarra was a Texas Ranger. At least, he thought he might be. He hadn't actually signed any enlistment papers. He had spent the past year with a Ranger Troop across the border in Texas, at first providing them with horses from his little *rancho*, then serving them as a horse wrangler, later as a scout, and finally as a trooper, fighting alongside other Rangers.

Members of the Texas Rangers wore no official uniforms. They provided their own horses and weapons. Any pay they might receive was erratic, but food was plentiful. The only means of identification with the Rangers was an official badge, and not all of them had those. Recently, a small shipment of badges had reached the Border. Nacho had been handed one. Did this mean he was actually a Ranger? Nacho wasn't sure, but, in any case, he kept the badge with him. It was in his pants pocket. He could feel it now, against his leg. That badge could be his death warrant, if it came to be revealed. No, this was no place for Nacho Ybarra.

No one seemed to be paying any attention to him. Yes, it would be best if he slipped away. Nacho took a tentative step backwards. He bumped into a man standing behind him.

"Ah, Nacho, step forward, my old *amigo*. Don Francisco has been asking for you."

Nacho did not need to turn around; he recognized the voice of Tomás. Something was poking him in the small of the back, possibly a finger but also possibly a *pistola*. He marched slowly across the patio, in the direction of Pancho Villa.

As he neared Villa, the bandit stared into the dim light. Conversation stopped. Suddenly, Villa rose from his chair, smiling, and extended his arms. "Ah, Nacho, Nacho, my old *compadre*. How good it is to see you again. I have asked my *muchachos* to look for you. And now Tomás has found you and brought you to me. Thank you, Tomás, for this favor. Nacho, come sit with me."

Nacho moved forward deliberately but carefully. This effusive greeting puzzled him; after all, he had only a nodding acquaintance with Pancho Villa. They had met on a few occasions, back in El Paso. Nacho didn't think that Villa had taken much notice of him.

The group of *dorados* parted to allow Nacho to pass through them. They watched silently as Nacho came to a halt directly in front of Villa. For a moment, the two men eyed each other, both expressionless. Then, with a large gesture, Villa grasped a rickety chair and set it down by his left side, near his own but lower down, beside the dais but not upon it. He grasped Nacho's right arm with his own, and with a smile indicated the chair with a wave of his left arm. Nacho cautiously eased himself onto the chair and looked up expectantly at Villa. He understood the significance of being seated on Villa's left. The bandit's right hand, his gun hand, remained out of sight. If Pancho Villa were a rattlesnake, he would be coiled to strike. Nacho realized he must act and talk carefully to avoid teasing the rattlesnake.

"How goes it with you, Nacho?" Villa reached his left hand down and placed it on Nacho's right shoulder. "They tell me you have been in this Lower Rio Grande Valley for some few years now. And you have aged, my friend. Tell me, how goes the *Revolución?*" Villa's grip tightened on Nacho's shoulder. It would have been difficult if not impossible for Nacho to draw his *pistola* under that pressure. Nacho hoped that Villa was following a usual procedure for his visitors, not one crafted especially for him.

"*Se va.* It goes well, Don Francisco," Nacho replied with a slight shrug, hoping to ease Villa's hand off. But Villa's grip was strong, and his fingers returned to dig into Nacho's shoulder. Nacho bit his lip and resisted the urge to flinch.

Abruptly, Villa removed his hand and looked outwards.

"Pancho, call me Pancho, old friend. Word reaches me that you have crossed the river into *tejano* country. Is this true? You have traveled in Texas?" Villa glanced sideways at Nacho and then looked away.

Again, Nacho shrugged his shoulders. "One does what one must," he replied, forcing a smile onto his lips. This was a dangerous area of inquiry. Nacho stopped himself from rubbing his hand across the Texas Ranger badge in his pocket.

"But of course! Each of us must keep his own council. And work for the *Revolución* in his own manner." Villa waved his hand, acknowledging a bandit who was joining the group of *dorados*.

These words of reassurance were welcome. But one must be cautious. Nacho followed Villa's gaze across the courtyard. The group of *dorados* had ceased to study him and was talking with the newcomer. Nacho decided to pursue the matter a little further.

"Don Francisco, I am surprised to see you here. We had heard that you were in Juárez, and then in Chihuahua City. Your army was famous in the State of Chihuahua. What brings you to the Lower Valley?

Pancho Villa turned and studied Nacho with a small, thin smile on his lips. His dark eyes narrowed, their gaze almost hypnotic. Nacho wondered if he had gone too far, become too familiar. But then Villa slapped him on the shoulder, playfully.

"What brings me here to the Valley? Why, the trains, the marvelous trains, they brought me here. They take me wherever I want to go. The brave trains. With some of my brave *muchachos*." Villa gestured expansively. "And, of course, their wives and children. The *Revolución* does not change."

It was common knowledge in Texas that Pancho Villa had suffered a crushing defeat in a battle with his rival, the strongman Carranza. Villa knew no military strategy, no history of battle tactics, no manual of arms. His only tactic was a head-on cavalry charge, and it usually carried the day. His advisors included some Americans who brought him light cannons. But recently he had been out-maneuvered. Could this pitiful little group be the remnant of his army?

Could this be a recruiting trip? Perhaps so. All over Mexico, little groups of *peónes* had started the revolution. Like the soft desert breeze arising in the early morning, it had started with a puff here, a puff there, coalescing until a major wind swept through Mexico. But, unlike the breeze, this wind had no direction. It was a whirlwind, sweeping everything from its path. Villa must have come to the Rio Grande Valley to collect whatever breeze might be stirring there.

Villa's next question proved that Nacho's surmise could well be correct. "Are you acquainted with a local revolutionary who calls himself Chulo Valdez?" Villa looked sideways at Nacho, and then stared out across the courtyard again. His hands rubbed slowly across the knees of his trousers as he stared quietly into the distance.

Nacho looked at his own hands, considering his answer. Chulo Valdez was no more than a common bandit who had taken to raiding aimlessly across the river in Texas. Valdez did not rustle cattle, except for an occasional beef for food. He tried to rob a bank on occasion, without much success. Valdez was short on planning. Waylaying travelers and cleaning their pockets was his main activity. By reputation, he was a murderer. Like all Mexican bandits, Chulo Valdez called himself a revolutionary. Was he, in fact, any different from Pancho Villa?

"Yes, Don Francisco, I know of Chulo Valdez. He is not an important man. He disturbs the Texans."

"That is not a good idea. We must keep the good will of the Texans and their colleagues in the *Estados Unidos.* Yet I want to meet this man. I think he might help me. I might make a withdrawal from the *Banco de Matamoros.*" Again, Villa glanced sideways at Nacho and quickly looked away.

Nacho's eyes widened; he understood the meaning of that remark. Pancho Villa's withdrawals were simply robberies. True, he never took all the money. He had explained that he needed the banks to survive, so he left enough money in them to keep them in business. He might need to make another withdrawal, at another time. For the *Revolución,* of course.

Nacho rose from his chair. This was the opportunity he had been hoping for. He turned to face Villa, who looked at him expectantly.

"Yes, indeed, I can find Chulo Valdez. I will ride into Matamoros and find him and bring him to you."

Villa's eyes lit up. For the first time in this interview, he seemed genuinely pleased. Nacho felt a sense of relief. He'd made the right choice.

"Nacho, my friend, I have always been able to count on you for help. Please bring him as soon as you can." Villa rose and reached forward to embrace Nacho. He then slapped him on the shoulders, nodded his head, and gave Nacho a small dismissive wave.

Nacho gave a small bow, hitched up his gun belt, turned, and started walking rapidly across the patio. He managed to conceal a smile, which forced itself across his lips. Actually, he had no intention of returning to the Villa camp once he got away from it. He would retrace his steps back across the border to re-join his Ranger troop. Villa would surely leave soon for his more familiar territory upriver in the state of Chihuahua. Once Nacho crossed the Rio Grande, things would be back to normal.

But before he could clear the patio, Villa called out again. "Tomás! Go with my old friend Nacho and be sure that he does not get into any trouble." The group of *dorados* broke into laughter. Clearly, Tomás was to be more than an escort. Pancho Villa was not going to be deceived easily.

Tomás fell in beside Nacho and matched his strides. Nacho glanced at him. Tomás wore a sinister grin on his face, a toothpick sticking from the corner of his mouth.

"Let us ride," he said and urged Nacho through the patio doorway into the night.

Nacho stopped in the darkness to rub Fogata's neck. She neighed softly and bobbed her head, recognizing Nacho's touch. Tomás halted beside him.

"Maybe we should wait until tomorrow, Tomás. My old horse, she is tired. It is fifty miles to Matamoros. Let us rest for this evening. *Por qué no?*"

"Because Don Francisco tells us to go now, not tomorrow. But do not fret. We will ride only as far as Reynosa; then we will take the train to Matamoros."

Nacho considered his options. He did not like being without his horse, since he still hoped to escape back to Texas. But there seemed to be no way to avoid this train ride. At least he could stable Fogata in Reynosa.

"Leave your horse," said Tomás. "I will give you one from the *remuda*. Paco will collect it tomorrow. Your old horse will be safe here."

This was even worse. Fogata would remain in the hands of Pancho Villa's outlaws. Nacho sighed and stroked the horse again. It seemed that he would have to return to Texas without the old mare. Well, it must be as *Dios* wills it. He waited quietly for Tomás to bring up a pair of horses. The one offered to Nacho was a lively gelding. Nacho swung into the saddle and grasped the reins, tugging them and digging in with his heels. The horse danced sideways and bobbed its head. Nacho pulled sharply on the reins. This would be no quiet ride to Reynosa.

The last-quarter moon had risen and cast faint shadows across the dirt road as they retraced their steps to Reynosa. Within a half-hour, Tomás pulled his horse to a stop beside the small railroad station. By now it was late in the evening; the platform was empty, and the station house was closed. The night air was deadly still. A small cluster of moths worked their way to their doom around a single electric light bulb peeking out from a battered fixture. A bat swooped in and out, seeking its dinner among the moths. Nothing else moved in the stillness on the station platform. Nacho could hear a dog barking in the distance and an answering bellow from someone's cow. There were no humans in sight.

Tomás dismounted and, collecting the reins, tied their two horses to a post beside a water trough. He swaggered across the railroad platform and swung himself up onto a baggage cart. With a crooked smile at Nacho, he lay down flat on his back.

"Who knows when the train arrives? We will wait for it here." Tomás turned on his side, propped his head on a saddlebag, and stretched his arms. With a deep sigh, he settled himself and closed his eyes.

Nacho hefted his saddlebags onto the baggage cart and eased himself down into a sitting position beside one of the cart's big wheels. The jolting ride into Reynosa astride that lively horse had given him a stiff back. He felt no need for sleep. Reaching into his pocket, he retrieved a small tobacco pouch and papers. Tomás vented a snort, the beginnings of a raucous session of snoring. Nacho rolled a small *cigarillo*. He struck a match to it and gazed thoughtfully down the railroad tracks. He sighed. It was amusing to him that the railway system had become so important to the rebels. Old Benito Juárez, Little Benny the rebel, would have been dismayed. After defeating the cursed French and liberating Mexico, Juárez had decreed "No Railroads!" He had feared that a network of railroads would allow the United States to invade Mexico. But *El presidente* Díaz, formerly a Juárez lieutenant, had thought otherwise. Díaz had brought the railroads and the accompanying foreign industry to Mexico. He had made many friends in North America and in Europe. *El presidente* and his high-placed friends had become *muy rico*. But Díaz had forgotten his peasant origins. Prosperity did not extend to the *peónes*. And now those peasants, in constant revolution, were using the railroads in their battles against their government. Little Benny may have been right, after all.

Nacho's thoughts wandered back to the Ranger camp across the river. During the past year, Company D of the Texas Rangers had become his family. They had accepted him without question, once he had proven his worth. Nacho smiled as he recalled his two comrades, Red Regan and Whitey Wilson. The Red and the White he called them, their nicknames coming from the colors of their hair. The two Rangers quarreled constantly with each other but were inseparable. They had accepted Nacho as a friend, and he enjoyed their company. He passed along to them some of the knowledge gained during his years of experience on the border. Had they noticed that Nacho was missing? He had told no one that he was leaving, but he had expected to return this night.

Tomás produced another snort and began snoring in earnest. Nacho looked down at him and then at the horses tied beside the station platform. Perhaps fate had offered him an opportunity. He might be able to slip away after all. If he could tolerate another ride on that frisky horse. Nacho rose slowly and carefully retrieved his saddlebags from the baggage cart, making as little noise as possible. Tomás stirred and seemed to wake momentarily but then settled himself against his saddlebags and began snoring softly. Well, thought Nacho, perhaps it would be best to wait for a while, until Tomás was sleeping more soundly. He sat down again and settled himself as comfortably as he could.

He was unaware that he had drifted into slumber until a sharp jab on his shoulder awakened him abruptly. "Nacho! The train arrives."

Nacho scrambled to his feet, looking around in confusion. Tomás forced his saddlebags into his arms.

"Come now! It slows down!"

It was a freight train, slowing for the town but maintaining its headway. Tomás ran beside an empty freight car, pacing himself beside the open door. With a two-armed effort he threw his saddlebags into the car and then propelled Nacho forward. With a leap Nacho gained the floor of the car, just barely, lying on his stomach with his legs hanging out and his arms entangled with his own saddlebags. Tomás sprang up beside him into the freight car, turned quickly, and pulled Nacho to safety.

"Ah, Nacho, you must learn the ways of the trains if you want to become a *villista* again. Have you not ridden our railroads?"

Nacho lay sprawled on the boxcar floor, his breath coming in gasps. He shook his head as he tried to get his breathing under control.

"Tomás, I have ridden many trains," he gasped. "But always, I bought a ticket."

Standing over him, Tomás jabbed Nacho in the ribs with the toe of his boot. "Today you do not need a ticket. Today, you are a guest of Don Francisco Villa."

Nacho propped himself up on his elbows and watched Tomás make himself comfortable beside the open door. He wondered what else rode in the boxcar. Any other passengers? The interior of the car was completely dark. Well, if he was sharing this trip with others, they had not made their presence known. Evidently Tomás was not concerned. The young man seemed to have dropped back into sleep, undisturbed by the rocking of the car.

What were his options? To escape he would have to step over Tomás to get to the open door. Suddenly alarmed, Nacho felt for his *pistola*. He was relieved to find it still secured in its holster, held in place by the small string across its hammer. He considered drawing the gun and holding Tomás at bay while he leaped from the train. But jumping from a rapidly moving train, into the unknown darkness, was not something he wanted to do. No, he would have to wait for a better opportunity. He settled his head against his saddlebags. Somehow, someplace, he would have to manage to escape from that determined young man.

CHAPTER THREE

U p the Rio Grande from Reynosa, a sudden gust of breeze blew from the west, disturbing the stillness of the late April night. Shadows of ebony trees were cast onto the river by the light of the last-quarter moon, cloaking the waters with darkness. Only the occasional leap and splash of a river perch interrupted the gentle flow of the stream. The quickening night breeze, carrying the smells of the river across its banks, sent the mosquitoes to seek shelter. Frogs continued to give urgent voice to their biological needs. Their high-pitched trills were accompanied by an occasional *"yo, yo"* call from a bullfrog. Someplace to the east, a toad joined the nighttime symphony with its rude utterance.

On the Texas side of the river, a large overgrowth of brushland nudged within twenty yards of the riverbank. The thick, twisted stems of shrubby vegetation reached twelve feet tall, most of them wielding thorns both large and small. The South Texas brushland formed an impenetrable mass of spikes and claws.

Standing at the edge of the brush, concealed by its shadows, two men studied the river. One man turned back toward the thorny patch and began to poke at the ground with a large stick, stirring the fallen debris.

"Dammit, Whitey," muttered the other man, "quit pokin' around with that stick. You're givin' me the willies."

"Well, Red, I thought I heard a rattler sneakin' through there. He ain't gonna catch me unawares."

"Just keep it quiet for a while, will ya?"

Whitey quit stirring the litter, but he kept the stick handy. Like many Texans, he worried about rattlesnakes. He'd seen them often enough. He knew that the Diamondback hunted mainly at night. Big rattlers could strike high on the leg, well above the top of the boot, and their bite could be deadly.

Both Whitey Wilson and Red Regan were senior Texas Rangers. They had chased rustlers, stagecoach robbers, marauding bands of ruffians, rioters, any lawbreakers whose capture called for men of determination. But they feared the rattlesnakes.

Regan now held the rank of sergeant in the Rangers. Whitey Wilson was still a private. On this night they'd been assigned to keep watch at a crossing in the Rio Grande, just below the Mexican village of Hidalgo. Although they could have alternated the watch, taking turns at napping, neither felt sleepy.

"What time you think it is?" asked Whitey.

"Lookin' at them stars, I'd say about four o'clock, wouldn't you?"

"Be glad when that buggy gets back in the mornin' to pick us up. What did ole Longhorn Maddox think we were gonna see, anyway?"

"The captain? He just said for us to watch the crossing. For whatever comes our way, I guess."

Red cautiously propped his Winchester among the thorny leaves of a yucca plant. He stretched his arms above his head and looked at the sky for any trace of morning light. None showed.

"You gonna take that promotion? To captain?" Whitey asked over his shoulder.

"Nope."

Whitey poked the brush with his stick. "It's due you, Red."

The pair had a long history of cooperation as a two-man team. Whitey was the bolder one, quick to take action, often too rash for his own good. Regan was more deliberate, a thoughtful planner. This difference in temperament had made them a formidable pair of fighters, the tall, rangy Wilson teamed with the stocky, muscular Regan. They had become a dependable, efficient fighting team in Company D.

"Why not?" Whitey continued to press the issue. "You'd be a natural as a captain. It'd suit you."

"I'd have to move to a troop up in Amarillo," said Regan. "Nothin' happens in the Panhandle any more. No more Indians. Just a few rustlers. Vagrants hoppin' off the train now and then. There's plenty of local law up there to handle those problems. No, I'd rather stay here on the border."

"Maybe Mabel would go up there with you."

Regan glanced at Whitey, trying to read his expression in the darkness. Maybe Whitey just wanted him out of the way, he thought. So he would have a free field with Mabel Steuben. A cute, vivacious blonde, Mabel had a reputation for quirkiness. She'd shopped in the Valley's best boutiques while dressed as a cowgirl. She had cheerfully encouraged Whitey and Red to compete for her attentions at Saturday night dances. Red Regan's interest in the girl had take a serious turn. Whitey Wilson took a lighthearted, casual attitude toward Mabel, but Regan knew him well enough to realize that he was serious in his own way. Mabel treated the situation as an amusing contest, but it was one that threatened to put an end to a long friendship between Red and Whitey. While on patrol they didn't talk about her, an unspoken agreement. Why would Whitey bring her up now?

Suddenly Red reached across and grasped Whitey by the arm.

"What is it?"

"Shht! The frogs."

The frog chorus had fallen silent. The two Rangers stared into the shadows across the river, searching for the cause of the sudden silence.

"There," whispered Red, but Whitey had already seen it. The red point of a cigarette glowed briefly in the shadows at the river's edge, then dropped downward and vanished. Regan felt for his Winchester, wincing when one of the yucca needles jabbed his hand. The two Rangers squatted low to the ground and waited.

A single rider emerged from the shadows and urged his horse into the river, stepping it carefully onto the gravel bar. In the fading moonlight, the rider looked to be little more than a shadow. He stopped near the middle of the river and turned the animal upstream, riding slowly for a few paces. Then the horse was turned and coaxed downstream.

"He's feelin' out the gravel bar," whispered Whitey.

Regan nodded to himself. "See anybody else?"

"Could be others back of the river bank. Don't see nobody." Whitey hefted his Winchester. "Clear field of fire. Why don't I just drop him?"

"Shit, no! Remember what the captain said. Watch and see what happens. No fights." Regan looked to be sure that Whitey lowered his rifle.

"What if a bunch of 'em comes splashin' through? They're sure to be bandits. What we gonna do then?" Whitey's whisper was getting louder.

"We'll melt back into the brush with those rattlers you keep talkin' about. Let's see what he's up to. Keep quiet!"

The rider finally crossed the river into Texas, reining his mount to a stop a mere ten yards from where the Rangers were squatting in their hiding place. Both men held their breaths. Regan reached across and placed a restraining hand on Whitey's arm. He could feel the tension; Whitey was a spring waiting to uncoil into action. Regan tightened his grip.

The rider walked his horse slowly along the riverbank. He stood in his stirrups and peered up through the open space beside the brushland. Finally, he turned his horse and walked it back across the river, disappearing into the night. The two Rangers waited silently. After some minutes, a lone bullfrog croaked, the first of an increasing chorus of clicks and trills. Regan put down his Winchester. He rose to his feet and stretched his arms above his head. Whitey stood up beside him.

"We got somethin' to report, I guess," said Whitey.

"Yeah, Pardner, I guess the captain knew somethin'. I figger this crossin' has now been duly scouted. Those *bandidos* over there must be lookin' for a river crossin' with a good bottom. Maybe tomorrow we'll get a passel of them usin' it."

"I guess the captain will have the Troop here waitin', do you think?"

"More likely he'll plan some kinda ambush." Regan punched Whitey playfully on the shoulder. "You're gonna get a chance to sling some lead outa that Winchester, Whitey, if I know Captain Maddox. He's been wantin' to get the jump on that bunch of bandits. Tonight he's had the Troop scattered along the Rio, scoutin' and waitin'."

"Well, I'm ready for mornin' and that buggy ride back to camp. Hope we get some sleep today, Pard." Whitey poked Regan playfully in return. "This night has tired me some."

"If I'd known you was so scared of rattlers I'd have brought old Nacho along instead. What happened to him today, anyway?"

"I think he slipped out yesterday. He's probably out chasing señoritas. You know Nacho, always got something going for hisself. Look, it's beginnin' to get light in the East. Why don't you hunker down for a little shuteye? I'll keep the watch."

"Holler if anything happens." Regan scooted down and propped his back against the trunk of a Mexican Olive tree, carefully avoiding the big yucca next to it. He settled himself and closed his eyes. He was tired, but sleep would not come. His thoughts ranged back to the question about the captain's commission he had been offered. Should he take it? The offer was a continuing bone of contention because nothing had been suggested for Whitey. Nothing at all, no promotion of any kind. Regan understood that decision. Whitey preferred to work on his own, as many older Rangers did. Aside from Regan and old Nacho, he had no close friends in the Troop. Whitey was a Ranger in the old, classical mode: self-reliant, resourceful and quick to act. Decades ago, when the Rangers were spread thin on the frontier, prompt individual action was the only means of survival. Move fast, go in shooting, don't stop to ask questions. Like they said of one old time Texas Ranger, "He'd charge hell with a bucket of water." Regan smiled at the memory.

Now, under today's conditions, group actions were the rule. Against organized bands of bandits, a lone fighter had little chance. Regan had learned the hard way. Leadership, experience in tactics, those things were necessary in this undeclared war. Captain Maddox had explained all this to the Troop. And he made it clear that he believed Regan had the ability to become a leader of men. If Regan would accept a captain's job in the high plains of the Texas Panhandle, said Maddox, he would learn leadership where the situation was less volatile. Once he proved himself as an officer, he would be eligible for a more challenging assignment.

Regan realized that his time had come. If he turned down the promotion, it would not be offered to him again. But he did not like leaving Whitey under these circumstances. Regan knew that Whitey depended upon him to act as a balance wheel against his abrupt decisions. The two men had developed a true partnership, in which each anticipated the other. What would happen to Whitey if Regan left?

Regan's thoughts turned back to Mabel. He frowned, faced with a difficult choice. Was he really in love? He'd had other romances, but with Mabel it seemed different. He opened his eyes and looked across at Whitey, who was now leaning on his Winchester and gazing out across the Rio Grande in the light of early dawn. Just how deeply did Whitey care for Mabel? Was it just the competition, the contest, that interested him? And Mabel—would she go with me to Amarillo? If she would, I might be willing to go. But probably she wouldn't want to live way up there in the Panhandle. Regan stretched his arms and yawned. Why am I worrying about these things? he asked himself. Maybe I'd better just stick here on the Border with Whitey. He had a feeling, though, that the old Ranger days were about to be over. Perhaps for him and for Whitey both. He scooted down further against the Mexican Olive tree and closed his eyes. He started at the sound of something scraping across the ground. Whitey had picked up his stick and resumed the rattlesnake patrol.

CHAPTER FOUR

The freight train stopped abruptly, jarring the boxcars so that each in turn gave a sudden jerk, passing a booming signal from one car to the next along the length of the train. Nacho's head was bounced from its pillow of saddlebags. He woke suddenly, confused by the unfamiliar surroundings, reaching for his *pistola*. He pulled himself erect, sitting up, shaking the fog from his brain. Awareness returned when he saw Tomás standing in the open doorway of the boxcar, where a few faint rays of daylight filtered in. The train sat motionless on the tracks, a few creaks and pops emerging from the boxcar's wooden floor.

Dawn was breaking. Nacho had surprised himself by falling into a sound sleep, lulled by the rattle of the boxcar. The few hours of deep slumber had refreshed him. He scrambled to his feet and took a moment to organize his thoughts. Was this the time, now, to escape back across the border into Texas? Tomás seemed determined to be Nacho's guardian and protector, as well as his jailer. He may have surmised that Nacho would escape at the first opportunity. Or perhaps, thought Nacho, he just believes I'm an incompetent *viejo*. Clearly, Tomás's loyalty was to Pancho Villa. Young though he was, the boy presented a dangerous complication in Nacho's life.

The memory of his meeting with Villa brought escape to the front of his thoughts. I must get away soon, he decided. What did Villa want with that little bandit Chulo Valdez, anyway? Why did he ask Nacho, of all people, to locate him?

Pancho had framed it as a request, but with Villa, requests had a way of turning into commands.

Moreover, Nacho's son-in-law presented a complication to his plans. Had that young man actually joined Chulo Valdez in his bandit raids? His daughter thought so. Nacho considered his options. Perhaps, for the time being, he would begin the attempt to contact the bandit leader. Maybe he could locate young Marco Luís and explain to him the error of his ways. In any case, the Texas Rangers would be grateful for whatever information he could give them about Chulo Valdez and his gang of bandits. And Pancho Villa, here in the Lower Valley. Nacho smiled, thinking of the excitement his report would cause among the Rangers. Yes, the thing to do now was to follow along with this plan of Villa's. Then he would escape back across the *río*.

Nacho realized that Tomás, standing in the doorway of the boxcar, was urinating outside into the dawn. With a sigh, Nacho decided to join him.

Tomás grunted a morning greeting. Nacho looked out of the boxcar door at the early morning light falling across the little city of Matamoros. He felt his spirits surge at the sight of this, a childhood home, the little city where he grew into his manhood. An early morning mist was lifting from the city, dispersed by the rising sun. He saw the twin spires of the cathedral on the plaza, looming above the low adobe buildings. The massive opera house, pride of the city, stood off to his left. Somewhere in the distance a rooster crowed, a faint cry into the dawn. A small flock of white-winged doves brushed past the boxcar's doorway.

The familiar surroundings of his boyhood lent confidence to Nacho. He straightened his shoulders and glanced at Tomás, who was carefully buttoning his fly. The train gave a sudden jerk, causing both men to feel for their balance. The boxcar began to move forward, slowly.

"Come." Tomás turned and began to gather his saddlebags together. "We should get off now."

"In a moment." Nacho leaned out through the door. The train was easing into position beside a freight platform.

"Now!" insisted Tomás.

"No, just a moment more. Ah, here we are." The train stopped again. Nacho picked up his saddlebags and hopped down onto the station platform beside the tracks. Bales of cotton, stacked two high along the platform, blocked his view as far as he could see. Tomás jumped down beside him.

"This way." Nacho pointed to a small gap between the bales, and led Tomás through it to the back edge of the platform, where the city again became visible.

"Why is all this cotton here?" Tomás frowned at the long row of cotton bales and then at Nacho.

Nacho laughed. "Ah, Tomás, welcome to the State of Tamaulipas! Cotton producer of eastern Mexico! This cotton will be shipped across to the *norteamericanos*, or perhaps down to the coast to be sent to Europe. Unlike your State of Chihuahua, eastern Mexico has some prime agricultural land." He pulled a wisp of cotton from a nearby bale and examined it carefully.

"Look," he said. "Long staple cotton. The best." He tossed it aside.

Tomás continued to frown. "Are the *peónes* enslaved, those that work the fields? Have they not heard of the *Revolución?*"

Nacho shifted his saddlebags on his shoulder. "*Sí,*" he said with a sigh. "The *Revolución* is here. Let us go and see if we can find it."

He began a slow stride down the platform, heading towards the passenger station.

"*Bien, viejo!*" Tomás hurried after him. "Don Francisco has sent me along to be sure that you do not fail in your task. Although why he did not send me alone, I do not know. I could surely find this *hombre* Valdez by myself. But I am here, and I will see that you do not attempt to evade your responsibility to the *Revolución*."

Nacho stopped abruptly and turned sideways, forcing Tomás to a sudden stop. Soon he must reach an understanding with the youngster. This was as good a time as any. Tomás was grinning at him and playing with one of his *pistolas,* pulling it partly out of its holster and then shoving it back. Nacho knew that this youngster's arrogance could get them both killed in these circumstances. He slipped his saddlebags from his left shoulder onto the platform and raised his left hand, thrusting it, palm outward, into Tomás' face. The boy rocked back on his heels, surprise in his eyes. Those eyes opened wider when Nacho lowered his left hand to reveal a revolver clutched in his right hand, and pointed directly at Tomás's face. Nacho raised the *pistola* until it nearly touched the boy's nose. He pulled back the hammer to the fully cocked position. The *click*! *click*! of the single action revolver rang loudly in the stillness of the morning. Carefully, his eyes fixed on the end of the pistol barrel, Tomás raised his hands into the air.

"Now, Tomás." Nacho spoke softly and deliberately. "Let us understand one another. Pancho Villa has asked me to find someone for him in this city. Chulo Valdez is a worthless bandit, but Villa asked it. He knows that I can do it because this city is well known to me. He has sent you along to assist me, if I need it. You are not my guardian or my jailer. Do you understand?"

Tomás remained silent, his wide eyes still fixed on the end of the gun barrel. He gave a tiny, slow nod. With a smile Nacho tweaked Tomás's nose with the end of the *pistola*. Twice.

"Good. Now we have an understanding." Nacho holstered his weapon and turned towards the station house. He straightened his shoulders and strode forward.

"Bring my saddlebags and follow me."

Without saying a word, Tomás reached down for the saddlebags, shouldered them opposite his own, and followed Nacho.

They stopped at a water trough beside the passenger station. No one was outside the station; the morning's railroad business had not yet begun. He gestured to Tomás for his saddlebags, which he opened and propped against the station wall. He retrieved a coarse brush and began vigorously to clean the straw and dirt from his clothes. Tomás watched as Nacho carefully cleaned his worn felt hat and re-creased it. He removed his spurs and tucked them into his saddlebag. Then he plucked a clean red neckerchief from the bag and tied it around his neck. Hands on hips, he turned to survey Tomás, who was staring at him suspiciously.

"Walk into Matamoros looking like that and you will be standing against a wall before sundown." Nacho stepped forward and removed Tomás's large sombrero from his head. He looked at it speculatively and then sailed it off down the alley behind the passenger station. Tomás reached after it ineffectually.

"You will not need that here. We will get you another hat. And remove those bandoleers. Put them in your saddlebags. Along with those big-rowel spurs. We do not want anyone thinking we are bandits."

"I am a revolutionary," muttered Tomás softly, "not a bandit."

"Today you are an *agricultór*." Nacho handed him the brush. "Clean yourself. As best you can."

The sun was well into the morning sky when the two men arrived at the main plaza in Matamoros. A thorough washing of head and hands had invigorated Nacho but merely irritated Tomás, who did not appreciate the rough soap which had appeared from Nacho's saddlebags. Both men had left their revolvers in their saddlebags, again over Tomás's objections. Nacho had taken the opportunity to conceal his Texas Ranger badge as well. He secured it in his hatband, the hiding place used by many of the Rangers for whatever small valuables they wished to conceal. In addition to his badge, Nacho's hatband hid several gold coins, his reserve of *dinero*. He had peso coins and a few American dollars crammed down into his pockets.

"First, Tomás, we will take a little breakfast at a sidewalk café on the main plaza. We must gather information before we can proceed." Nacho suddenly realized that he had begun to form a plan, of sorts, for contacting the bandit Chulo Valdez. Last night, his only concern had been to escape back to Texas, with his horse Fogata if possible but without her if necessary. The familiar surroundings of his favorite Matamoros had helped to change his mind. Also, he felt an increasing curiosity about the bandit leader. Chulo Valdez was a sworn enemy of his Texas Ranger Company. Did he count Nacho's son-in-law among his fighting men? Nacho silently rehearsed the comments he would make to that lad if—when!—he found him. Marco Luís was a good boy, just very young, who needed his responsibilities explained to him. Nacho intended to do just that. Primarily, he reminded himself, he must keep from getting entangled in any kind of bandit activities, despite Pancho Villa's request. He was, after all, a Texas Ranger, a man who wore a badge of honor. But I do not wear it on this side of the border, he thought with a smile.

The main plaza, the social and cultural center of the city of Matamoros, was beginning to come to life. The warm April sun was drying the dew from the grass beside the bandstand. Where the wispy leaves of the ebony trees cast their shadows across walkways and flowerbeds, the coating of dew was slow to evaporate. Flocks of pigeons mixed with white-wing doves, mingling in the street, jostling each other in their search for breakfast in the debris of the gutters. Only a few people were visiting the plaza this early in the morning. A handful of early worshipers climbed the steps towards the massive cathedral doors, still in the shadows of the tall twin spires. A cart pulled by a burro moved slowly past the tavern where Nacho and his companion had seated themselves.

The *Taberna Calle Amistad* was not yet open for business, but Nacho was content to wait. He and Tomás had found chairs upended on one of the little tables on the sidewalk outside the building. They had turned the chairs upright and seated themselves. This tavern was a central meeting place for certain important *hombres* of the city. Hector León, the owner, was a boyhood friend of Nacho's, and he hoped that his old *amigo* would share some information about the local bandits. *Por cierto*, Hector should be good for a little breakfast.

"Down there, Tomás." Nacho pointed down a side street. "Down that street was my uncle's house. I played with my friends here in this plaza, chasing pigeons and scaring the girls." He laughed at the memory. "Later, of course, we joined the Sunday afternoon parades, boys circling around to the left, girls to the right. Always with their chaperones. Those old crows! I was hit several times with their little fans. Did you play these games in the plazas of El Paso or Juárez, Tomás?"

"I do not like this place!" Tomás squirmed in his chair and attempted to adjust the torn straw hat that Nacho had found for him under one of the tables. He frowned and pointed across the plaza at a pair of soldiers patrolling the sidewalk. They were dressed in rumpled khaki uniforms and scuffed black boots. Neither of them wore a cap. Rifles were slung from their shoulders and cartridge belts circled their waists. They nodded to passersby on the sidewalk but maintained a brisk pace, almost a military march.

"Who are those *hombres*?" Tomás fretted. "Whose soldiers are they? Suppose they challenge us? What shall we do?"

"Contain yourself, Tomás. Those men must be part of *general* Blanco's forces. We will stay clear of them. I do not think they will bother us. Do not call attention to yourself."

"Who is *general* Blanco?"

Nacho rolled his eyes and sighed deeply. He settled himself to a more comfortable position in his chair, and leaned across the table to engage Tomás's attention. With his forefinger he tapped Tomás on the wrist.

"Tomás, you surprise me. But I forget, my friend, that you are from Chihuahua and are not familiar with local politics here on the lower *río Bravo*. Last year, *El presidente* Huerta sent *general* Blanco up here with an army. He was supposed to occupy Matamoros and squelch any revolutionary spirit. Matamoros resisted and there was a bloody battle. I saw it myself. I watched from the railroad bridge over the *río*, on the *americano* side. *General* Blanco's troops prevailed. They continue to patrol the town. Now, *general* Blanco thinks perhaps he should be *presidente* himself, since Huerta has been deposed."

"These troops are enemies, then?" Tomás continued to watch the two soldiers as they reached the far edge of the plaza and turned towards the tavern.

"I suppose they consider themselves to be *federales*, true soldiers of the Government of Mexico. The revolutionaries helped to install President Huerta, remember? Now he has been removed and *general* Carranza has become the tyrant in Mexico City. These troops should answer to him. Perhaps they do, perhaps they do not. Does not your own leader, Pancho Villa, fight against Carranza?"

"I do not think about these things." Tomás turned his attention to Nacho. "Don Francisco knows what he is doing. We fight when he tells us." He leaned forward and pointed a finger under Nacho's nose. "And you, Nacho," he scowled, "for whom do you fight? Are you a revolutionary or not?" His eyes bored into Nacho's.

Nacho threw a quick glance towards the two soldiers, who were now approaching the tavern and were slowing their stride in order to inspect them. This was not the time to enter into an argument. He pushed back from the table and gave forth a burst of laughter. Tomás stared at him in amazement.

"Laugh, you young fool," Nacho said in a low voice. He reached across and slapped Tomás playfully on the shoulder. Comprehension suddenly struck Tomás. He joined Nacho in gales of laughter. A quick glance to the side showed Nacho that the soldiers had picked up their pace and had begun to move on down the sidewalk.

"Tomás, I will try to answer your question. About the *Revolución*. I am a child of the Lower Valley of the *río Bravo*." He gestured with his arm to indicate the town. "Here we used to be isolated, both sides of the river, cut off from the *norteamericanos* and from the rest of Mexico alike, until the railroads came. We lived with the *americanos* and they lived with us. When they had troubles with their government, things such as heavy tariffs, they moved their businesses across the river—they call it the Rio Grande—and joined us here in Matamoros. And in Matamoros, if oppressive taxes were imposed, we moved ourselves across the river—our *río Bravo*—to the *americano* side. Many types of businesses made these transfers, back and forth. Many Mexicans had *americano* partners. The river was our link to the sea and our route of commerce. We took little notice of the fact that the river was a border between countries. Last year, after the battle, many Mexicans transferred themselves across the river to Brownsville."

Tomás frowned in confusion. "I do not understand. You are Mexican. The *americanos* are not our friends. Are they?"

"No, you really do not understand." Nacho sighed and stared out across the plaza. "Nationalities are blurred here on the lower *río*. I swam in that stream. So did the girls. I could tell you—." Nacho stopped himself. "But you see, here in the Valley, we did not act as if there were two countries. We moved freely. We were remote from our governments. Sometimes there was a footbridge. Always there were the boats." He sat back in his chair. "And now it is even easier, with the railroad bridge on which many people cross every day. And it is well that there is such a bridge. With all this fighting in Mexico—well, as I said, many Mexicans have simply moved across the river to live. Perhaps someday they will return. Perhaps not."

Tomás stared into Nacho's face, with a simple curiosity plain on his features.

"So, Nacho. Does that make you a Mexican? Or a *norteamericano?*"

Nacho studied his hands, flexing his fingers, considering how to answer. In truth, he did not actually know what he was. He could not remember his parents, only his uncle and aunt. As a young boy he had lived on both sides of the river. Nacho had papers proving he was American, and a different set proving he was Mexican. Both sets were forgeries. He was almost never required to produce them. Until two years ago, the border was crossed freely in either direction, without any questions being asked.

Nacho stared out across the plaza. How could he explain this to Tomás?

"As I said, Tomás, I am a child of the Valley, the Lower Valley of the river. The *Revolución* did not affect us. Not until *general* Blanco attacked Matamoros. And the bandit raids into Texas began."

It was not a satisfactory answer, he knew. Where were his loyalties? He loved the border towns and villages, both sides of the river. The Texas Rangers claimed his allegiance as well. His heritage was Latino—Spanish and Indian—but this was also true of the *tejanos*, those of Latino heritage who were Texans by birth. Perhaps, he thought, I am more than one thing. Or maybe I am trying to be too many things. He shook his head and shrugged his shoulders. Perhaps it is better not to dwell on these thoughts.

Tomás was looking at him quizzically. Nacho smiled weakly, not knowing what further to say.

Behind him the door to the tavern opened. The proprietor, Hector León, stepped outside, wiping his hands on his apron as he surveyed the morning. He almost stumbled backwards when he saw Nacho smiling up at him.

"Ygnacio! Have you lost your mind?" He looked quickly to both sides to be sure that they were not being observed. "Come inside—get out of sight!"

"Hector, it is good to see you, too. What is this commotion?" Smiling, Nacho rose and offered a handshake, which the proprietor ignored.

"You *estúpido*," he hissed. "Don't you know there is a price on your head? Inside, inside! Quickly! The *federales* seek you. You will be shot!"

CHAPTER FIVE

Q uickly! Follow me." Hector León led the way through the tavern, weaving between the empty tables, hurrying towards the rear of the dining room. Nacho could see that the tavern was preparing for its morning business. A young man was arranging chairs around the tables. Another stood aside with an armload of tablecloths. Hector strode past them.

"This way." Pushing open a swinging door, Hector entered the kitchen, with Nacho and Tomás hurrying to follow him. Breakfast preparations had begun. A woman in a print dress was heating tortillas on a griddle. Hector stepped to one side and stopped beside a small door, thrust it open and gestured through the doorway.

"Inside. Hurry!" He took Nacho by the elbow and guided him through the door. Tomás was propelled through it with a shove in the back. Hector entered behind them and pulled the door shut. For a moment all was darkness, then a bare electric bulb hanging from the ceiling flashed on. Nacho quickly glanced around, shielding his eyes from the glare with his hand. He saw that they were in a small storeroom. Canned goods lined the shelves. Packing crates were piled on the floor. Tomás stumbled against a mop and bucket and righted himself by grabbing Nacho's arm. Nacho shook him loose. Both of them turned to stare at Hector, who was standing with his ear pressed to the door, listening.

Nacho leaned back against a stack of crates and studied Hector. He pulled a splinter from one of the wooden crates and stuck it in his mouth.

"What is it, my old *amigo*? Why are you so alarmed?"

Hector turned to face Nacho and held up a cautionary hand. "You are a wanted man. There is a price on your head. Why did you come back to Matamoros?"

Nacho frowned. He hadn't been in Matamoros for ten years or more. Even if it became common knowledge that he was a *tejano* Ranger—well, that was not a crime. An indiscretion in some quarters, perhaps. But a crime? No.

"Nacho," Hector continued. "You were seen. At the bridge. Helping the wounded."

"Ah." Nacho stared at Hector as a slow realization progressed through his thoughts. "The bridge across the *río*. It is true. I was there."

"And you were seen. And identified." Hector glared at him.

"What is this?" interjected Tomás. "What bridge?"

"Who is this youngster?" asked Hector.

Nacho frowned and closed his eyes. So, this was what it was about. Yes, he had helped refugees escape from Matamoros across the railroad bridge to safety in Texas.

"What is it?" insisted Tomás.

Nacho lifted his hands, palms outward. "During the siege of Matamoros," he explained to Tomás. "Last year. The fighting was bloody. *General* Blanco's troops were forcing their way through the streets, winning the battle. A few wounded men tried to cross the railroad bridge into Texas, where they would find sanctuary. Some of us watched from Brownsville, on the bank of the river, right across from Matamoros. I was one of those who watched the battle. And it is true, I got onto the bridge itself and assisted some *hombres* to safety. We were fired upon." He smiled. "Fortunately, those *federales* were not very good shots."

"But someone recognized you, Nacho, they must have," insisted Hector. "*General* Blanco has listed you among the enemies of the Republic. If you are captured, well, recently *general* Blanco has been executing some of those he considers his enemies. He is ruthless. Furthermore—but who is this *joven?*"

Hands on his hips, Hector now frowned at Tomás, who drew himself up to his full height and scowled in return.

"I am a revolutionary," began Tomás, but Nacho placed a hand on his arm and silenced him.

"*Señor* Hector León, may I present *señor* Tomás Aguilar."

Hector looked Tomás up and down, and then returned his attention to Nacho.

"Tomás is a *soldado de primera* in the army of Pancho Villa," Nacho continued.

Tomás lifted his chin and rocked back on his heels. He hooked his thumbs into his belt. He offered a little smirk to Hector, who gaped at him open-mouthed for a moment.

Hector turned back to Nacho. "*Dios mío!* What have you done? Have you brought another battle upon us? For the love of God, Nacho!" Hector raised his eyes skyward and gestured towards heaven with closed fists. He took a deep breath, reached across and grasped Nacho by the shoulders.

"Please understand, old friend. We are all trying to be very quiet here in Matamoros. *General* Blanco is out of the city these past few weeks. His army waits. If there is no one to fight, no insurrection to put down, he will take his army elsewhere. Maybe he will try to become *presidente*, now that *general* Huerta is no longer in power. We just want him to leave."

"Relax, Hector. Do not be concerned. We have only a simple mission to perform. We wish to contact your notorious bandit leader, Chulo Valdez, that is all. *Nada más*"

Hector turned his head and spat noisily. "That *pendejo*. Who knows where he is hiding? I think he may have gone south of here."

"And," continued Nacho, "I want to find my son-in-law. He is supposed to be riding with the *pendejo*. You know him, I think."

Hector stared at Nacho for a moment and then looked down at the floor.

"Marco Luís. Yes, I know him. *General* Blanco has put him in prison." Hector straightened his shoulders and looked away. "Marco Luís shot and killed an army officer. I think they will execute him. I am sorry, Nacho."

Wide-eyed, Nacho looked at Tomás and then back to Hector.

"What did you say?"

"They have arrested Marco Luís. He is imprisoned in the old jail down on *calle Guerrero*. They say he shot and killed one of *general* Blanco's favorite lieutenants."

"How did this happen?"

"They say—well, they say he just walked into the Laureles Bar and shot him."

"That old bar down by the *Mercado*? Market Square? That one?"

"That's right, Nacho. We have heard these things discussed here in the *Taberna*."

"Discussed by the soldiers?"

"By the soldiers, the *federales* who come in from time to time."

Nacho sat down heavily on a packing crate. He studied his hands, tops and palms. Hector and Tomás stood beside him, waiting silently. Finally Tomás began to shuffle his feet.

"Nacho…"

"Yes, Tomás, I must do something. I must find a way to help Marco Luís. And find Chulo Valdez. It all seems part of the same puzzle, Tomás. We must find this Chulo Valdez if we are going to help Marco Luís."

The three men stood silently, looking at one another. Nacho stared at the floor. He searched his mind for possibilities; no plan of action suggested itself to him. Hector nervously wiped his hands on his apron, waiting for Nacho to speak. Tomás shifted his weight from one foot to the other, eyeing the two others. Finally, Tomás spoke again.

"Nacho," he said softly. "Nacho…"

Distracted, Nacho answered abruptly. "*Sí*, Tomás. What is it?"

"I am hungry."

Nacho looked up and began to chuckle. "So am I. So am I." He punched Hector playfully on the shoulder. "Hector, will you offer us some breakfast? I think the *joven* has the right idea. One does not make good plans on an empty stomach."

Hector opened the storeroom door and peered outside. "You must eat in the kitchen. Then, please, you should be on your way."

Nacho stood quietly inside the Laureles Bar, trying to be inconspicuous. He admonished himself for acting in haste. Coming here had been a mistake. Nacho had advised his young Ranger friends, always consider the consequences of your course of action before you begin. Then move ahead deliberately; you will be prepared for whatever difficulties arise. The younger

Rangers were apt to barge headfirst into trouble with little thought of where it might lead them. Well, thought Nacho, I have acted like the youngsters. I should not have come into this bar without a firm plan. Worries about Marco Luís and his fate had clouded Nacho's judgment. His daughter would depend upon him to rescue her husband.

Nacho had left Tomás to his own devices, in the company of Hector who, reluctantly, would try to keep him out of trouble there at the restaurant. Perhaps Tomás would return to Pancho Villa. At this point Nacho did not care. Tomás would only be in his way. Nacho needed to discover what he could, to think, to decide on a course of action.

He had wanted to see the barroom for himself, ask some questions, and maybe find a witness or two. There might not be much time left for him to get his son-in-law out of the clutches of the *federales*.

Where to turn, where to begin? Think like a Ranger, he told himself. Hector had reminded him that he was wanted by the *federales*. Why was there a price on his head? Few in Matamoros would recognize him, after all these years. He must try to be inconspicuous. If he was recognized, he might well be joining Marco Luís in the *calabozo*. Especially if his relationship with Pancho Villa should be discovered. That alone would be sufficient to land him in prison.

Nacho had cautioned Hector not to mention the presence of the *villistas* in nearby Reynosa. He knew it was only a matter of time. Hector, owner and operator of the *Taberna*, was well known as a source of news. A rumor about the presence of Pancho Villa in the Lower Valley would just be too good to keep. Whether such a rumor would be believed—well, Hector was, after all, a confirmed gossip.

Nacho had staked out a position at the far end of the bar. From where he stood, his field of vision swept over the entire barroom. Not that there was that much to see. One by one, customers had drifted out into the street. By now it was mid-afternoon, and he was the only patron still standing at the bar. Across the room, several Mexican army officers occupied two of the tables. They had been drinking for several hours. Playing cards were scattered across the tables haphazardly; the games were over. The air was thick with laughter and acrid cigar smoke mingled with the background odor of stale beer. Half-empty bottles of whiskey stood on each of their tables. Behind the bar, the bartender polished the same glass over and over, watching the officers with furtive glances.

Nacho had nursed his bottle of beer for more than an hour. No one had paid any attention to him. He flicked his forefinger at a fly crawling on the bar, and watched as it circled back to land again several feet away. The soldiers were getting louder as the whiskey bottles emptied. Their outbursts were friendly laughter, not drunken anger, and were accompanied by good-natured back-slapping. They had become more raucous as the afternoon wore on. Occasionally someone from the sidewalk would start to enter the barroom, but the spectacle of the loud party would cause him to turn prudently away.

The afternoon sun shone warmly through the open door. Nacho could see across the street into the tree-shaded Plaza. Except for an occasional wagon or motorcar, there was little activity outdoors. After all, it was the time of the *siesta*. Most businesses were closed until later in the afternoon. The barroom where Nacho waited would be closed now, were it not for the presence of the army officers.

The volume of laughter began to diminish. Perhaps the whiskey was taking effect. Nacho shifted his feet and tapped the beer bottle gently on the bar. Would the bartender talk with him, at last? Without looking at him, the bartender produced another bottle of beer and slid it down the bar. He continued watching the soldiers.

Nacho did not want another beer. He had questions for the bartender, but it seemed that he was not going to have an opportunity to ask them. The bartender refused to be distracted from his vigil. It would be a mistake to interrupt him because Nacho needed his full cooperation. With a sigh, Nacho tasted the second bottle of beer. Well, perhaps he should leave now and return at a later time. This evening? Perhaps that would be better.

He was turning towards the door when two men burst in, loudly stomping their way across the barroom.

"Barkeep," shouted one. "Your best tequila! Pronto!"

Nacho realized that the men were Americans. The soldiers had fallen silent, staring at the two men. Each wore a black leather vest over a flannel shirt, tailored trousers tucked into knee-length boots, and a gray felt hat. The clothes and boots were clean and looked to be new. They must be newcomers to the Valley, thought Nacho, young men playing at the game of cowboy. Just tourists. One of the two men turned towards the soldiers. With a grin, he gestured a toast with a shot glass of tequila. They continued to stare at him.

Nacho eyed the door, wondering if he could get there before the trouble started. But after a tense moment, the officers returned to their conversation and the American turned back to his friend. After all, *presidente* Carranza had decreed that the Americans were his friends, ever since the American *presidente* Wilson had decided to support him. The Mexican Army was dependent upon the *americanos* for military supplies. *General* Blanco would frown upon any trouble between his officers and *americanos*.

Nacho suddenly realized that one of the Americans was studying him closely.

"Say," he said, "ain't you a Texas Ranger?"

Nacho almost stumbled in shock. How did he know?

"Naw," said the other American. "He ain't a Ranger. He's a Mex. Ain't no Mexican Texas Rangers."

"He is, too! I seen him last week when we was at that Ranger camp. I wondered about it then, him bein' a Mex and all. He's the one, all right. You are a Ranger, ain't you, Seen-yore?"

Nacho shifted his beer bottle into his left hand. He felt along his right hip, before remembering that he had left his *pistola* behind. Once again. This could be very serious. He glanced quickly toward the tables, where the officers had fallen silent, watching the action at the bar.

"I'm talkin' at you, Mex," continued the American, pointing at Nacho with his index finger.

"There is no need to shout, *señor*. I am not deaf."

Nacho tightened his grip on the beer bottle, as the American started to walk towards him. Abruptly, the man stopped. The bartender had reached across the bar and blocked his progress with a small bat, which he held across the American's stomach. His other hand slowly appeared, holding a small sawed-off shotgun. He placed the weapon flat on the bar.

"*Señores*, I think you should leave now." The bartender spoke quietly but with authority. He gave the Americans a steely glare. Both Americans looked at the shotgun, its barrels turned towards them. One of them slipped his fingers slowly into the pocket of his trousers. He returned the bartender's stare.

"C'mon, George, let's get outa this firetrap," said the second American.

"Yeah. I'm tired a this place."

Without another glance at Nacho, the two men stomped out of the door and turned down the street.

Nacho and the bartender stared at each other. The bartender placed his bat and shotgun back under the bar.

One of the officers suddenly appeared at Nacho's side. When Nacho turned towards him, the officer searched his face. The Mexican was a slight, thin man with a neatly trimmed black mustache. An officer's cap hid most of his short black hair. His tailored khaki shirt was soaked in sweat. Captain's bars were pinned to its shoulders. His breath was strong with the smell of whiskey, but his black eyes were bright with the light of intelligence.

"*Señor.* Are you a Texas Ranger? As he said?" The officer looked intently into Nacho's eyes.

Nacho managed a smile. "No, *general.* I am a cotton buyer, from *ciudad* Victoria. The *americano* was mistaken." Nacho held perfectly still, his mind racing.

The officer studied Nacho carefully, noting the straw hat, denim shirt and chinos, the absence of badge or gun. His glance lingered on Nacho's boots for a moment. But then he smiled at Nacho.

"Yes," he said. "You are not an *americano* Ranger. And I am but a mere *capitán.*"

Abruptly, he turned to his companions and gestured towards the door. "*Vámonos.*" Without a word, the other officers rose and left the barroom, walking through the door, single file. The bartender put down his glass and bar rag. He and Nacho eyed each other. Finally, Nacho spoke.

"I am grateful to you, *señor.*"

The bartender shrugged his shoulders. "I did not want to have to clean up another mess."

"You refer to the shooting that happened here two days ago?"

The bartender leaned across the bar towards Nacho.

"Who are you, *señor*? I do not know you."

Nacho placed his hands flat on the bar. He spoke softly.

"Your friend Hector is also an old friend of mine. He told me that I could trust you. I have some questions about that killing. I hope you can help me."

Nacho lifted his right hand, to reveal a small gold coin. He pushed it slowly towards the bartender.

The bartender studied the coin without touching it.

"You have observed," he said, "that my bar is a favorite with the officers of *general* Blanco's army." He thought for a moment. "I am a prudent man," he continued, "attempting to make a quiet living. It would be unwise to involve myself in the troubles of others."

The bartender leaned on his elbows and looked Nacho up and down.

"I do not think that you are a cotton buyer. The *capitán* did not think so, either. Look at your boots, *señor*. Do you wear spurs in the cotton fields?"

Nacho glanced down at his boots. He had removed his spurs, of course, but the marks they had made were clearly visible on his boot heels.

In for a *centavo*, in for a *peso*. Again, Nacho gently pushed the coin forwards until it rested between the bartender's elbows.

"I only wish to hear what happened, *señor*. As you saw it."

Suddenly the coin disappeared into the bar rag. The bartender looked around, verifying that the barroom was empty. He looked back at Nacho.

"I will tell you. Some officers were at the tables, as they were today. I wished to close the bar at two o'clock, as is customary, but they did not leave. Like today. *Bueno*. This young man came in, dressed like a *bandido*. He had a broad sombrero, *charro* trousers with conchos, big silver spurs, and two *pistolas*. You know, like he was ready for a *baile*. But the soldiers did not want to dance. I tried to warn him away, but he ignored me.

"Two of the officers got up and grabbed him by the elbows and walked him over to their table. With much laughter, they sat him down and began to tease him. I do not know if they were going to arrest him or not. They had every right, him coming into town like that, pretending to be a bandit, but he was young. They were teasing, pulling at him.

"There was a shot. A young *teniente* fell out of his chair, to the floor."

"And who fired the shot?" Nacho interrupted.

"*Señor*, I did not see. I do not know. They immediately captured the young *charro*."

"Did he still have his *pistolas*?"

"I did not see. They hurried him away."

"And there was no one else in the bar?

"Just the officers." The bartender hesitated. "And the *indio*."

"The Indian?"

"*Sí*. He cleans the floors, cleans up the messes. He was here when it happened. I remember seeing him scurry beneath a table."

Nacho stared across the room.

"Where would I find this—*indio*?"

The bartender smiled at him. "*Señor*, it is *siesta* now. And he drinks. He might be here, asleep in the back room. I will see." The bartender turned away and removed his apron, which he hung carefully on a wall hook. "He is *un sordomundo*" he said, and disappeared through a curtained door.

So, there it was. The only eyewitness is both deaf and dumb. And an Indio as well. A wry smile crossed his features. What can I do?

A skinny form suddenly emerged from the back room and stopped at the far end of the bar, looking toward Nacho. Thick black hair hung over his forehead. His clothes were dirty and worn. Probably castoffs, Nacho thought. So this is my witness. The Indian leaned against the bar, waiting.

Nacho had some proficiency with the sign language of the Lipan Apaches, signs he had learned in West Texas. He tried gestures of greeting and indicated friendship and his desire to talk. The *indio* stood unmoving, elbow on the bar, staring at Nacho without any indication, any expression or shifting of eyes, that would suggest he had understood.

What to do? After a moment, Nacho pointed towards the table where the officers had been sitting. And then he extended his forefinger and made a shooting motion, like a pistol. He looked at the Indian. The man's head slowly nodded; his expression did not change. He continued to stare at Nacho.

So far, so good. Nacho repeated the shooting motion, then shrugged his shoulders, palms outward, a universal gesture of interrogation. What did you see? Who was it?

After a moment, the Indian stood erect and raised his right hand. With his index and second fingers, he tapped his left shoulder, near his neck. Twice.

Nacho repeated the gesture. The Indian slowly nodded.

Aha! The Indian was mimicking *capitán's* bars. One of the army *capitán's* had shot the lieutenant. Nacho studied the table, trying to picture the scene. But he did not know who was sitting in what chair, or exactly where Marco Luís would have been standing.

When he looked back, the *indio* had disappeared. Clearly, this interview was over.

Nacho left his bottle of beer on the bar.

CHAPTER SIX

The afternoon sun beamed down from a cloudless sky, its light reflecting off of the white buildings on the other side of the narrow street where Nacho trudged slowly along. It was deserted, praise *Dios*, except for a skinny, dirty mongrel dog that slinked down the sidewalk, tongue hanging from the side of its mouth. It walked carefully with a slow sideways pace, as though each footstep was painful. The dog paid no attention to Nacho. Good, he thought. He wanted to be as inconspicuous as he could. He had borrowed some shapeless trousers and a battered *serape* from Hector, along with some *huarache* sandals and a broad-brimmed straw hat. He walked on the right side of the street, staying in the shadows and keeping as close as he could to the walls of the buildings. His saddlebags he kept slung over his right shoulder, towards the walls, so that they concealed the pistol crammed beneath his rope belt. Nacho kept his face down, partially concealed beneath his tattered straw hat. He had adopted a slow shuffling walk, and dust from the adobe brick sidewalk slipped into his *huaraches* and settled between his toes. He hoped that his guise as a poor *peón* would allow him to blend into the background, at least until he had found his uncle's house. Of course, if anyone examined him closely, they would see that he was no *peón*. What would a *peón* have to do with big leather saddlebags? Were they stolen? Nacho bit his lip, forcing himself to amble slowly in spite of his feeling of urgency. He wanted to get off that street as soon as he could.

Clearly it was necessary for Nacho to shift his base of operations away from the *Taberna*. The tavern was far too public, and Nacho's presence was making Hector nervous. So Nacho had decided to look for his uncle's old house. Hector told Nacho that his aunt and uncle had died. He thought the house now belonged to Nacho's cousin Paulo. Would Paulo still be living there? Hector became evasive and would not discuss Nacho's cousin. Nacho had no place else to go.

A shaft of sunlight illuminated a large cloud of swarming gnats floating back and forth across the street. Nacho took pains to avoid them. He shuffled past a pile of garbage that had been unceremoniously dumped into the street; the sour-sweet smell caused him to wrinkle his nose in disgust. This was not the Matamoros he remembered from his childhood. The city he recalled was a lively place of pleasant avenues filled with cheerful people. Today he walked along a deserted, filthy, narrow passageway between high-walled buildings. He quickened his pace in hopes of finding a cleaner, more pleasant part of the street.

The encounter with the army *capitán* at the cantina had unnerved Nacho. The more he thought about it, the more worried he became. *Por Dios*, he might have been apprehended right there in the cantina and might be keeping Marco Luís company in the military prison this afternoon. And it could happen at any moment, although he felt that it was unlikely that he would be noticed at this time of day. No one was about on the street, and besides, it was the time of the afternoon *siesta*. Nacho hoped that any *federales* he encountered would not recognize him in his *peón* garments. Furthermore, when he was last seen on the bridge during the battle of Matamoros, he had a full gray beard and shaggy hair. Now his face sported only a small Van Dyke beard, and his hair was shorter. Soon that would change even more. The beard would disappear altogether, if he could find his uncle's house and had a chance to shave. In the meantime, his main worry was that some old acquaintance might recognize him and ask questions Nacho would rather not answer.

To make matters worse, Tomás had disappeared. Evidently, he had simply walked away from the *Taberna* before Nacho returned from his visit to the cantina. Hector said that Tomás had badgered him with a number of questions about the city and the bandits who might visit the *Taberna*. Hector, preoccupied with his duties, had answered in an offhand manner. The next thing he knew, Tomás was gone. Where? Hector had no idea; he didn't know when Tomás left. Would the boy search for Chulo Valdez all by himself? Nacho was beginning to regret that he had not kept Tomás with him, although it had seemed a poor idea earlier. After all, the youth was not familiar with Matamoros. He did not know how to behave in the city, how to avoid the *federales* or how to pretend a subservient attitude. He had slipped away on some errand of his own. Tomás was filled with the revolutionary spirit; riding with Pancho Villa had given the boy a confidence he did not deserve. More than likely, Tomás would bustle about the city calling attention to himself. Well, it could not be helped. Not now.

The fate of Marco Luís worried Nacho above all else. If not for him, Nacho would be content to slip out of Matamoros and rejoin the Ranger troop. He could continue down the narrow street to the river, locate a rowboat, wait until nightfall and simply row two-dozen strokes across the Rio Grande. He would be back in Texas. A tempting idea, but he could not abandon his son-in-law to his fate at the hands of the *federales*; his daughter Rachel would be devastated. Could he help Marco Luís at this point? Nacho had only a vague idea of how he might, perhaps, introduce some confusion into the question of the murder. Was the Indian *mozo* at the Laureles Bar a credible witness? If Nacho could muddy the waters, scramble the *huevos* so to speak, perhaps he could keep Marco Luís alive for a while, at least. Until the *Revolucíon* took another twist and the current hierarchy was upset.

Right now, the pressing need was to alter his appearance even more. To help Marco Luís, Nacho needed to be able to move around the city freely, without fear of recognition. First, though, he must locate the house of his uncle.

Nacho stopped on the sidewalk and tried to get his bearings. His musing had left him somewhat disoriented. He thought he might have entered a better neighborhood. The street did not look that different—framed on both sides with high walls of adobe blocks cemented together irregularly and covered with peeling gray plaster. But it did seem cleaner. He no longer noticed the odor of garbage or waste. Nacho counted the massive wooden doors and tiny windows, barred and boarded, set well back into the walls. Was he nearing his uncle's old house? How many windows did it have? He couldn't recall. There was no sign of movement anyplace on the street, but Nacho could hear a piano playing softly behind one of the windows. He recognized a Mozart etude, played slowly and badly. Nacho smiled; some child was having a piano lesson. This must be the neighborhood he was seeking. Within those walls would be the haciendas of middle class Matamoros, presenting a cold, anonymous face to the outside world but concealing comfortable, even luxurious, dwelling places.

Nacho stepped carefully into the middle of the street and studied the walls along the sidewalk. It had been many years since he had visited his uncle's house. He tried to visualize his cousin Paulo as a grown man, presiding over a hacienda. The image would not come to him.

His eye was caught by a clump of prickly pear cactus growing atop a tin roof and trailing down the wall from above, halfway to the street. That scene looked somehow familiar. Could this be the place? It was worth trying, as good as any. Nacho stepped up to the large oaken door in the wall and rapped on it softly, then again and a little louder. There was no response. He recalled that it was still time for *siesta*; families might be reluctant to answer a knock at this hour. Again Nacho tapped on the door. He glanced up and down the street. He saw no one, but who knew when a patrol of *federales* might appear? He slipped his pistol from the saddlebag and used the handle to pound loudly on the door. *That* should awaken someone.

Suddenly he became aware that a faint voice was speaking to him from behind the door. *"Quién es?"* came faintly to his ears.

"Ygnacio. Nacho Ybarra. Open the door," he said in a hoarse whisper.

"Quién es?" came the question again. A child, he realized. A little girl, perhaps. Would no one else answer?

"Open the door, *niña*. Let me in." Nacho tucked the pistol into his belt and placed his hands flat against the door, willing it to open.

Abruptly, a small window beside the door was pulled aside. A man's face appeared back in the shadows. Brown eyes studied Nacho carefully.

"Who are you? What do you want?"

"I'm looking for my cousin Paulo." Suddenly, Nacho was overcome with fear. This was a mistake. He didn't know who he was talking with. The man might be an off-duty officer. "I have made a mistake," he said. "Please excuse me, *señor*. I apologize for disturbing your rest." And he backed away from the door and began walking rapidly down the street.

Behind him, he heard the creak of the door opening and the sound of footfalls on the brick sidewalk. Nacho slipped his pistol from his belt and whirled around. A short man was following him. The man frowned at the pistol.

"Is that the way you greet your cousin, the son of your favorite uncle, after all these years?" The man raised his hands in mock alarm, smiling broadly. "Have you become a revolutionary, or even worse, a *bandido*? Well, I am your prisoner then. *Mí casa es su casa*, as always, Nacho my old *amigo*."

Nacho hurriedly returned his pistol to his belt and stepped forward, to be embraced by his cousin.

"Paulito! What a pleasure it is to see you again!" Nacho planted a kiss on his cousin's cheek.

"Ugh!" said Paulo, wiping his cheek with the back of his hand. "You need a good scrubbing. But come into the house; it is not safe on the street these days."

As Paulo closed and secured the large door, Nacho stared around the courtyard, drinking in the old images—the walls, the cactus garden, and his aunt's herb garden, still growing by the door to the kitchen. Nothing had really changed, except that it seemed smaller now. And the cactus plants were larger. The giant prickly pear in the corner of the courtyard was covered with bright red blooms. How his aunt had treasured that unusual plant. Each April it favored the patio with its large, odorless blooms, much brighter than the yellow ones on the usual prickly pear.

Several rooms opened directly onto the patio. Nacho remembered roofs made from tightly woven palm leaves, but now he saw that those had been replaced with sheets of tin. The same heavy timbers still framed the dwelling. He could see into the kitchen with its large, wall-to-wall fireplace. Ah, the kitchen. Nacho stopped and broke into a broad grin. Many times he had sat near that fireplace, listening to his uncle tell tales of French and Spanish soldiers.

"*Siéntese*, Nacho. *Aquí.* You look tired, my old friend. Let me get you a cooling drink." Paulo indicated a bench by the door as he hurried into the kitchen. Nacho sat down heavily on the old bench, a rough wooden frame with a rawhide seat, stains revealing its age. This was the peaceful garden of his childhood. He felt his body begin to relax. The past two days had kept him continually on the alert, and now he realized what a toll the strain had taken. He reached across the back of the bench and rubbed his hand across the snow-white plastered wall. The patio brought back memories of playing tag with a youthful Paulo and his sister Ninfa. What had become of her? He rubbed the toe of his sandals across the worn brick flooring. How many times had he skinned his knees on those bricks? And flinched when his aunt carefully applied iodine to the scrapes?

He felt a tug on his pants leg and looked down at a little dark-haired girl in a many-colored dress who looked up at him soberly. "*Quién es?*" said the child in a soft voice.

"Violeta, this is Nacho, your—well, he is your uncle. He will be staying with us for a while. And—he will tell you some stories." Paulo appeared beside the bench and handed Nacho a glass of cool buttermilk. He picked up his daughter in both arms. "But now, my child, we will let your uncle Nacho rest for a while. Let us see what we can find for you in the kitchen. And then, my daughter, back to your *siestita.*"

Alone now, Nacho sipped his buttermilk. He stretched his legs out in front of him. The ragged trousers exposed his bony ankles. He swung his dirty feet from side to side, examining his toes, which reached out the ends of his *huaraches.* Paulo must have many questions. Thankfully, he'd postponed them.

What should he be told? Could Nacho trust his cousin with the full story of his predicament?

Suddenly, a deep tiredness fell across Nacho's shoulders. He carefully set the glass of buttermilk onto the floor. Before he realized it was happening, his head bowed and he drifted into a light slumber.

Half awake, he heard Paulo and his wife, Consuela, walk lightly up and stand in front of the bench, looking down at him. They made a pudgy pair, neatly dressed after their short *siesta*, ready for their usual quiet family evening

"He looks terrible." Consuela stood with her arms folded across her chest, her neat apron unstained by kitchen duties, her red toenails peeking from her sandals.

"He is not so bad. Let him bathe and change clothes. You know, *querida*, Nacho is wanted by the *federales*. When he awakes he will explain why he has sought us out."

Consuela frowned and continued to study Nacho. "Indeed, my husband, I know that he is a wanted man. No doubt there is a good price on his head. I do not like having him here. Suppose someone sees him? We have been fortunate in that the *federales* have left us in peace. We must think of the children. How long does he plan to stay?"

"I suppose he will tell us. Now, let us leave him to sleep for a while." He took Consuela by the arm and turned her back towards the kitchen. "My dear, it will soon be time to feed the children."

Consuela shook her arm free. "My husband, when will the servants return? When will I be freed of these duties— cooking, washing and cleaning? I get so tired."

Paulo sighed. "I will help you, *querida*. As always. When *general* Blanco returns and gathers up his *federales* they will all leave, and we will resume our lives. In the meantime, we must cope." In fact, the number of federal troops in Matamoros was falling already, and the whereabouts of *general* Blanco were unknown. Perhaps, thought Paulo, he could manage to get some of the old servants to return.

Consuela had managed very well at first. Taking over the kitchen duties was like a game, a return to her younger years. But after the household chores became a dull routine, her meals became slipshod affairs. Paulo had taken on more and more of the duties. He, too, longed for a return to more normal conditions in Matamoros.

Paulo was arranging the kitchen table for the children's meal when a shadow fell across him. He turned with a start, to see Nacho standing in the doorway.

"Come into the kitchen, old friend," said Paulo, "and tell me what you are about."

"It is you who must tell me things," replied Nacho. "What is going on in this city?"

He turned to see Consuela and smiled a greeting towards her. "And Consuela. You have grown from the little girl I remember into a fine woman. It is such a pleasure to cast these old eyes upon you again."

Consuela drew herself up to her full height. "I remember you, too, Ygnacio. Yes, I was only a little child when you left us. You were a troublemaker then, and evidently you still are. You are a danger to my family. We do not want you here." Consuela's dark eyes flashed fire; her jaw muscles clenched. She banged her spatula on the top of the iron cook stove, emphasizing each word as she spit them at Nacho.

"You—must—leave—immediately!"

The image in the mirror returned Nacho's gaze without flinching from his scrutiny. *Dios mío*, Consuela had performed a miraculous change in him. She had cut his scraggly gray hair to a short stylish length and colored it black with some of her own hair dye. His small gray beard was gone; only a thin mustache remained, dyed to match his hair. Even his eyebrows were trimmed and tinted so that they matched the color of his mustache. The effect gave him the appearance of a man thirty years younger. Nacho studied himself, turning his head from side to side. He mouthed a few words, *"Buenos días, mis amigos,"* testing the action of his new face. *Maravilloso!* Who would have thought it? He actually felt younger. The *federales* would not recognize him now.

Nacho straightened his spine and stepped back from the mirror, studying the effect of his new jacket on his image. Not a new jacket, really, but a good one that had belonged to his uncle. The black woolen coat with its white piping along the lapels looked, not exactly new, but fresh and well cared for. The white shirt with a large collar and the string tie completed his ensemble. Nacho turned to the side and watched his image as he tugged at the lapels. He raised his hands and looked at his fingers, cleaner than he had seen them in years. A slow soaking in a warm bathtub and plenty of soap had transformed him.

He grasped the front of his black trousers and gave them a tug. His uncle's pants were too large for him. Consuela had put tucks in the back of the waist but they were still loose. One of Paulo's belts fitted him loosely also. In all, though, the effect was good, from his hair down to a pair of Paulo's polished dress boots. Truly, he could pass himself off as an *abogado*, a lawyer. He reached across to the dressing table and picked up his uncle's broad-brimmed black felt hat, complete with tassels on the brim's edge. Carefully, he set it on his head and adjusted it across his brow. He had argued with Consuela about the tassels, asking that she cut them off, but she insisted that he must wear the hat with tassels or not wear it at all. Well, he was no longer trying to be inconspicuous, as he had been in the peasant costume. He laid the hat aside, for the moment at least.

Paulo's image appeared in the mirror behind Nacho's. He, also, was dressed in a formal suit similar to Nacho's.

"I don't know what you did to charm Consuela, my friend. I thought she was going to chase you from our house with that spatula. *Claro*, Nacho, in these past years you have learned much about the ways of women."

"*Ay*, Paulito, that it were true! I know so little. You are the fortunate one, my cousin. Consuela is a jewel. Guard her well."

"Truly, I am fortunate. But what did you say to her? She is like a new person. She orders you from our *hacienda*, and then, before I know it, she has taken you in to barber and to clothe. And, unless my nose betrays me, she will feed you as well." He took Nacho by the arm and led him towards the door.

"Come, Cousin, before we go in to dine, tell me. How did you persuade her to accept you into our house?"

"Consuela followed me to the gate. But before she could open it I sat down on that rawhide bench and invited her to join me. After a moment she did. And then..." Nacho paused and smiled at his cousin.

"And?" insisted Paulo. "And? And?"

"And then," continued Nacho, "And then—I listened to her."

Paulo stopped dead in the doorway. "You—listened? You just listened?"

Nacho waved his hand in a deprecating gesture. "This much I have learned about women, Paulito. Women such as Consuela have much to say, if you will but listen."

"Amazing." Paulo put his hand to his forehead. "But— what did she say? What did she tell you, my friend?"

"Consuela bore a grudge from our childhood days, Paulito. Do you remember? It was nothing of any consequence, just a misunderstanding between a teenager and a child. She used to follow me around, and I teased her. Then one day my little jokes went too far. An imagined slight, not anything I had intended, but I insulted her. You know the deep thoughts of children? Once she described it to me, put it into words, it seemed of little consequence. And then, all was forgiven.

"She had many things to tell me," Nacho continued. "Her life here, the children, the hardships since Matamoros was occupied by the *federales*. I think she has become lonely, my friend. Have so many social contacts disappeared?"

As they reached the threshold of the dining room, Paulo grasped Nacho's elbow and turned him aside, stopping him short. "You should know, Nacho, that Consuela has laundered the clothes you brought with you in your saddlebags. And she has discarded your old peasant clothes and your dirty straw hat and your *huaraches*."

"What?" Nacho gasped. "My hat?"

"It is all right," Paulo said hurriedly. "She remembered the old habits from our childhood. She remembered that we used to hide our *dinero* inside our hatbands. She searched yours before she discarded your straw hat."

Paulo took a handkerchief from his pocket. Holding it in his palm, he carefully unfolded it. He lifted the handkerchief and held it close to Nacho's face. It contained a dozen gold coins. And there in the center was Nacho's Texas Ranger badge.

Nacho held his breath. Suddenly his mind went blank. What could he say, how to explain it?

But Paulo merely chuckled softly. He folded the handkerchief and handed it to Nacho. "My cousin," he said, "I think you have some interesting things to tell us. Over dinner, perhaps? Now, let us go into the *comedor* and see what Consuela has prepared."

Nacho preceded his cousin into the brightly lit dining room, his thoughts racing. Must he continue this charade even further, involving his cousin in a chain of lies? Seeing Consuela seated at the table, smiling at him, Nacho hastily crammed the coins and badge into his jacket pocket. For now, he would continue to be a Mexican gentleman. His stomach urged him to the table.

CHAPTER SEVEN

The oil-burning torches on the back wall of the patio cast a dim pattern of light and shadow, a quiet setting after the hectic hours of the day. Crickets chirped noisily in the lantana bushes. Someplace in the distance, a whippoorwill sang its mournful song. For Nacho, the peaceful scene evoked memories of a happier, simpler time. He leaned against the open doorway of the dining room, a position that allowed him a clear view of the entire courtyard. He took a deep breath and relaxed, enjoying the serenity.

He suddenly realized that he had been unconsciously surveying the courtyard for possible places of concealment or any indication of intruders lurking in the corners. Old habits die hard, habits arising from his carefully honed survival instincts. As his eyes searched through the patterns of light and shadow, his night vision slowly improved. There, in the back corner—was that a figure crouching in the shrubbery? He stepped further into the courtyard to escape the influence of light from the fireplace in the room behind him. He moved slightly to one side, craning his neck and peering more closely into the corners. Nothing there, just the shadows among the flowering shrubs. Nacho stepped back to lean against the wall beside the doorframe, a position where he would no longer be silhouetted against the light. He inhaled deeply, breathing in the mixed perfume of the flowers and the smoke from the torches. He looked up, expecting to see a starry sky, but the haze of smoke and the lights of the town, dim though they were, obliterated the heavens. He started when a night bird swooped low across the patio and quickly vanished over the walls.

Paulo had left him a short time ago, excusing himself with a vague mention of errands that must be done. Nacho was glad to be alone for a few hours. It was a chance to review the day's events and to plan for tomorrow. He had not had the opportunity to explain to his cousin the problems he was facing. How could he manage to get Marco Luís freed? What was to be done about the request of Pancho Villa, that he find the bandit Chulo Valdez? Would Paulo be able to offer any assistance? And Tomás. He'd disappeared, and who knows what mischief the youngster might fall into, given his tendency to sermonize about the *Revolución?*

Nacho turned his thoughts to the dinner that he had shared with Paulo and Consuela. The plump little child who had followed in his young footsteps had metamorphosed into a vibrant young matron, dark eyes flashing in contrast with her bright red lips. She used her makeup well. A careful look at Paulo raised the good possibility that she colored his locks as well as her own.

The evening meal had been a pleasant one, the three of them dining together in a formal setting. Consuela had skillfully directed their conversation. She had diverted their discussions away from the controversial matters of economics and politics and turned them towards the recounting of memories of happier times. Nacho was relieved when he realized that the purpose of his visit, and his presence in Matamoros, were not going to be dinner table topics.

As the meal was served, a young Indian girl had appeared at the table, bearing the main course of beef *asada.* Paulo had gasped in surprise. Consuela silenced him with a shush and a frown, turned to Nacho and continued her commentary on the new planting in the courtyard.

Later, over cigars in front of the fireplace of the *sala*, Paulo had explained his surprise. The *indio* woman was a servant he'd dismissed some months previously. He did not know how Consuela had managed to persuade her to return. Nacho had started to tell Paulo about the arrest of Marco Luís, but Paulo had interrupted him. Later, he'd said, at the moment there was a small errand he must attend to.

Paulo's *cigarro* was flavorful, and he had enjoyed it, but Nacho had come to prefer the bitter little *cigarillos* made from the Bull Durham tobacco favored by the Rangers. Left alone, he carefully measured a little tobacco into a paper, closing the pouch strings with his mouth as the Rangers did. With the pouch still dangling from his lips, he rolled the little cigarette into an irregular tube and moistened it with his saliva. He twisted the end so that the finely ground flakes of tobacco would not fall out. Finally, he struck a match across the plastered wall and lit his cigarette. He took a deep drag, sucking the acrid smoke into his lungs and then exhaling it towards the center of the patio. The smoke drifted slowly away, rising slightly in the still air.

The memories of his childhood in this house kept surging into his consciousness, and he welcomed them as a diversion from the dilemma he was in. There, that back wall, that was the place he could climb and escape into the alley, with the aid of an old mesquite tree now long gone. Young Nacho had learned the silent ways of the *indio* children who were his sometime playmates. Learned, as well, to keep his senses alert and to listen to their messages.

Nacho tugged again at his coat lapels. His uncle's clothes felt good on his body, even the smallish jacket. Perhaps this was where he belonged, a *caballero* in a fine *hacienda* in a small city. A man of respect, a man with an established place in society. As he adjusted the jacket, he was aware of the weight of the revolver he carried in his right coat pocket. It was a small thirty-eight-caliber pistol, gunmetal gray, that he kept as a backup weapon. He had retrieved it from his saddlebags earlier in the evening. Did a weapon such as that one belong in the pocket of a *haciendero*? Perhaps not, but Nacho felt uncomfortable without a firearm, even dining with his cousin's family in his uncle's old house.

The thought raised an issue, one that had lingered in the back of Nacho's mind for the past few hours. What, exactly, was Paulo's position in the society of Matamoros? Consuela complained about the lack of domestic help, but Paulo himself seemed adequately attended. The house and the courtyard were well cared for. Earlier, Nacho had watched two small boys scurrying about in the patio, lighting the lamps. The lack of servants did not seem to extend to the needs of the husband. Well, that was not unknown in Mexican society. And Consuela seemed well prepared to take care of her own position, despite her earlier complaints.

Did Paulo have a profession? Was he a lawyer or an accountant, perhaps? Nacho had not asked, and Paulo had not volunteered anything about his habits. Perhaps his uncle had left Paulo with enough resources that he did not need to earn an income. Was Paulo a *rico*, one of those fortunate few who had now become the targets of the *Revolución*? Suppose I had not decided to leave this home. I might find myself living here, or nearby, in such a house, with my wife and children. A sudden vision of his wife, Gloria, deceased these many years, forced itself to the front of his mind. He reminisced briefly about his house in El Paso and the pleasant hours spent there with his wife and daughter.

Nacho sighed deeply and rubbed his chin with the back of his hand. He forced his thoughts back to the present day. There was more to this household of Paulo's than appeared on the surface. Nacho realized that his cousin was no longer the fat little *muchacho* so full of laughter that he remembered from his younger days. Now he was a grown man. *Un hombre* in his own right. *Ay, ya no más.*

Nacho shrugged his shoulders, readjusting his jacket. Perhaps the open life of the Texas Rangers was his true calling, after all. The camp under the stars, the companionship of like-minded men of purpose, the culture of horses and firearms and the law, the constant sense of danger, all combined to provide a life that was satisfying to a man of action, an *hombre* such as he thought himself to be. But he was getting older, and the life of a Ranger was a dangerous one. Perhaps it was time for him to change professions once again.

He felt again in his pocket for the badge, and caressed it between his thumb and forefinger. During the evening meal, Paulo had wanted to talk about that badge, how Nacho had acquired it, but Consuela had stifled that conversation, *gracias a Dios.* He still did not know how much he could tell Paulo, how far he could be trusted with information that could place Nacho in great peril here in Matamoros. First, he needed to discover Paulo's attitudes towards the *Revolución.* He felt a brief twinge of guilt as he realized that he was planning to deceive his cousin. Nacho would prefer to keep his own council and let others assume what they would. In his present circumstances that did not seem possible. Each must play the cards fate deals him.

The feel of the circle-star badge between his fingers brought back the memory of the two *americanos* in the bar that afternoon. *They were wrong*, he thought. 'Ain't no Mex Rangers,' one had said. There certainly had been, and were, Texas Rangers who were Mexicans. Not citizens of Mexico but *tejanos*, Texans of Mexican descent. Why, there had been *indios* who were full-fledged Texas Rangers. An *indio* once held the rank of captain. The *americano's* remark had annoyed Nacho, even though he felt uncertain about his own situation. Exactly when had he ceased to be an employee, a horse wrangler and cook, and become a regular Ranger? Perhaps when he first drew his Colt *pistola* and fought with the troop, riding hard to pursue a small party of *bandidos*. For Nacho, becoming a Ranger had been a gradual process, not a matter of enlistment. And it had culminated when the captain had handed him his badge. No ceremony, no handshake, he just handed over a badge and said, "Here."

Nacho straightened his shoulders. He dropped the remains of his cigarette into a flowerbed and started to turn back into the room. From the corner of his eye, he saw a small movement in the courtyard, a little rustle of foliage behind the hibiscus bush growing against the wall. He was right! Earlier, his instincts had told him that someone watched from the shadows in the patio. Nacho leaned forward, away from the wall beside the doorway, crouched down, and slipped his small *pistola* from his jacket pocket. Now his senses were at full alert. Survival instincts took over. He scanned the patio, looking for other places of concealment. He quickly considered and discarded several potential routes that he might use for an escape. He was crouched beside a wall between two lighted doorways, and if he moved in either direction, his silhouette would offer an easy target.

Nacho concentrated on the hibiscus bush and the shadow behind it. Now that he was sure someone was hiding there, he was able to make out more of the figure. It was not a large man. Indeed, it was not a man at all, but only a boy! Nacho lowered his revolver. His eyes scanned the patio wall, and he saw that there was a large chinaberry tree growing in the alley, a tree with branches hanging close to the patio wall. He smiled to himself as memories of his own escapades in this house returned to him. More than once he had returned from a late night adventure by climbing into such a tree and dropping over the patio wall. That boy was surely Paulo's son Mauro. The boy had slipped over the wall into the patio and landed behind the hibiscus bush. Now he was waiting for Nacho to disappear, so that he could scoot quickly across to his room. Nacho smothered a chuckle. He straightened up and returned the *pistola* to his pocket.

Nacho teased the boy. He took a few slow steps forward towards the center of the patio and yawned expansively, stretching his arms. Slowly, he walked across the patio towards the guest bedroom, taking care to step noisily as he passed the big hibiscus bush. After he passed it, he slowed down, listening carefully, and was rewarded when he heard the faint rustle of leaves. Mauro must be hastening off towards his room. Nacho did not have to look over his shoulder. He laughed to himself.

Once he reached the guest room, Nacho took the pistol from his coat pocket. Well, now it seemed unnecessary. He returned it to its small holster in the bottom of his saddlebags. As he turned to retrace his steps, he noticed his gun belt, hanging on a peg beside the mirror. On an impulse, he reached for it and strapped it on, pulling the belt tight against his trousers. The tails of his jacket covered the holster, but the big handle of the Colt made an obvious bulge. Nacho examined himself in the mirror and smiled in satisfaction. He judged it to be an imposing image, a blend of the city *don* and the *caballero*.

His reverie vanished when he heard the big outer door swing open. Someone entered the patio, coming from the street. He slipped out of the room and into the shadows of the patio. What now? But it was merely Paulo coming home. Nacho frowned; Paulo was followed by three other *hombres*. What was this?

Paulo gestured towards the dining room, and the group moved in that direction. They spoke softly; Nacho could not distinguish the words. He crouched, back to the wall. His hand found the butt of his Colt, and he loosened it in its holster, ready to bring it into action. What was Paulo doing? Had Nacho been betrayed by his cousin? A sudden feeling of panic swept over him. It would be best to take no chances, to slip from the house into the night. Staying in a low crouch, he started to creep along the wall in the direction of the main doorway. The group of men went into the dining room; now he could hear Paulo calling his name.

Nacho reached the corner of the patio. Another twenty feet straight along the wall and he would reach the big door to the street. He slipped carefully through the shrubbery. His attention was on the dining room; he was startled when he suddenly bumped into somebody directly in his path. His gasp was met by another one. He looked down into the eyes of the boy Mauro, who was cringing away from him in the darkness. Nacho grabbed the boy's arm with one hand and lifted the other to his lips, a finger signaling for quiet. The boy nodded. They exchanged a long glance; now they were co-conspirators in this game.

Paulo stepped out into the patio, calling Nacho's name over and over. Well, Nacho thought, this particular card would have to be turned. He didn't want to put Mauro in danger. At least they would not expect him to be well-armed. He patted Mauro's shoulder and slipped out into the faint torch light. Mauro obediently remained crouched beside the wall.

"Ah, there you are, Nacho. Come. I have some *hombres* I wish you to meet. Come inside."

Nacho stopped just inside the room, squinting into the light. Through lowered eyelids he looked carefully at the newcomers. Two men stood facing him. They were dressed in simple brown woolen suits, the customary garb of businessmen. Each wore a white shirt with the collar closed by a black string tie, and formal boots peeked out from their trouser legs. They might indeed be businessmen, thought Nacho, but one never knew. They had no obvious weapons. If they had come to capture him, they must mean to do it by stealth; they did not appear imposing. The third man had stationed himself by the fireplace. He was a tall *hombre* dressed in gray coat and slacks over a blue shirt open at the neck. He stood with folded arms, watching the others.

Paulo directed Nacho's attention to the two in front. "Nacho, may I present *señor* Ortíz, *presidente del Banco de Matamoros.*" The small man bobbed his head in response, hat held in front of him in both hands. Nacho nodded, his attention fixed on the hat. Both of the man's hands were visible on the hat brim. No *pistola* was concealed within the hat, pointed towards him. The man seemed nervous but otherwise harmless.

Paulo stepped over to stand beside the other man. "And this, this is my friend *señor* Riviera, who is *principal del consejo.*"

Riviera scowled at Nacho from beneath large black eyebrows that matched his heavy mustache. His hands were clenched into fists, and he shifted from one foot to the other. He did not bow or acknowledge the introduction in any way. Neither did Nacho. This one would bear watching.

"And finally, Nacho, meet *señor* Steiner." The third man nodded and smiled as though amused by the proceedings. He was leaning against the edge of the fireplace, his right elbow on the mantle, his left hand thrust into his trouser pocket. His manner was relaxed. He was hatless, and his brown hair was neatly trimmed. He was clean-shaven. Nacho gave Steiner a long look, appraising him carefully. Of the three, this man seemed to be the most dangerous.

These would appear to be *hombres muy importantes*. Nacho waited for Paulo to explain the reason for the assembly. His cousin was smiling broadly, his hand on Nacho's shoulder, obviously enjoying himself. Nacho kept his attention centered on the visitors.

"And, *señores*, this is my cousin Ygnacio Ybarra. He may hold the answer to our problems. He is a well-known fighting man. Recently, he has killed one of the hated *rinches*."

Nacho stared at Paulo, wide-eyed. What was he saying? Killed a Texas Ranger? Nacho swallowed and licked his lips, but he found himself speechless. He turned back to face the newcomers. Their eyes now seemed menacing, and he nearly flinched under the intensity of their stares. What in the world was Paulo trying to do?

Paulo grinned broadly. "It is true. Nacho, show them the badge you have taken from the Ranger you killed." He turned to his companions. "It is truly said, no member of the *rinches* would ever give up his badge unless he was dead."

Paulo held his arms out toward Nacho, palms open wide. "My cousin," he said with a broad smile. "Show them the badge!"

The circle-star badge made the rounds, each man examining it closely, turning it to catch the light from the fireplace. The silver badge was new, unscratched by wear, with the words "TEXAS RANGER" engraved on the outer circle. Inside the circle was the plain five-pointed star, the symbol of the State of Texas. The letters "Co. D" were centered within the star itself. The circle-star badge was a mark of distinction. The man who wore it was automatically set apart from other lawmen. Each Ranger carried the reputation of the entire force upon his shoulders, and he was expected to keep that reputation intact through brave and prompt action in the face of danger. In Mexico, the circle star badge was a different kind of symbol. It spoke of deadly gunplay, of violent outbursts directed against any Mexican who was so unfortunate as to be in the wrong place when the hated *rinches* opened gunfire. The Rangers' unofficial creed was "Shoot first and ask questions later." Mexicans translated this motto as "Shoot and then see who you killed."

Finally, Paulo returned the badge to Nacho, reaching out his arm and holding it carefully between thumb and forefinger. He stepped back to join the others as they stood in a row staring at Nacho. Slowly, Nacho slipped the badge into his jacket pocket. He felt relieved to have it out of sight. He didn't want to respond to Paulo's conclusion that he'd murdered a Ranger. After a period of silence, the question he got was of a different sort.

"*Señor* Ybarra, what brings you to the streets of Matamoros?" The tall man, Steiner, had offered the question. He unfolded his arms and stood erect, a slight smile curling the corners of his mouth.

Nacho met his gaze and forced a smile of his own. This area was one he could discuss without straying too far from the facts.

"I have a relative, a son-in-law, imprisoned here. I have come to see about getting him released. Into my custody."

"Aha! So that is why you have come to my house." Paulo waved his arms with enthusiasm. "I had wondered what brought you back to see me, after all these years." Nacho looked thoughtfully at Paulo. What did he mean?

"That is very noble of you." Steiner folded his arms and leaned back against the fireplace mantel. "Especially considering that you are a wanted men here yourself. I am told that *general* Blanco would execute you if he captured you. You are indeed a brave man, *señor*."

Nacho frowned at Steiner. His Spanish was soft, strangely accented and somewhat hard to follow. Had he just been threatened by this man? Nacho took a step towards him.

Paulo moved forward and stepped between the two men. "That is true, *señor* Steiner, and Nacho is well aware of it. You should have seen the disguise he wore when he arrived here this afternoon." Paulo forced a chuckle, then turned towards Nacho. "What is the name of this unfortunate man, your son-in-law? I will see what I can do."

"Indeed, *señor* Ybarra, you are most fortunate yourself in the choice of relatives." Smiling, Steiner gestured towards Paulo. "It is not difficult to get a prisoner released, when your cousin is the police commissioner himself."

Nacho rocked back on his heels, taking in a deep breath. His thoughts whirled. Paulo the police commissioner! So that is what he meant. Suddenly Nacho considered that he might have stepped into the lion's den. Here he was, a wanted criminal with a price on his head, asking help from the person responsible for the police department. He glanced quickly at Paulo, unsure what to do. Could this be a trap after all? Perhaps police officers had slipped into the patio while his attention was diverted. And he was standing with his back to the open doorway into the patio. Move! Move! He took a quick step to the side and eased back against the wall. His right hand moved of its own volition, loosening the pistol in its holster.

"Although his powers are limited under the present..." Steiner stopped himself and peered closely at Nacho. Then he pointed at him, turning to the others.

"Look at him, *señores*. He did not know! We have surprised him."

Nacho glanced from man to man, breathing heavily now, every sense at full alert. Possible actions sprang to mind but were immediately discarded. He was well and truly trapped. He focused his attention on Steiner, feeling sure that the action would center on him.

He slowly became aware that Paulo was speaking to him, softly.

"...and of course you are welcome here, Nacho, and please be assured that you are in no danger from me or from my friends. I have brought them here to talk with you about our own problems here. Please, Nacho, we mean you no harm."

The big man Riviera spoke for the first time, his head lowered, eyes glaring through his heavy eyebrows. "You should understand, *señor*, that you are wanted by *general* Blanco and the military, not by the civil authorities."

"True, true," exclaimed Paulo. "As I said, you are perfectly safe in this house with me and my friends."

"In fact, *señor*, we have a proposition to discuss with you." Riviera looked at his colleagues. Ortíz nodded his encouragement. "We are looking for a bold leader," he continued. "Paulo tells us that you are such an *hombre*. We have a plan," said Riviera. "Permit me to explain it to you."

"*Señores*, a moment. Let us consider this further." Steiner shuffled his feet and pulled a large white handkerchief from his pants pocket. He shook it open and dabbed at his forehead with it.

"I find it warm in this room, sorry." Steiner continued patting his forehead, his eyes downcast. "Perhaps we should reconsider before we involve this *hombre* in our plans."

Suddenly, Nacho found himself on familiar ground. Steiner was wiping his forehead with his left hand. His right had moved out of sight, behind his back. *Por Dios*, this was a game Nacho knew well. Always watch for the gun hand. That right hand was feeling for a weapon concealed in back of the man's trousers.

Nacho wasted no time in pulling his Colt. He thrust the barrel at Steiner and cocked the hammer. Steiner froze. When Nacho gestured upwards with the barrel of his gun, Steiner slowly raised both hands above his head.

"Nacho, what are you doing?" Paulo started towards him, but Nacho waved him back, gesturing with his left hand as he kept his attention fixed on Steiner's face. "Turn around, *señor*," he said.

Steiner started to pivot slowly, his hands held aloft. Nacho stepped forward and grasped his shoulder, spinning him around. Beneath the back of Steiner's jacket Nacho found what he was looking for. It was a pistol, one of a design not familiar to him. He examined it briefly and then thrust it into the top of his trousers.

"Now, *señores*. Are all of you armed as well?" He spoke without taking his eyes from Steiner, who stood still, facing the fireplace, his hands well above his head.

"Only a fool ventures out on these streets at night without a weapon." Riviera slowly opened his jacket, revealing a small pistol in a holster under his armpit. When Nacho gestured with the barrel of his Colt, Riviera slowly withdrew the pistol and placed it carefully on a small table beside him.

Suddenly, Ortíz began fumbling with his trousers. He extracted a pistol from his pants pocket and laid it down beside Riviera's. His hands in front of him, palms outward, Ortíz stepped away from the table.

Nacho kept the Colt leveled at Steiner. He glanced over towards Paulo and raised his eyebrows. "And you, my cousin?"

"Nacho, I have no weapon concealed. This is my home. There is no need. Besides, Consuela would not permit it."

"*Ay*, did I hear my husband speak my name in a disrespectful tone of voice? But what is this?"

Consuela swept into the room, followed by the Indian serving maid who carried a tray with glassware. Consuela still wore her long dinner dress. Chin up, carriage erect, her small figure made an imposing image.

"I have brought brandy for you and your guests, Paulo, and I find this display of guns. I have asked that you not bring guns into this house. I have made an exception for Nacho, but now I see he is abusing my hospitality."

"*Lo siento. Discúlpeme, señora.*" Nacho holstered his *pistola*. He added Steiner's pistol to the other two on the side table. Steiner, his back still turned, watched over his shoulder. Not until Nacho deposited the pistol on the table did he turn around.

"Now, *señores*, share a glass of brandy and dispense with these silly guns." Consuela gestured to the maid, who carried the tray to Paulo. As the brandy was poured and the glasses passed around, the men eyed each other. Then, upon Paulo's gesture, they raised their glasses in a mutual salute towards Consuela. With a smile and a nod, Consuela turned and marched from the room, with the maid close on her footsteps.

Nacho carefully placed his glass on the table. He turned his attention to Steiner. The tall man was now facing him, hands at his sides. He no longer wore a sarcastic smile.

Nacho picked up Steiner's pistol and turned it over in his hands. "*Señor*, I have seen many pistols, but this design is not familiar to me."

"It is a German Pistole '08. You may know of it under the name of its designer, Georg Luger." Steiner started to reach for the weapon but changed his mind under Nacho's glare. "It is an automatic pistol, firing a nine-millimeter bullet from a clip in the butt."

Nacho hefted the pistol, feeling its weight. It was much lighter than his Colt. He sighted along the barrel.

"Keep it. As a gift."

"I have no need of it." Ammunition would be a problem anyway, thought Nacho. He started to return the weapon to Steiner but abruptly changed his mind. Steiner made an abortive reach towards the pistol but stopped when Nacho tucked it into his trouser band.

"*Señores*, let us put these *pistolas* away." Nacho's Colt was now holstered, but he kept his hand near the butt and continued to watch Steiner. He felt in control of the situation, but he still did not trust the tall man. The other two Mexicans stepped forward, retrieved their pistols and slid them into pockets.

"Good, good." Paulo clapped his hands. "Now tell us, Nacho, the name of your son-in-law who is in prison. I'm sure we can be of assistance in this matter."

Well, why not? Sooner or later this issue would have to be resolved.

"He is Marco Luís Gonzales. I do not know where he is being held."

"I do." Paulo gave a sigh and looked down at his hands. "He is being held for murder, in my jail. But the military authorities are holding him, not the police. They will probably execute him. It is out of my hands." Paulo looked up at Nacho, squared his shoulders and thrust out his chest. "I will, however, see what could be done."

"He will not be executed anytime soon." Steiner was smiling again. "No one can be executed without *general* Blanco's direct order. And *general* Blanco is out of the city."

"What is this?" exclaimed Riviera.

"You see, *señores*, my friendship with the officers of the army has its rewards. I have discovered that *general* Blanco has gone to *ciudad Victoria*, supposedly in pursuit of some kind of military adventure."

"You know this for a fact?" Riviera asked.

"It is a fact that Blanco has left town, whether to *ciudad Victoria,* I do not know. Captain Arredondo has assumed command. But he will do nothing without orders from Blanco. *Señor* Ybarra, your son-in-law is safe for the moment."

Nacho rubbed his chin while he digested this information. He was not surprised to hear that Marco Luís was a prisoner of the military, at least that military represented by *general* Blanco's army. If Steiner was correct, there would be no execution anytime soon.

A vague plan that had been tugging at Nacho's brains was beginning to take form. Possibly, he could use Pancho Villa and his rebels to get Marco Luís freed. Without its strong leader, Blanco's army would begin to dissolve. The officers would contend among themselves for command. The soldiers would take the opportunity to desert and slip away towards their homes. Perhaps, he thought, just perhaps, Pancho Villa could do me an enormous favor. On an impulse, he pulled the strange little revolver from his trousers and turned it over in his hand. He looked expectantly at Steiner.

"As I said. Keep it as a gift. You will find it a more effective weapon than that antique weapon you carry."

"I thank you." Nacho tucked the little *pistola* into the top of his trousers. As for his antique weapon—well, the Colt was an old model, a single action Peacemaker, but it had served Nacho well.

"*Gracias,*" he repeated. He would take the little pistol to Villa who, he knew, would be pleased with the little toy.

"*Está en buenas manos,*" said Steiner.

"And now," Nacho said, his gaze sweeping across the group of men. "And now, you were going to ask my assistance in some matter." He looked squarely to Paulo. "How may I help you?"

Paulo drew himself up. "Nacho," he said forcefully, "we wish you to lead our armies in the invasion of Texas." Nacho, surprised and astounded, looked at the others. Ortíz and Riviera returned his solemn gaze. Steiner, the smile still on his lean face, gave a little snort. Nacho was speechless.

CHAPTER EIGHT

Our plan will take the *Revolución* forward!" Paulo's eyes sparkled with excitement. He waved his hands, fingers outspread, and looked back and forth at his colleagues, who returned his agitation with silence. Paulo had brought chairs from the dining table, wooden ladderback chairs with rawhide seats, and arranged them in a circle. Nacho sat facing Paulo and two of his friends. Steiner had ignored the chair offered to him and remained standing near the fireplace. Nacho watched him out of the corner of his eye. Steiner seemed displeased by Paulo's enthusiasm. He continued to shift his position, now leaning on the fireplace mantle and then standing erect. He kept folding and unfolding his arms. Perhaps, thought Nacho, the *señor* Steiner is unhappy with the direction in which Paulo is taking this conversation. Perhaps he is not pleased that these *hombres* are involving me in their plans. Nacho was not so pleased about it either. He returned his attention to Paulo.

"Here in Matamoros," Paulo continued, "we are in a position to expand the State of Tamaulipas to its original size. Perhaps it could become Nuevo Santader again, as it was before the *americanos* took it away from us."

Nacho's full attention was now focused on his cousin. What was this? What was he trying to say? Restore Nuevo Santader? The old Spanish colonial province that included northern Mexico and modern Texas? How could this happen?

"It is time…" Paulo looked around at his companions, seeking their agreement. "It is time to restore the disputed lands to our country. I am speaking of the territory between the *río Nueces* and the *río Bravo*."

Riviera held up a hand to interrupt Paulo. "It was stolen from Mexico more than sixty years ago." The big man leaned forward, hands on his knees, his eyes boring into Nacho's. "Ybarra," he continued, "We intend to recover the Nueces territory. We think…" He sat back in his chair and looked at each of his colleagues. "We think we should set up a new State, with territory reaching from the *río Nueces* west across to Laredo."

"At least we should recover the Nueces territory." Paulo glared at Riviera. "How it is added to Mexico, how it would be governed, need not be decided now." Riviera returned Paulo's glare but settled into his chair in silence.

"You see, my cousin, that the time—the timing is right for such an action." Paulo, eyebrows raised, waited for a reply, a comment, any thought from Nacho.

Nacho bit his lip and stared at his cousin. This was worse than mere stupidity. This was madness. The *hombres* were waiting for him to comment on their scheme. He did not know what to say. He looked at each of the men in turn, trying to evaluate their moods. What could they possibly expect from him?

The Nueces territory, he knew, had been claimed by both Texas and Mexico following the Texas revolution. Texas had claimed the Rio Grande—which Mexico called the *río Bravo*—as the border between the two nations. Mexico had insisted that the Nueces River, some 150 miles to the north, should be the border. Between the Nueces and Rio Grande rivers was a desolate, barren stretch of land—the Wild Horse Desert. General Zachary Taylor took an American army south to Corpus Christi, a little seaport at the mouth of the Nueces, to protect the U.S. claim to the territory. Then, when ordered by President Polk, Taylor had marched south and defeated a Mexican army near the Rio Grande. This war, and the Treaty of Guadalupe Hidalgo which followed it, firmly established the Rio Grande—the *río Bravo*—as the border. The United States had extended its territory into New Mexico, Arizona and California as the result of that conquest. The most disputed area was still the Nueces strip, between the Rio Grande and Nueces rivers.

Like other ranchers, Nacho's ancestors had found a good grassland in the Nueces territory, despite the low rainfall. Land along the two river valleys was productive. The lower Rio Grande valley, in particular, was well suited to agriculture. Americans had been moving into the valley during the past two decades. Nacho had seen farms, orchards, and small homesteads develop among the former ranching country. The new railroad lines provided a means for shipping fruit and vegetable harvests, and these had been abundant in the past few years. And now? To try to recapture the territory for Mexico—what were these *hombres* thinking? This seemed to Nacho to be a wild dream, not the culmination of a revolution. It could not possibly succeed. He could not think what to say. What was their motive for such a brash suggestion? What could they gain from such a plan, even if by some wild chance it succeeded?

Ortíz leaned forward and engaged Nacho's attention. The little banker raised his hand, palm outwards.

"Already the *yanquis* are leaving the valley of the *río Bravo*. We can chase out the rest of them. Mexicans now living in Texas will join us."

"There is only a small garrison of *soldados* across the river in Brownsville," Riviera interrupted, silencing the banker with a hand on the little man's knee. "We can easily defeat them," he continued.

"And the *rinches*," Paulo added. He punched Nacho on the shoulder, a playful gesture from childhood days. "Nacho, you have shown that you can defeat them. They are not very numerous anyway. Those Texas Rangers could not stand up to our numbers."

Nacho slowly pulled his tobacco pouch from his shirt pocket. He needed time to think how to answer these arguments. There was some truth in them, he knew. Americans were beginning to leave the Valley because of the bandit raids. The army was undermanned and ineffective. The Texas Rangers were few in number. Nevertheless, this effort, this silly war, could not possibly succeed. Paulo and his friends watched quietly as Nacho went through the ritual of making a Bull Durham cigarette, lighting it, and taking a deep draw of smoke into his lungs.

As he exhaled, Nacho looked carefully at the conspirators, each in turn, while he considered what he might say to them. Paulo, Riviera and Ortíz silently waited for his comments. Their eyes searched his face. Steiner, still standing at the fireplace, ignored them. He had added nothing to their arguments. What was his part in these proceedings? Nacho studied him for a moment.

Finally, Nacho waved the cigarette smoke away from his face. "*Señores*, you will need an army. I do not see it. Where will you find *soldados*?"

"But it is all around you." Ortíz waved his arms in the air. "The bandits of the border will be a formidable army. They only need the leadership of a strong man. A true *macho*. Then they will sweep across the river and destroy the *norteamericanos*."

"They are a rabble. Not an army. They would not know how to behave in a military operation." Nacho sat forward in his chair, leaning towards Paulo and Ortíz. "These border outlaws are not truly revolutionaries or soldiers. They are jackals. They raid only the weak, unprotected farmers and storekeepers. When they meet any resistance they ride for the border and slip across to Mexico. You would need *leónes*, not *chacales*. Here in Matamoros you have not even been able to displace the army of *general* Blanco." He sat back and took another drag on his little *cigarillo*.

"The soldiers of Blanco's army are deserting." Steiner spoke for the first time, softly, head down, speaking into the fireplace. "Every day that army becomes smaller. They have no leadership." He turned to face the others. "I do not think Blanco's army would offer much resistance. They could be persuaded to join us."

"And," offered Paulo, "we could ask one of the revolutionary *generales* to join us. Perhaps we could ask Pancho Villa. Why, he might come down from Chihuahua to fight with us."

Nacho stared at Paulo. Had he heard that Villa was in the area? This plan had the potential to escalate rapidly, in a different direction. If Villa knew of this plan, he would not only be interested, he might take command, whether or not he was invited to do so. But Nacho doubted that Villa would attack the United States. He was in debt to his American friends, some of whom fought with his army. No, this was not likely. If Villa could assemble a large army here on the Border, he would march it towards Mexico City, not across the Border.

He was glad that he had not brought Tomás with him to Paulo's house. He hoped to keep Villa's presence a secret from these *hombres*.

"We have a leader here in Matamoros." All heads turned towards Riviera. "He is a local chieftain, Chulo Valdez. You may have heard of him." Nacho glanced over Riviera's shoulder at Steiner, who was smiling his amusement.

"The name is familiar to me." Nacho continued to look at Steiner, who turned back to the fireplace. "From what I have heard, I would think he is just another border bandit." He turned back to Riviera. "*Señor*, you would need more than men. Artillery. Cannons. Certainly, modern arms and materiel for your army."

"That," said Paulo, "that is where *señor* Steiner can help us. He is a German national. A representative of the government of Germany."

Steiner turned away from the fireplace and looked toward the courtyard. "Well, *señores*, let us just say that I am here in an unofficial capacity. I offer my friendship, and perhaps my services, to aid neighbors in distress. Some assistance with armaments can be arranged." He smiled at Nacho. "Just as the Americans have been assisting Pancho Villa. Not officially."

Nacho frowned at Steiner. "I believe, *señor*, that such assistance has come to an end. The *Estados Unidos* no longer supports Villa; they have come to an accommodation with *presidente* Carranza. Or so I am told," he added. Had he said too much? Steiner continued to smile at him.

Nacho rose to his feet. He adjusted his clothing and walked slowly over to the fireplace to stand beside Steiner. He must consider his next comments very carefully. There was opportunity here, a chance to help Marco Luís and to make contact with the bandit Chulo Valdez and thus keep the promise he had made to Pancho Villa. Perhaps this would all work out to his advantage after all. He would need to move carefully, so as not to become involved in an unfortunate military adventure.

Nacho straightened his shoulders and turned away from the fireplace. "*Señores*, I must think on these matters." He directed his attention towards Steiner. He was beginning to think that the German was the true instigator of this strange plan.

"*Señor* Steiner, I cannot believe that the *yanquis*, or the *tejanos* either, would not put up a massive resistance to your efforts. You would be stirring up an ant's nest." He gestured towards Paulo and his friends, still seated in their chairs. "You would bring disaster upon these people."

"*Señor* Ybarra. I have reason to believe that the Americans will become occupied elsewhere." Steiner lowered his voice. "Soon, I hear, the United States will enter the war to fight against my country, Germany. But their military is not prepared for it. I do not think they can fight two wars. No, *señor*, you would not meet a massive resistance from the *yanquis*."

Nacho took a deep breath as the implications of Steiner's comments settled into his thoughts. This, then, must be Steiner's motive. He wanted to create a border diversion that would occupy the armed forces of the United States. Their capacity to make war on Germany would be reduced. In fact, they might prefer to fight in North America and stay out of Europe altogether. The impetus for this rash plan was beginning to come clear. Very likely, Steiner was indeed the guiding force behind this misguided attempt at a border war.

Nacho doubted that the border bandits, Chulo Valdez and his kindred, would be able to mount a significant military threat, even with modern weapons. But Pancho Villa was another matter. Nacho looked into Steiner's impassive face and decided that he would do whatever he could to see that Steiner and Pancho Villa did not meet and come to some arrangement. In Villa's present state of mind, his losses to Carranza, his loss of face in North America—well, Villa might try something outrageous.

He raised another objection. "Such a war would require a large amount of *dinero*. Where would you find it?"

Paulo laughed. "As I told you, Nacho, *señor* Ortíz is *presidente del Banco de Matamoros.*"

Nacho stared at his cousin. So this is the motivation for Ortíz. Funding a war is always very profitable for a *banco*. He himself had profited well from the sale of weapons to the *villistas* when he made his home in El Paso. No doubt Steiner and Ortíz had cooperated in planning the financial details of traffic in armaments.

"And you, *señor* Riviera, what do you stand to gain from this conquest." Nacho smiled at Riviera, who scowled at him for a moment.

"The Riviera family owned large grazing lands across the *río Bravo*," he said. "I simply wish to see my lands recovered from the *norteamericanos.*"

So, the motives for this trio of conspirators were now clear. Nacho felt his confidence soaring. This was no patriotic upwelling, no surge of passion for the *Revolución*. It was a play for power and, of course, *dinero*. Always, money would come to the surface, even in a city suffering occupation by a hostile army.

Except for Paulo. His cousin, ever a romantic, would truly believe in the cause, the plan they had devised. *Ay*, Paulito, you are in over your *cabeza*. Must I extricate you as well as myself from this strange predicament?

Nacho turned aside and spoke directly to Paulo. "This is a matter for careful consideration. You realize, my cousin, that my heart is heavy with the knowledge that Marco Luís lies helpless in your jail. Helping the boy must be my most important consideration." There, he thought, that lays it out for all of them to understand. The four men exchanged looks. Riviera nodded at Ortíz, who then nodded at Paulo. The message had been plain, and it had been understood. First, before anything else, Marco Luís must be set free.

After a moment, Paulo squared his shoulders. It would be his responsibility.

CHAPTER NINE

The campfire had burned down to a bed of coals. A big enamelware coffeepot snuggled among them. Red Regan squatted beside the little fire, one booted foot beneath him and the other extended. Breakfast was over, but his hand still cradled a tin cup of coffee, now grown cold. Behind him he could hear his small squad of Texas Rangers grumbling to each other as they worked to erect a barricade of logs from palm trees. Regan watched the coals slowly cool into white ashes. He rubbed his chin, a wry smile on his face. If this was what he could expect in a leadership role, well, the Rangers should look elsewhere. As their sergeant and leader of the squad, Regan was expected to oversee their activities, but he would have been more comfortable if he were actually doing some of the work.

Regan could sympathize with the youngsters. The Rangers as a group were experienced in the rough ways of outdoor camps. Each maintained his own equipment, including his mounts, his weapons and other gear. A Ranger must be prepared to be self-sufficient, to prepare or arrange for his own meals, to travel alone on assignments when necessary. A Ranger would swing an ax for firewood or shelter. But the menial labor required for construction of an extensive barricade fell outside the usual activities. Regan's squad was not enjoying the experience.

He turned to look when he heard Whitey's voice giving instructions about construction of the barricade. When Captain Maddox had put Regan in charge of the squad, Red had worried about Whitey's reaction to his field promotion. They had operated as a team for years, somewhat balancing each other's strengths and weaknesses. Whitey was a man of instant action, whereas Regan tended to be more thoughtful, evaluating first and acting later. Regan thought of Whitey as the ultimate Texas Ranger: a superb horseman, a crack shot with rifle and pistol, and a determined fighting man with a strong sense of duty. So he was relieved when Whitey simply accepted Regan's promotion. In fact, once Regan had made it clear what had to be done, Whitey had led the others down to the river, where they chopped down palm trees and hauled the logs back to the site Captain Maddox had selected.

Once the captain, in his own terse manner, had explained his plans for a barricade, Regan could see the logic behind it. The barricade was located well up slope from the river crossing that Red and Whitey had scouted the previous evening, a site where bandits might be expected to cross into Texas. A narrow meadow of prairie grasses led up a steep slope away from the river. It was flanked on both sides by thorny, impenetrable brush. A hundred yards up the slope, the grassy meadow took a dogleg turn towards the west. It was there that Captain Maddox had selected a site for a barricade. The location was not visible from the river, but any traffic crossing the Rio would be funneled up to the site. A Ranger squad forted up there would surprise any bandit raiders who used the crossing.

This barricade was a new development for Captain Maddox and Company D. They had ranged up and down the Valley, responding whenever bandit activities were reported. As a mobile force, the Rangers were not very effective on the Border. In the Indian Wars, the Rangers would set out to pursue hostile raiders as far as they could. Sometimes they managed to overtake their quarry. At the very least, they dispersed the band of Indians. These tactics were not effective in dealing with the bandits of the Border. Once the bandits had crossed the Rio Grande into Mexico, they were safe from further pursuit by the Rangers. On occasion, an individual Ranger had been known to cross into Mexico, but not an entire troop.

If Captain Maddox intended the Rangers to man a number of little barricades, then their forces would be spread too thin. Regan did not know if this was to be a temporary arrangement or a permanent one. Captain Maddox kept his own council and did not share his plans with members of his command.

Regan set his coffee cup down beside his boot and carefully flexed his hand. A sharp pain shot up his arm, causing him to wince. Earlier he had attempted to help set a palm log in place and had caught his hand under it. The damage did not seem to him to be serious; he could move all his fingers, but bruising was beginning to appear on them. Regan frowned; it was his right hand, his gun hand. None of the others had seen what had happened, but Whitey had looked at him quizzically when he retreated to the campfire. He flexed the hand again. He doubted that he could hold a pistol with it.

Behind him, a horse gave a loud whinny. Regan turned to look. Whitey's big red horse, Cimarron, was calling for attention. Cimmie towered over the other horses in the *remuda*. Most Rangers preferred the smaller, more agile mustangs to the big eastern horses. The mustangs, wild horses taken from the prairie grasslands, were relatives of Indian ponies. They could forage off the native grasses, subsist on little water, and carry their riders on hundred mile treks. Each Ranger had a string of several mustangs. Whitey was the only Ranger in the group to ride a big war horse. The two of them, man and horse, made an effective fighting unit on the Border where chases needed bursts of speed rather than endurance. However, Cimmie needed his oats; grass would not support his metabolism for very long. He whinnied again.

Regan looked across the campfire towards the jumble of blankets, saddles and baggage that marked the campsite. Perhaps this would become a more or less permanent site. The Rangers might have to spread canvas and settle in. If so, Regan thought, the little squad would enjoy the chance to rest for a few days.

A loud "Gawdammit" shifted Regan's attention back to the squad. Dolph Krieger hopped on one foot, holding the other one. Krieger was a recent recruit, a local boy from further up the Valley. A lanky youngster with a shock of black hair, he had proved to be a good horseman and a good pistol shot. Like the other men, he was dressed in broadcloth trousers and a loose shirt covered by a black leather vest. His pants legs were tucked into his knee-high leather boots, footwear that protected the lower legs during rides through the brush country. Evidently, the boots didn't offer much protection from dropped palm logs.

The Rangers had no official uniforms, but they managed to dress in a similar style. Their most individualistic feature was the condition of their hats, which ranged from almost new to badly worn. Each man wore a cartridge belt, which carried a sheaf knife on one side and a holstered revolver on the other. The short-barreled, double action Colt 45 was the pistol carried by most of them, although some older men still used the long barreled, single action Colt Peacemaker. Most Rangers had given up the practice of wearing paired revolvers on their belts. When they were fighting Indians on the High Plains, two Colts were a necessity. On the Border, one pistol was sufficient.

For rifles, the Rangers preferred the Winchester 95 rifle in carbine length, firing a thirty-caliber round. A lever action weapon with a box-style magazine, it was well suited to their needs. On the trail, they wore a second cartridge belt which held rifle ammunition. Like most Ranger captains, Maddox had instructed his troops to dismount before firing their carbines. Blazing away with six-guns during a horseback pursuit of bandits was usually a waste of lead. A few Rangers were dead shots with six-guns, horseback or not. Whitey Wilson was one of these.

Dolph Krieger finally resumed work on the barricade. Regan did not know him well enough to evaluate his capabilities. He was a flashy horseman and a loud talker. He had not yet proved himself in a fight.

Harold Johns, an older and more experienced Ranger, laughed at Dolph's expense. A quiet man, short and thin, Johns seemed fearless, calm in battle, and a good shot with a carbine. Regan looked down the barricade to the end where Whitey and two others were shoving a final palm trunk into place. Gerald Sailer and Tommy Mabry had been with the troop for two years. Both had joined in San Antonio, and they had worked as a pair from the time they enlisted. Each had received a serious wound during their first fight with bandits, but that had not discouraged them. The two had developed into first-class Rangers. All in all, Regan was pleased with the makeup of the squad he had been given. Except for Dolph, they were seasoned fighters. He smiled when he realized that he and Whitey could have been Sailer and Mabry ten years ago. Ten years! Regan shook his head at the thought.

Suddenly, he realized that all work had stopped. The men were standing still, looking past him towards the top of the slope. A big automobile appeared on the trail, chugging through the mesquite brush. Abruptly, it swerved and headed directly towards the Rangers' camp. It rumbled down the slope and skidded to a stop just short of their fire. Regan stumbled backwards out of the way, kicking over the coffeepot in the process. The car's motor died with a cough.

The Rangers stood open-mouthed and stared at the automobile. Bright green with yellow stripes, the car was open-topped. Dust swirled around in front of it. Regan tossed his coffee into the remains of the campfire. He looked disgustedly toward Whitey, who was striding up to the automobile.

Whitey removed his gloves and tucked them under his armpits. He wiped his hands across the seat of his pants.

"What the gawdamn hell is goin' on here? Who's handlin' that rig anyway?" Whitey stopped beside the driver's door. It opened to disgorge a small man wearing a gray uniform. The man stood erect on the running board of the car, which elevated him to Whitey's height.

"This, sir, is a Packard Touring Car, property of the Saint Louis, Brownsville and Mexican Railroad Company." The little driver gestured towards his passengers. "Congressman Black here has been offered its use by this gentleman, Mr. Edelberg, for the congressman's tour of investigation in the Rio Grande Valley. And I am chauffeuring them during this trip. Can you direct us to the headquarters of a troop of Texas Rangers who are rumored to be in this vicinity?"

Two men sitting in the back seat of the car inspected Whitey, who returned their stares.

"What's he want?" Regan called to Whitey.

"Didn't follow him," replied Whitey. "He talks funny." This brought a round of laughter from the other Rangers, who were walking up to the big automobile. Whitey brushed the dirt and splinters of palm wood from the front of his trousers.

He pointed to the coffeepot, now lying on its side in the ashes. "Look at this mess, Red. I was ready for a cuppa java. I've ventilated hombres for less."

The other Rangers crowded around the car, stroking the paint and staring at the passengers. Whitey scowled fiercely at the driver, who was grinning at him.

"Damn you, you little jackass, I'll give you somethin' to laugh about." Whitey reached towards the driver, grabbed his coat with his left and cocked his right arm. Regan, who had come up beside him, reached out and took hold of Whitey's free arm before a blow could be struck.

"Leave him be, Whitey. He didn't mean no harm."

"Well, he oughta learn some manners, drivin' like that."

"Yeah, but if you put him outa business, well, one of us gotta get rid of that car."

"I guess that's so." Whitey turned away, still grumbling under his breath.

"I apologize for any inconvenience." The driver removed his short-billed cap and wiped his forehead with the back of his hand. "If one of you gentlemen will be so kind as to point me in the direction of Ranger headquarters, we'll be on our way."

"I guess you're smack dab in the middle of it, Mister." Red looked into the back seat. A large white canvas top had been folded back, leaving the back seat open. It held two men, who sat quietly watching the proceedings. Both turned their attention to Regan. He touched the brim of his hat and returned their stares.

"What can I do for you gents?"

The man closest to Regan reached up and touched the brim of his white straw hat with his finger, in return. "I am Congressman Harvey Black. Are you a member of the Texas Rangers?" The congressman was clothed in a blue woolen suit, white shirt and black string tie. His portly figure exuded confidence when he smiled and leaned over towards Regan. "Well?" Red realized that the congressman was used to having things go his way. He could be in for some surprises on the Texas-Mexico Border.

"Yes, Congressman, I'm a Ranger. You've located part of Company D of the Texas Rangers. We're kinda busy here."

"And where, Ranger, is your troop's headquarters?"

Regan considered his answer. "I guess our headquarters is wherever Captain Maddox happens to be at the moment."

The second man in the car leaned forward and peered around the congressman.

"Edelberg. Milt Edelberg." He extended his hand. "I'm a member of the City Commission of Harlingen. About forty miles east."

"I know where Harlingen is." Regan removed his glove and shared a brief handshake with Edelberg. He glanced at the congressman, who had made no moves towards shaking hands. Regan replaced his glove.

Suddenly Regan noticed that Whitey had approached the car from the opposite side, and he was still wearing his fighting expression.

"Where can I find this Captain Maddox?" continued Congressman Black. His smile had disappeared. He gave Regan a stern, no-nonsense look. "Where is your headquarters building, Ranger? If you are a Ranger," he added under his breath.

"We ain't got no buildin'," said Whitey with a snort. Heads swiveled towards him as he continued. "Rangers don't do too well in buildin's. Or behind desks, neither. And 'specially not in big motor cars."

"What Whitey means," Regan interrupted, "is that we spend our time out here in the brush, settin' up a defensive perimeter." He slapped his hand down on the edge of the car door, redirecting their attention towards himself. "We're scattered along the river, in the brush, hopin' to intercept any Mexican bandits who try to cross."

Congressman Black cleared his throat. "Hell of a way to fight these bandits," he said to Edelberg. "No wonder you people have troubles down here."

Edelberg ducked his head, as Whitey Wilson stepped up to his side of the car and stared at him. Edelberg reached over and tugged the congressman's coat sleeve. "Sir, maybe we should be talking with the captain of this troop," he said.

"Good idea," said Whitey. "Here he comes now."

Congressman Black looked over his shoulder just as Captain Maddox came clattering down the slope in a buckboard, pulled by a pair of black, lathered horses. With a strong pull on the reins, he brought the buckboard to an abrupt stop. He sat, still holding the reins, and stared at the shiny automobile.

"Red, what in the name of Jesus have you got here?"

Whitey answered for him: "A durn congressman, a gent from Harlingen, and their little popinjay driver."

Maddox swung down from the buckboard and waved Whitey away as he strode over to the automobile. "Whitey is a little touchy, seein' as how he ain't shot anybody in a few days. Now, what do you men want?"

Congressman Black took a long look at Captain Maddox. He was not impressed. Maddox was tall and thin, with long angular arms held out from his body. His stringy black hair hung almost to his shoulders. Piercing eyes peeked out from beneath heavy black eyebrows. Black stubble covered his face. His dusty clothes were shapeless, his knee-high boots worn and nondescript. Maddox brushed the dust from his sleeves and returned the congressman's stare.

"Are you indeed the Ranger captain?"

"I am, sir, Captain Maddox of Texas Ranger Company D. Are you indeed a congressman?"

Black leaned towards Maddox and pointed his finger at him. "Don't be impertinent. I am here in an official capacity, to investigate the problems created by bandits raiding across the Border. Citizens of Texas—" he gestured towards Edelberg— "Citizens of Texas have requested federal assistance to deal with these bandits. I am here to investigate."

Maddox turned his head to the side and spit into the dirt, then continued to offer Black a fixed stare.

The congressman coughed to clear his throat. "Captain— what is your assessment? Is Mexican banditry as bad a problem as I've been told?"

Maddox spit again. "We got plenty of bandits awright."

"And what are the Texas Rangers doing about it?"

Whitey stepped forward again. "Mister, we're shootin' 'em as fast as we can."

Maddox held up his hand, stopping Whitey's outburst.

"Seeing as how you're here to investigate—well, let me tell you what it's like here, Congressman." Maddox gestured toward the west. "We got a Border here of a good 150 miles all the way to Laredo. On the other side of the river are about five thousand Mexicans, armed and in a mood for a revolution. They ain't got no idea where they're goin', except they don't like their government." Maddox turned his head to spit into the dust again. "Can't really blame them for that." He turned his stare back to the congressman.

"Are all of them really bandits?" Black shifted in his seat.

"Nossir. I'd say that about a thousand of 'em are true, died-in-the-wool bandits. The others are revolutionaries. Right now, they got nothin' to revolt against except each other. And

Congressman, they don't like us *gringos*. They blame Americans for a lotta their troubles."

Black held up his hand, palm out, a gesture he used to assume command of conversations. "People tell me,"—he glanced towards Edelberg—"My constituents tell me that people here are afraid for their lives. Americans are being forced to pack up and leave their homes here in the Rio Grande Valley. What's being done about that?"

Maddox continued to fix the congressman with his steely-eyed stare, his scowl daring Black to start any kind of an argument. The captain was not accustomed to being questioned in such a manner.

Red Regan pushed his way to stand between Maddox and Black.

"Congressman, it ain't that bad. Sure, some people have pulled out or been burned out. Lotsa cattle been rustled off the ranges here. But most people are stickin' it out."

"Yeah," added Whitey, "the ones willin' to fight back."

Black turned his head towards Edelberg. "It appears to me, Sir, that your request for federal aid was most timely. Evidently, the bandit problem transcends the abilities of these Texas Rangers."

"What did he say?" asked Whitey

Maddox grabbed the congressman's arm, causing Black to gasp and jerk back towards the captain.

"I'm gonna explain somethin' to you, Congressman. I want you to listen real close now." He continued to put pressure on the arm. "I'm gonna explain what this situation here is, so you can go back and tell them in Washington."

Maddox released his grip; he had the congressman's full attention. Black rubbed his forearm and stared at Maddox, a heavy frown on his face.

"Now Congressman, I'm an old timer. Been with the Rangers more than thirty years. When I started ridin' with the Troop we were fightin' Indians. We fought Comanche raiders who came down from the High Plains. We learnt our lessons the hard way, bein' outrode and sometimes outshot. I know..." he raised his hand when Black started to interrupt. "I know it ain't Indians you're askin' about, but you'll see how it all ties together."

"In the Eighties," he continued, "along about the end of the Indian troubles, the Rangers had to protect settlers along the frontier from raidin' bands of Comanches. Now Comanches were the meanest, most vicious murderin' skunks there ever was. When they quit their reservation over across the Red River, they raided all the way down into Mexico. The army couldn't stop 'em."

"But I thought..."

"Hold yer water, Congressman. The army couldn't stop 'em because the Comanches just thinned out. When the soldiers chased 'em, they split into a bunch of small parties. Cavalry couldn't ketch 'em because they couldn't follow 'em."

Maddox gestured towards the little *remuda* of the Ranger's horses. "See them ponies, Congressman. That's what the Comanches rode—prairie bangtails, scrawny ponies that could do a hunnert miles in a day. Big ole oat-burner roans like that one of Whitey's over there couldn't keep up. We Rangers learned to use the prairie ponies. Still do."

"Now the other thing..." Maddox turned back to confront the congressman. "The other thing was we could chase 'em until they found us. We'd haul off and follow a group of Comanche raiders, usin' Tonkawa scouts to trace 'em. All of a sudden, up there in the High Plains, they just showed up, ridin' back and forth in front of us and whoopin' it up. So we'd make a stand and shoot at the skunks. And then, all of a sudden, we'd be surrounded by Comanches. Now that's a bad feelin', them weavin' in and out on their ponies and darin' us to come out. Lotsa old timers never made it back."

"What finally skedaddled 'em was this." Maddox pulled out his big Colt Peacemaker and held it under Black's nose. The congressman recoiled at first but then leaned forward for a closer look.

"This, Mister Black, was the six-shooter that gave the Rangers the edge. The Comanches soon learned to stay clear of it. We could sling more lead than they bargained for." Maddox holstered his revolver. "But then, thanks to some no-good traders, by the time I joined up, Comanches had firearms too. I'm getting to it," he added when the congressman attempted to interrupt.

"Ancestors of these Mexican Border bandits had to fight Comanches just like we did. For near a hunnert years. And they learned Comanche tricks. The *rurales* couldn't stop the Indians, Comanche or Apache or Yaqui or whoever. No army could. Now, they can't stop these bandits either."

"Indians raided in small groups," he continued, "groups of one-two dozen. They stole horses, took captives and booty, and rode a hunnert miles by the next day. No army troop could catch 'em."

"Wait a minute." Black had heard enough. "Everybody knows the army cleared the hostile Indians out of our western plains."

"The army never won a battle with Comanches," insisted Maddox.

"That's silly. The army slaughtered hostile Indians."

"Tell that to George Custer," Whitey interjected.

"You ain't listenin', Congressman." Maddox waived his finger in Black's face. "I said they never won a battle. The

Comanche ran too far, too fast. Colonel Ranald McKenzie defeated 'em by takin' their horses away. First time he found their herd, he captured their horses. Indians just stole 'em right back. Finally, he flat shot them horses. Killed 'em. Hunnerts of 'em. The Comanches couldn't live in the High Plains without horses. McKenzie put 'em on foot. They surrendered."

"Their horses?"

"Yessir. McKenzie found the tribe in the Palo Duro. They skedaddled up the canyon walls on foot, leavin' the horse herd behind. Them horse skellytons is still out there on the prairie. You see, soldiers didn't defeat Comanches in no battle."

"No, I still don't see…"

"Here's the size of it, Congressman. Fightin' the Mexican bandits is like fightin' Comanches. They raid in small groups, take a little booty, and slip back across the river. They don't stand and fight. If a small group gets surrounded they'll shoot it out, but they don't stick around for a proper battle. You never know where they're gonna show up next.

"So you see, Congressman. We got that 150 miles of Border I told you about and less than two dozen Rangers. These men you see here…" Maddox gestured with his arm. "These Rangers are givin' the bandits hell."

The group of Rangers muttered their agreement. The younger ones had not heard some of this Ranger history. Congressman Black clearly hadn't either, and they were enjoying his discomfort.

"Captain, the army could be patrolling the Border."

"You'd just get a bunch of soldier boys killed." Whitey offered his opinion. "They wouldn't know what to do."

"I reckon Whitey's right." Maddox stepped back and put his hands on his slender hips. "Here's what you can tell 'em in Washington. The first thing they need to do is put pressure on the Mexican government. The Mexicans can do something about them bandits over there in their own country."

"The second thing…" He shifted his weight to the other foot. "The second thing to tell 'em is, if they send a big army down here, they're gonna start a war. Sooner or later the army's gonna want to chase bandits back across the river. They'll invade Mexico."

Maddox walked back to his buckboard. He stopped and turned for a final word. "And when they do—they ain't gonna ketch 'em."

Congressman Black sat, considering the captain's lecture. Finally he leaned to Edelberg and spoke in a soft voice. Edelberg, in turn, leaned forward to instruct the driver.

The automobile's starter gave a prolonged whine and the engine began to fire, to the amusement of the group of Rangers. The congressman gave a wave of his hat towards Maddox. The driver coaxed the Packard around and turned it back towards the trail.

Regan and Whitey walked over to the buckboard where Maddox was waiting for them.

"Damn, Cap, you really gave it to 'im." Whitey slapped his hands on his thighs. Regan studied Maddox, who looked back at him expectantly.

"Captain, do you really think the army would be of no help here?" Red asked.

"Hell no," exclaimed Whitey, but Maddox raised a hand to silence him.

"Red, today's soldiers ain't much. They got no experience and not much in the way of trainin' either. Look at those yahoos layin' around Fort Clarke and Fort Brown. Those *bandidos* could squash 'em like wood ticks.

"But right now I got a job needs to be done. A buncha citizens up at Lyford caught themselves a bandit, or so they say. A Mexican was drunk and shootin' up the square, or somethin' like that. I got a telegram that was kinda vague. Seems they caught a bandit and made him prisoner somehow." Maddox pointed at Whitey. "Now Whitey, saddle up and go get that bandit. Put him on the train and take him to the courthouse in Brownsville. Then get back here."

Whitey broke into a broad grin and punched Regan on the shoulder. "You betcha I'll get 'im. Right away."

Regan frowned. This meant that Whitey would have a chance to visit with Mabel Steuben. Alone, without Regan around. Maddox was continuing. "Dammit, Whitey, I want that bandit to get to Brownsville all in one piece. None of this 'shot trying to escape', not this time. Get him to the court alive. We need the County Court to see what we're up against, what kinda people we're dealin' with." He looked back and forth at the two Rangers, who were still eyeing each other. "In fact," he decided, "Red oughta go too. Red, you ride along with Whitey and see that he don't unlimber his iron 'less he has to."

Now the grin was on Regan's face. "Right away, Cap."

"I want you boys back here tomorrow night. I don't expect no bandit trouble in the daylight, and there ain't no moon 'till late tonight. But I don't wanna leave these youngsters here by themselves for too long."

CHAPTER TEN

Captain José Arredondo rubbed the back of his neck and studied Karl Steiner through squinted, watery eyes. Steiner, seated across the table from him, wore a sarcastic smile that seemed to Arredondo to be a permanent fixture. Somewhere in the distance, a rooster greeted the morning with a drawn-out cry. Arredondo did not feel like crowing. He shook his head carefully, massaging his neck. His temples throbbed. Fog seemed to fill his brain. He smacked his lips together and swallowed carefully. *How much did I drink last night?* he asked himself, sitting at the table in only his underwear and his stocking feet. When he stretched his arms and yawned, another wave of pain erupted behind his eyes and surged through his forehead. He slumped further down in his chair. What the hell did Steiner want, this early in the morning?

Time seemed to pass slowly for José Arredondo these days. There was little for the army to do in Matamoros, only routine patrols of the city. There were no general orders. He simply waited for the return of *general* Blanco. At first Arredondo had enjoyed the power of command, but it had become an empty chore. He was drinking more than usual.

He blinked his eyes several times and carefully focused again on Steiner's face. How did the man get in here, in the captain's personal quarters, at this time of day? Steiner seemed able, somehow, to gain entrance wherever he wished. Later, Arredondo would punish the corporal of the guard for admitting a civilian to the post without authorization. Especially a foreigner.

Arredondo yawned again, this time less painfully. He picked up the stub of a *cigarro* from an ashtray and immediately discarded it; he had lost his taste for tobacco. He looked back over his shoulder towards the bedroom where the woman still slept. The proprietor of the Yellow House occasionally sent girls for his pleasure. Last night's woman had been unusually energetic. Arredondo preferred his lovemaking to be leisurely, with a passive partner. This one had exhausted him, and he wanted her out, removed quietly, as soon as he could arrange it.

He looked up as his corporal slipped in silently through the door, with a large coffeepot and a single china cup. The corporal set these in front of Arredondo and departed as quickly as he had entered. With a shaky hand Arredondo poured the steaming liquid into the cup. He made no move to offer any to Steiner. After a slow, careful sip of the scalding coffee, Arredondo set down the cup and looked expectantly at his visitor.

"Well, *señor? Qué pasa?*"

"*Capitán*, there is a problem which only you can solve."

Arredondo sighed. Steiner had been helpful to him in the past weeks, helpful with advice about his command, with gifts of small arms and promises for more weapons that were as yet undelivered. Recently, Steiner had begun to speak of his plans for the future of Mexico, only vaguely and never directly involving him, but Arredondo was beginning to feel that he was being pressed into some kind of plot. That in itself would not be surprising; Mexico was inflicted with a variety of plots and schemes, all set against the background of the *Revolución*. Arredondo did not care what plans Steiner was proposing. Up until now, he had not paid much attention to the man's darkly vague comments about battles and invasions. But this morning, he realized, Steiner was about to ask for a favor. *Now comes the request for payment for those little gifts of arms.*

Arredondo sighed again. *"Señor,* what problem is this? What must I do?"

"You must release that young *charro* you have in the *calabozo.* The one you are holding for the murder of the *teniente."*

The captain sipped his coffee, now cooled enough to be drinkable. He stared through the dirty window into the courtyard. Soldiers were beginning to stir in the barracks. Some were drifting outside onto the parade ground, where they gathered in small groups. It would soon be time for their morning meal. The *soldados* were becoming disgruntled over the decline in their rations, a decline that was inevitable unless more vegetables could somehow be imported. Today, Arredondo had planned to investigate the activities of his quartermaster. In fact, he thought, today would be a good day to evaluate his entire officer corps. And to reassess his own plans.

He turned back to look at Steiner, who was watching him expectantly.

"As you know, *señor,* I am required to keep the man in custody until *general* Blanco returns."

"The order was to hold all executions until his return, was it not? There was no order concerning trials or the release of any prisoners."

"You seem to know more about *general* Blanco's orders than I do, *señor.* I will wait until his return. He can hold a trial if he wishes to do so." Arredondo picked up the *cigarro* stub again and looked around for a match. The coffee was beginning to clear away his hangover. Tobacco seemed attractive again.

Steiner leaned forward. His little smile changed into a deep scowl. "Blanco will not return," he snarled through his teeth. He shook his finger under Arredondo's nose. "You know that as well as I. *General* Blanco is involved in an attempt to assault the federal government. He leads a corps of *federales* for First Chief Carranza. He has no interest in things here in Matamoros. He has another army now."

"That may be. But I have no authority to act in his absence." Arredondo ignored Steiner's wagging finger. He put the cigar stub between his lips and continued to look for a match among the debris on the table. Steiner reached in his shirt pocket and retrieved a box of matches, which he tossed across to the captain. Arredondo realized that Steiner was struggling to regain his composure. The German produced a bandanna and mopped his brow with it.

"Arredondo, you have all the authority you need. You should be *general* Arredondo now. The army is yours. We can do important things with this army." Steiner leaned back in his chair, holding his bandanna to his mouth.

The captain raised his eyebrows. "We?" He drew a mouthful of smoke from the cigar stub.

"*Amigo mío,* there are great things afoot here in Matamoros. You yourself can take the first step, set things in motion. You must release the youngster to the custody of *señor* Paulo DeLeón."

"Ah, the police commissioner. Well, perhaps. I will consider it." Arredondo decided that a tentative agreement was the best course for now. His headache was beginning to pound again, even more fiercely. He wanted to return to his bed as soon as he could usher the woman out through the back. And he wanted Steiner to leave him alone for now. Later, he would give careful consideration to this strange request.

Arredondo rose unsteadily, leaning against the table for support. Steiner leaped to his feet, started to take Arredondo's elbow, but then thought the better of it when he noticed the deep frown on the captain's face. He started to leave but turned back at the door.

"Remember what I have said. This is important. For all of us."

"Capitán. Sir, you have visitors."

Arredondo opened his eyes without lifting his head from the pillow. He recognized the voice of his corporal. What now? Had that fool Steiner returned?

"Capitán."

"Ay, pues, bueno. Quién es?" Arredondo rolled his legs off of the narrow bed and scowled at his corporal.

"It is the police commissioner. And another *señor."*

Arredondo gestured towards his trousers. He stood, shakily, as the corporal brought them to him and held his elbow while he pulled them on. He sat down again on the edge of the bed, letting the corporal kneel and help him don his boots. Arredondo grabbed his jacket and stalked from the bedroom, feeling his way at first but gaining confidence as he strode. The corporal followed silently, close behind him.

"Hay más de desayuno?"

"Sí, Capitán, your breakfast awaits you."

"Corporal, let us then go to breakfast. Our visitors can wait." Arredondo lengthened his stride. He thought he knew what the commissioner wanted. Surely it was the favor that the man Steiner had already asked of him. But why? What were Steiner and DeLeón plotting, this early in the morning? Arredondo needed time to think. He decided to indulge in a leisurely breakfast. Anything to postpone the moment when he would have to make a decision in the matter of his prisoner. He sensed that whatever decision he made would mark a turning point in his army career.

"You did not have to accompany me, Nacho." Paulo stared out the window at the group of soldiers assembled for a morning muster. "I am simply going to request that Marco Luís be placed in my custody. I expect the request to be refused. It is only a formality at this point. It is merely a means for opening negotiations. You know," he continued, "this might be dangerous for you. If you were recognized."

"We agreed that I could accompany you," said Nacho after a moment's hesitation. "I do not think that I will be in much danger, since I have changed my appearance. I will pretend to be a lawyer hired by his family. You will need some reason for the request. The presence of the family lawyer will provide such a reason."

In fact, Nacho did not think that Paulo would be effective with his request. Paulo stood with his shoulders squared and his chin up, but Nacho could see the perspiration on the side of his neck. Was Paulo able to stand up to this *capitán?* Evidently, Paulo's determination was about to be tested. Nacho wanted to see what course the discussion might take. He had donned his uncle's suit again, so he thought that he looked the part of a *haciendero* from the south.

The web of deception was beginning to make Nacho uneasy. He did not like to misrepresent himself, but it had become necessary the moment he was taken into Pancho Villa's camp. In the past two days, he had passed himself off as a horse wrangler, an agricultural worker, a murderer of Texas Rangers, and now as a lawyer. In an attempt to help his daughter, he had agreed to work first for Pancho Villa and then for a trio of unlikely revolutionaries. At the moment, he needed to focus on freeing his son-in-law. If he could do that, and get the youngster out of Matamoros on any pretext, he would be able to cross the Rio Grande and return to the Rangers.

Someplace in Matamoros, Tomás Aguilar was running free. Nacho hoped that Tomás would not present a further difficulty or make trouble for himself. He was a stranger in Matamoros, a young man unfamiliar with the ways of this Border city. If Tomás were lucky, he would find his way back to Villa's camp. Pancho Villa was out of his usual territory. Surely the bandit would soon return to more familiar ground in Chihuahua, south of El Paso. As he thought about it, Nacho began to doubt that he would ever see either Tomás or Pancho Villa again. It was a thought that lifted his spirits, even in these trying circumstances.

Paulo turned away from the window. "He is making us wait. Well, let us see who we have in the civil cells. The *calabozo* has been separated into civil and military wings," he continued. "I still have control over the civil part." He led the way down the hall and stopped at a gate, which was guarded by a jailer lolling on a stool. The man was dressed in ill-fitting dirty white canvas trousers and a khaki shirt unbuttoned to his waist. He wore a military capi, shoved carelessly askew on top of his tangled mat of black hair. As Paulo approached him, the jailer scrambled to his feet, the chair tipping over with a clatter. Rolling his eyes at Nacho, Paulo pushed the jailer aside and entered a narrow hallway with cells on one side.

"As you can see, my cousin, we are having difficulty maintaining a reasonable discipline among our civilian employees." Paulo led the way down the corridor, peering into the cells. "But we are resuming many of our former duties in policing the city. The army has lost interest in keeping the civil order. We collect the petty thieves, the drunkards, and the brawlers. I myself have the authority to assign penalties, since our municipal judges have fled the city."

"Do you enjoy that responsibility?"

"I do. Perhaps, when the *Revolución* is over, I will become a member of the judiciary."

Nacho stopped to stare into a dimly lit cell containing a single figure seated on a low metal cot. Could it be? His eyes widened as he recognized the battered form of Tomás Aguilar. Tomás sat with his head in his hands, unmoving, his face turned away.

Abruptly, Paulo turned and started back down the corridor. "Come, Nacho. Perhaps we should return to the offices and await the *capitán*."

Nacho turned quickly, but not before Tomás had struggled to his feet.

"Nacho? Is it you?" Tomás stumbled forward to grasp the bars on the door. Nacho seemed rooted in place. What could he do? It was too late to pretend that Tomás was a stranger to him. Paulo returned to stand beside him. He looked at Nacho quizzically.

"Tomás, what are you doing in jail?" Nacho hoped that Tomás would use some discretion. Paulo was watching them closely.

"*Ay*, Nacho, it was only a little fight. I was winning when two *policías* interfered."

"If that is so, Tomás, I would not like to see you after you had lost a fight."

Tomás was squinting through his left eye; his right one was closed. The right side of his face seemed to be one gigantic bruise. His right ear was torn and bloody. His shirt was torn half off of his body. Grime coated the exposed areas that Nacho could see.

"Do you know this youngster?" Paulo was grinning at the spectacle.

"Yes, I do indeed. He is—well, he is an associate. I will pay his fine." Nacho was beginning to wonder how far he could stretch his remaining gold pieces.

"Oh, I do not think there will be any fine. I will arrange for him to be released to you. After we have concluded our business concerning your son-in-law." Paulo gestured towards the jailer and pointed into the cell. "Feed him and give him a wash basin."

"I am grateful, Paulito." Nacho hoped to avoid any further explanations. He was relieved that Tomás had not tried to mention his association with Pancho Villa.

Paulo started back down the corridor. Nacho and Tomás stood looking at each other.

"I am sorry." Tomás shuffled his feet. "I was only trying…"

"Never mind." Nacho raised his hand, hoping that Tomás would recognize the signal for silence. Evidently he did because Tomás turned and made his way back to his rusty metal bunk.

Captain Arredondo sat behind his desk, leaning back in his chair with one foot propped on the desktop. The breakfast and another cup of coffee had completely cleared his head. All of his senses were alert. Arredondo studied his two visitors. He did not like what he saw. The two men were seated across from him, each on the edge of his chair, and they were clearly very tense.

"*Capitán*," Paulo began, but Arredondo silenced him with a wave of his hand. He puffed on his *cigarro* and continued to stare at Nacho.

Nacho was attempting to keep his expression neutral. Paulo had introduced him as a lawyer, but Arredondo had abruptly stopped all conversation. The two men locked eyes. Nacho searched his memory. Had he met this man before? Not that he could recall. He mentally reviewed the arrangement of the building, in case he was forced to make an escape. The thirty-eight revolver in his jacket pocket was a comfortable weight. Nacho forced himself to breathe normally under Arredondo's intense stare.

Abruptly, Arredondo sat forward, his booted foot hitting the floor. "So you are a lawyer."

"*Sí, capitán*. My name is Villareal. *De ciudad* Victoria. I have been retained…"

Arredondo stopped him with a wave of his hand. "Today you are a lawyer. Yesterday you were an *agricultór*."

That was it, Nacho realized. His eyes widened. This was the *capitán* who had confronted him in the bar yesterday. Nacho had thought that the change in clothes, the trim and dye in his hair and beard, would disguise him. He had been wrong. This was serious. Nacho's hand started a slow, careful movement towards the jacket pocket that held his pistol. Did the *capitán* have a weapon concealed? His left hand held the *cigarro*; his right hand was concealed in his lap.

"Be at ease, *señor*." Arredondo held up both his hands, palms outwards, showing them to be empty but for the *cigarro*. "It does not matter to me. I do not care who or what you are. You have changed your hair and your clothing but not your boots."

It was true. Nacho had worn his own boots this morning because his uncle's footwear pinched his feet. Involuntarily, he glanced down at them.

"Yes," continued Arredondo, "I remember them because they bear the distinct marks left by the wearing of spurs. I did not think you were an agriculturalist. Now I am sure you are not a lawyer. Their spurs are only verbal, and such spurs do not mar the polish on their footwear."

Nacho lifted his left hand as he attempted to frame a reply. No words came to mind. He stared hopelessly at the *capitán*. His right hand slid into his jacket pocket and found the little revolver.

Arredondo leaned back, smiling, waving his *cigarro* in the air. "I think I would have recognized you anyway. Your face and your eyes are distinctive."

Nacho looked over at his cousin. What to do now? How to proceed? Paulo took the cue and began his plea once more.

"*Capitán*, we wish to arrange the release of the señor Gonzales. Marco Luís Gonzales. Please, *capitán*, we request that you give him his parole. Into my custody, of course."

"Impossible." Arredondo took a short puff from his cigar and placed it on an ashtray. He leaned forward. Nacho gathered himself together. But Arredondo then leaned back again and smiled at them.

"*Señores*, the *joven* is being held as a murder suspect. I must keep him in custody until the return of *general* Blanco. As I explained to your friend, *señor* Steiner."

"Steiner was here?" asked Paulo.

Nacho found his voice. "May I inquire, *capitán*, what is the evidence of this young man's guilt?"

"Paugh!" Arredondo waved his hand in a dismissive gesture. "He is not guilty. His only crime at this point is stupidity. He has committed no murder, at least none known to me."

Nacho and Paulo stared at each other and then at the captain.

"No, no," continued Arredondo. "I examined his *pistolas* when he was taken and brought before me. They had not been fired." He shook his head. "He did not shoot anybody."

"But why are you holding him?" Paulo raised his hands and shrugged his shoulders.

"Because he has been accused. *Señores,* two of my officers brought him to me, accusing him of shooting and killing my *teniente.* Of course I had to take him into my custody. And I must keep him until a trial is held. When *general* Blanco returns."

"And then will he be released?" Paulo persisted, mindful of the fact that Nacho was staring intently at Arredondo, a dark frown on his face.

"I cannot say. Perhaps Blanco will release him; perhaps he will execute him."

"But if he is innocent..."

Arredondo held up his hand, palm outwards, to silence Paulo. He stared out of his window and considered an idea that was beginning to form in his mind. Carefully, he drew on his *cigarro* and blew the smoke towards the ceiling. Perhaps there was a way out of this *acertijo.* He turned back to face his visitors.

"*Señores.* I have a suggestion." Arredondo smiled broadly, showing his white, even teeth. "Bring me a better suspect, an *hombre* who is more likely to have committed this murder, and I will release your friend to you."

Nacho and Paulo exchanged glances, as Arredondo continued.

"*Señor* DeLeón, you are the commissioner of police, are you not? Well, I hereby authorize you to undertake an investigation of this matter. I transfer authority for the investigation from the military to the civil authorities. I suggest you act promptly. I wish you good luck in your efforts."

Arredondo rose to his feet. "*Corporal,*" he called out. "Bring me pen and paper! I will write out this authority for you," he said to Paulo. "Now, *señores,* if you will excuse me."

Nacho strode rapidly down the middle of the dirt street. Paulo hurried to keep up with him, breathing hard. Nacho kicked ineffectively at a clod, raising a small puff of dust. He was relieved to find that Marco Luís was in no immediate danger of execution. Also, he himself had not been arrested, even though Arredondo was not fooled by his disguise. But Arredondo had angered him. The *capitán* was arrogant. He kept Marco Luís in prison while admitting that he was innocent. And had put the boy's salvation in the hands of Paulo. Clearly, Arredondo believed Paulo to be incompetent. Nacho suspected that the *capitán* was right.

With Paulo tugging at his coat sleeve, Nacho slowed his pace.

"Nacho, Nacho. This is wonderful." Paulo grasped Nacho's arm and turned him around. "Do you see what this means? It means that I have been returned to power as commissioner of police. I can reorganize my police forces. I will send a message across the river into Texas. Some of my men fled across the river. Now, they can return. We will be a police force once again."

Nacho rubbed his chin as he considered his cousin's enthusiasm. Had he misjudged Paulo? Perhaps now Paulo would give up his silly idea about a revolution to capture part of south Texas.

"What will you do, Paulo? How will you proceed?"

"My cousin, I will investigate the shooting. I will locate witnesses. I will—I will develop an inquiry. I will find the motive for this crime. I will find a suspect, so that Marco Luís will be released."

"Of course," said Nacho, "that is exactly what you should do." Since the *indio* had told him that a *capitán* was the killer, Nacho doubted that Paulo could accomplish much. At least, he thought, an investigation would keep Paulo out of the way. He turned and started down the street, resuming his rapid pace.

"Nacho, what are you going to do now? Will you help us with this investigation?"

"No," said Nacho over his shoulder. "I must follow my own path." Nacho was devising a vague plan, an idea that would bring Pancho Villa and his revolutionaries into the city. He had noticed the poor discipline in the army. With surprise on his side, Villa could take the city. And free Marco Luís. Then, thought Nacho, I can introduce Villa to *señor* Ortíz, *presidente del Banco de Matamoros.* He could not suppress a grin at the thought of Pancho Villa personally making a withdrawal of funds from pompous little *señor* Ortíz. That possibility in itself might be enough to lure Villa into the city.

Nacho slowed his stride and waited for his cousin to catch up with him. "Please, Paulito," he said, "will you release the *señor* Aguilar to me? And send him to the *Taberna* on *calle Amistad.* I think he will know where it is. Tell him I will find him there. Now, I must hurry to your *casa* and retrieve my saddlebags."

"Immediately, my cousin."

As Paulo started away, Nacho called after him. He suddenly thought of the local bandit leader, who might now prove useful to him.

"One more thing, Paulo," he said. "I need to contact that bandit, Chulo Valdez. Can you help me? How may I find him?"

Paulo turned with a smile. Good, very good. Nacho intended to pursue their invasion plans. The others would be pleased, especially the *señor* Steiner. This was all working out better than expected.

"I will get a message to him," he said. "Where should he meet you? At the *Taberna*? Would that be satisfactory?"

"*Sí*, my cousin, let us establish that as our meeting place. Hector León will not be pleased, but he will help us."

"*Bueno*. And Nacho, I will bring your saddlebags for you and meet you there this afternoon." Paulito scurried away. Nacho rubbed his chin and watched his cousin hurry down the dirt street. He turned his footsteps towards the *Taberna*.

CHAPTER ELEVEN

The two Rangers walked their horses, side by side, along the wagon trail that skirted the railroad tracks. On Captain Maddox's orders, they were headed to the town of Harlingen, where they were to catch a train north to Lyford, one of the new little villages that had sprung up along the railroad. Longhorn Maddox had made it clear to them. He had spoken slowly and carefully, his rheumy eyes moving back and forth between their faces. Go to Harlingen and take the train. Collect a bandit held in Lyford and transport him, again by train, to the Cameron County seat in Brownsville. Alive and in good condition.

Both men were operating under the general orders of the Texas Rangers. They were expected to adapt to changing situations, using their judgment and experience as guidelines. Captain Maddox had been definite about the need to get the bandit to Brownsville, and he had twice mentioned the railroad as the means of transport. The captain had spelled out the result he expected. It was up to the two Rangers to deliver.

They moved at a leisurely pace. Regan rode on the left side, next to the tracks; Whitey paced beside him on his right. This was their customary arrangement. Their eyes searched the distance constantly. During their years as partners, the two had developed a pattern of shared vigilance. It had served them well in the past. They had no reason to expect trouble, but each was prepared to meet it if it arose.

They rode in silence. Their feelings for the same woman had strained their partnership. Both men were infatuated with Mabel Steuben, the vivacious blond, the beauty of Brownsville, Texas. And their interest in her seemed to be growing by the minute.

Regan studied Whitey with sideways glances. The tall, slim Ranger sat erect in his saddle, left hand holding the reins of his big red gelding, right hand resting on his hip. He was stylishly dressed, Regan thought. Whitey wore new form-fitting denims tucked into his high top boots. A black leather vest covered his buckskin pullover shirt. The circle-star badge was displayed on the left side of his vest. Like Regan, he wore a Stetson "Texas" hat of the narrow brim style recently adopted by many of the Rangers. A bright blue bandanna was loosely tied around his neck. Regan could not see Whitey's sidearm on his right side, but the scabbard holding his Winchester carbine was in plain view, tucked in front of his saddle. A large Green River knife in a tooled scabbard hung from his belt and swung over his left hip. A second belt held cartridges for the carbine.

Regan himself was dressed in his best clothes: Dark woolen coat and trousers with the legs covering his boots, a dark plaid shirt buttoned at the neck and fitted with a black string necktie. He wore his Ranger badge pinned to his coat pocket. His hat was a high-crowned felt one. He wanted to present his best appearance, but he thought Whitey had outdone him. His conservative clothes compared poorly with Whitey's more colorful ones. Regan's only weapon was his forty-five-caliber revolver, which he wore on his left hip, rigged for a cross-handed draw, which he found easier when on horseback. Regan did not carry a large knife. Instead, he favored a backup pistol, a thirty-eight tucked into his right boot.

Riding in an alert silence wasn't unusual for the duo. Rangers looked for anything out of the ordinary, some disturbance in the normal pattern of nature. The sudden appearance of a stranger, movements of wildlife, the flight of a covey of quail, even unexplained silences might indicate trouble ahead. Bandits usually presented no danger during daylight hours, except when they traveled in large bands.

Regan flexed his right hand, testing the sprained fingers. The hand was still weak, and his fingers hurt when he moved them. He did not think anything was broken, but that dropped palm log had caused some severe bruising. He was not sure he could draw and hold his weapon. He had not mentioned his injury to Whitey.

Regan couldn't help daydreaming about Mabel. Her father maintained several farms near Lyford, one of which was her favorite springtime getaway. Would he have a chance to visit her during their trip up the Valley? Could he manage to separate himself from Whitey for that visit? He looked up into the clouds, imagining her laughing face.

Regan had reached a decision. He planned to tell Mabel that he loved her. He wanted a more formal relationship. He wanted to call her "My Girl." Did Whitey want the same thing? He was always joking with Mabel, kidding around with her. It was difficult to tell what Whitey was thinking, but it was clear to him that the competition for Mabel's attentions was more than just a game between friends. Regan sighed. He felt torn between his affection for Mabel and his long friendship with Whitey Wilson.

The tension between the two men was beginning to affect the behavior of their horses. Both mounts were familiar with the moods of their riders. Regan's muscular little pony was displaying a tendency to step sideways. Whitey's big horse

Cimmie had started to pace nervously. When a covey of quail burst noisily into the air directly in front of them, both horses and their riders started in alarm. Regan tugged the reins to bring his pony back under control; he realized that he was handling the pony with his left hand alone. His right had drawn his pistol. After looking around himself carefully, he returned the pistol to its holster. His hand hurt but he had been able to hold the pistol. He glanced at Whitey. Had the Ranger seen him draw?

Whitey was having even more difficulties with the big roan. Cimmie reared and spun on his back legs. Regan watched as Whitey urged the big horse into a circle and finally coaxed it to a standstill. The two men looked at each other and simultaneously began to laugh. The tension spilled from them and vanished into the morning breeze.

Whitey threw a leg over his saddle horn and pulled his tobacco pouch from his shirt pocket. "How 'bout it, Pard?" he said.

Regan shrugged. "Okay, I guess. How 'bout you?"

Whitey poured tobacco into a paper and carefully rolled a smoke. "Tell me somethin'," he began. "Old Longhorn sent two of us on a mission that either of us could do blindfolded. How come?"

Whitey offered the tobacco pouch to Regan, who waved it away.

"You know," he continued, "we gotta be real careful with that bandit. Don't make sense but that's what he said. The captain seemed real determined about it. Said he didn't want no *ley fugua* stuff. You know, shot tryin' to escape. I guess he figgered both of us wouldn't accidentally back-shoot 'im. He wants that bandit to reach Brownsville still kickin'."

Whitey struck a match against a stud on his denims and set fire to his little cigarette.

"Now, that ain't right. Maddox oughta know that two of us is about as likely to shoot a bandit as one of us is. And he knows we ain't gonna do it if he says not to." Whitey looked expectantly at Regan. "And somethin' else. I woulda thought he'd want us to help out if bandits hit that new barricade."

"I expect Maddox'll throw 'em off with campfires," said Regan.

Longhorn Maddox had brought with him to the Valley several tricks he had learned in the Indian wars. One was to build a number of large cooking fires. Then, after dark, the troop could slip away, leaving the fires burning and the hostiles thinking the Rangers were still in camp.

"Yeah, I guess you're right. Old Longhorn will move most of the troop on down to the Hidalgo crossing. Besides, we're gettin' into the dark of the moon. Them bandits seem to like moonlight for raidin'. Still, I'd feel better if old Nacho had come back. Some of them young'uns ain't been properly blooded yet."

"Mebbe he'll show up. Unannounced. Like he usually does."

Whitey inspected the end of his cigarette. "All the same. Don't see why Maddox wanted both of us on this little jaunt."

Regan thought for a moment.

"Well," he said slowly, "Maddox did say somethin' about us workin' it out between us."

Whitey took a deep pull on his cigarette and blew smoke high into the air.

"I reckon he's right. Red, we gotta settle this business about Mabel."

Regan was taken by surprise. He hadn't expected anything quite so direct. He glanced at his partner. What did Whitey have in mind, exactly? Some kind of contest? He shifted in his saddle and turned his body so that he was facing Whitey. Still puffing his cigarette, Whitey stared off into the distance.

Regan took a deep breath. "I intend to ask Mabel to marry me."

As soon as he had said it, Regan bit his lip. He had not intended to say anything about marriage. It had just risen from his chest and emerged from his mouth without his control. The thought frightened him. He looked at Whitey, who was now staring at him, wide-eyed.

"Red, that's the stupidest goddam thing you ever said. And you've come up with some dillies before. That one's out there all by itself." Whitey flipped his cigarette across onto the railroad track. "What the hell's got into you? You got no more sense than a horny toad, sometimes."

Regan picked up his reins and dug his heels into the pony's sides. The little animal abruptly started forward, trotting along beside the railroad tracks. He could feel Whitey's eyes boring into his back. He kept the pony at a trot. Soon he heard the clomp of Cimmie's hooves, catching up to him. Regan kept his attention fixed on the road.

"Dammit, Red," called Whitey. "Think about it. You're a Ranger. You ain't got no prospects. Mabel's papa has gotta be one of the richest men in town. He ain't gonna like this one bit."

Regan urged his pony forward into a gallop. He had surprised himself and he wanted to think. Why'd he say such a screwy thing? Did he really mean it? Was he ready to take a wife? Raise a family?

Whitey appeared beside him again, the big horse matching his pony's strides. Regan sneaked a look at him. This is foolish, he decided. I can't outrun that big oat burner. He eased his pony out of the gallop. Whitey matched his slower pace.

"Mabel's a lotta fun. Yeah, and a lotta laughs, too. What makes you think she'd marry you, anyway?"

"Don't know that she will. She'd probably rather marry you, anyway. You're excitin'. I'm kinda stodgy."

Whitey snorted. "I ain't the marryin' kind. And you ain't, neither. Give it up, Pard."

Regan looked out across the railroad tracks. He didn't answer. Finally, he spurred his pony into a brisk trot. This time Whitey trailed behind him.

Further down the track, Regan halted again and waited for Whitey to catch up with him. He was perspiring now, as the day warmed. He removed his coat.

The two rested their horses, giving their mounts a moment's breather. They watched a group of men busily working in the brushland across the tracks. They worked in a row, cutting brush with machetes, moving steadily forward. Neither Ranger spoke. They watched the laborers.

Finally, Regan broke the silence himself.

"Looks like another farm bein' cleared. Where do all these folks come from?"

"You can thank the railroads. And the goddam land speculators." Whitey spit in disgust. "Most of these people got no business tryin' to farm here. They don't know what they're doin'."

"Whatcha think this one is gonna plant? More sugarcane? He's too far from the river to irrigate his new field."

"Hell, there'll be another pump station before long. This whole Valley is gonna be one big goddam sugarcane field before long."

"Look what's comin' here." Regan pointed to a man riding a mule, who approached the workers and began haranguing them. The man was waving his arms, pointing up and down the rows, and then pointing towards the sun, which was reaching its zenith. The guy was trying to give some kind of instructions. He didn't seem to be getting his point across.

"Must be the supervisor," said Whitey, "or maybe the owner of the outfit. Poor bastard don't speak much Spanish, does he? He ain't gettin' very far. He better get hisself a field boss, pronto."

Regan laughed. "Wonder if he knows they're Mexicans and not Americans? These Yankees don't know real Mexicans from *Tejanos*. Think they're all the same. That sodbuster's gonna curse at them, but he won't find anybody else who'll clear that brushland for him. Only *peónes* from over the river will work those brushlands."

The big horse Cimmie began to pace nervously, and as Whitey gathered in the reins, Regan turned and started his own pony down the track. They rode in silence for a moment.

"Wonder if he knows that them brush choppers by day might turn into bandits by night?" Whitey urged his horse forward, skirting a large ebony tree at the edge of the railroad right of way.

"Yeah, it's a mess, ain't it? It's not just the clearin' of the grazin' lands for new farms. It's these new people themselves. They don't understand Tex-Mex people and how they work. We were gettin' along pretty well here in the Valley."

"Don't matter," said Whitey. "Bandits are bringin' it to a boil. You know, Red, we gotta do somethin' about them Mexicans. We oughta get the Rangers together and go across the Rio and teach 'em somethin'. We could do it."

Regan didn't reply. He was thinking of Mabel again, and the future of the Valley, and how he might fit into it. A farmer? A grower of sugarcane? He didn't think so.

"'Course," Whitey continued, "Bandits are chasin' a lotta these folks back north. Maybe they ain't all bad."

"Well it ain't all the fault of the Mexican bandits. Crop failures got a lot to do with it. Come on, we better light a shuck."

Regan urged his pony into a brisk walk. It was still a good thirty miles to Harlingen.

"Convenient of 'em to put the Empire Hotel halfway between the stables and the train station." Regan gestured towards a two-story building rising above the clapboard structures down the street. "'Specially since its got the best barroom in town."

"Just about the only one left," muttered Whitey. "This town is growin' up fast."

The two had followed the spur railroad line right into Harlingen, where it joined with the main north-south roadway of the St. L., B. and M. Railway. The men had stabled their horses and walked carefully along the new sidewalk. Commerce Street itself was unpaved, but the board sidewalks had recently been replaced by concrete ones. Whitey dragged his boot heel across the sidewalk surface, a scowl on his face. Regan grinned at him. Whitey hated concrete.

The Rangers had studied a timetable and found a seven o'clock northbound train, one which they could take up to Lyford. They strolled slowly, side by side, looking into the storefronts and making eye contact with everyone they met. They carried their saddlebags slung over their shoulders. Whitey's carbine dangled down from his right hand. Men who approached them on the sidewalk gave them a broad berth.

Regan finally slowed to a stop and looked up and down the street.

"Look at all them motorcars," he said, standing with his hands on his hips. Automobiles chugged along in both directions, slowly negotiating the deep ruts left in the street by the winter rains. Several cars were parked at different angles in front of the Empire Hotel. Regan counted several Franklins. He pointed out an old Maxwell touring car parked at the curb. Whitey coughed; the smell of gasoline was unfamiliar and hard on their senses.

"Yeah, things is changin' fast. Harlingen's becomin' a major city here in the Valley. But looky there," Whitey pointed. "There's one o' them old Mex water carts."

A mule slowly pulled a two-wheeled cart equipped with a large barrel down the edge of the street, under the supervision of a white-bearded Mexican man dressed in dirty white shirt and pants. Head down, he plodded along, bare-footed.

"It's a mixture of the new and the old, right here on the main drag. I guess not everybody's got their own water supply yet." Reagan watched the old man urge his mule forward.

"Red, we got plenty of time. Over an hour. I could use a cold beer."

Regan considered. A cold glass of beer did sound good.

"You think old man Corbin really got that ice machine to work?" Regan asked. "He kept sayin' he was gonna make enough ice for the whole Valley. Remember?"

"Let's find out."

Whitey pushed his way through the doors and into the barroom, with Regan on his heels.

"Looks like half the durn town is in here," Whitey said over his shoulder. The room was filled with shouting, laughing, arm-waving groups of men who appeared to be a mixture of Harlingen's citizenry. A few wore coats and ties, probably local men of some importance. Others wore greasy overalls: railroad men preparing themselves for the trip north. Several cattlemen gathered at a round table in the corner. Most of the men were dressed plainly, in a variety of unmatched shirts and pants.

There were no women in the barroom. Tobacco smoke rose toward the ceiling, its aroma competing with the sharp smells of sweat and booze.

Whitey pushed his way through the noisy throng, squeezing between the crowded tables and dodging around groups of standing men. He used his Winchester to separate a space for Red and himself at the standup bar. He placed his carbine carefully across the bar. The men he had shoved aside frowned at him at first, but after taking a good look at Whitey they turned their attention elsewhere. The Winchester looked serious, and Whitey was wearing the circle-star badge. Regan nodded to the man standing next to him.

"Harmon! You got any cold beer?" Whitey rapped his knuckles sharply on the surface of the bar.

"Well, if it ain't them two rascal Rangers. What brings you boys into Six-shooter Junction?" Laughing loudly, the big bartender set two mugs of beer on the bar. He leaned forward, propped himself up on his elbows, and smiled a broad grin across at the Rangers.

Harmon was a tall, muscular man with gray hair and mustache on a head the color of polished ebony. His white shirt, open at the throat, displayed his coal black chest. Harmon was well known for his complete bar service, one of the few left in town now that a mysterious fire had destroyed the clapboard building that formerly housed his main competitor. Harmon kept an orderly place. Anyone starting a fight or a shooting scrape in his bar found Harmon's double-barreled shotgun under his nose. He served as an unofficial lawman in Harlingen, joining with deputies whenever a posse was called into action.

"We're takin' the night train up to Lyford." Regan took a sip from his mug of beer. "Looks like quite a party goin' on in here."

"Always is at five o'clock." Harmon stood erect and walked quickly towards the end of bar to serve another customer.

Regan took another sip of beer. He looked at Whitey, who returned his glance. "I'd call it cool," Whitey said in a low whisper. "But it ain't cold."

"Better drink it anyway." Regan turned his back to the bar and looked out across the room, searching the faces carefully.

"Lookin' for Nacho?" Whitey was surveying as well, using the big mirror behind the bar to study the faces in the crowd.

"Thought he might be here. This is kinda the crossroads of the Valley. Don't see him, though."

"Probably in with some señorita, fallin' down drunk." But both men were aware that Nacho was not a heavy drinker.

"Hey there, Rangers. Remember me? Congressman Black?" A deep voice shouted above the roar of the barroom.

Regan's eyes searched the crush of people for the disembodied voice. He found the congressman seated alone at a table back in a corner, a bottle of bourbon in front of him. Regan noticed that the bottle was half empty. Congressman Black swept his arm in a broad arc, the gesture pointing to the empty chairs at his table.

"Join me. Join me," he shouted.

Whitey and Red exchanged a quick look, and together they pushed away from the bar and carried their beer mugs over to the congressman's table.

"I'm glad to see you gents. I hope you can help me."

The congressman was wearing a black three-piece suit, white shirt and black string tie. His face had a reddish hue and was covered with droplets of perspiration. He dabbed at his forehead with a handkerchief. Regan glanced quickly at the bottle of whiskey. Black had had enough to drink.

"How come they call this place 'Six-shooter Junction?'" The congressman picked up the whiskey bottle, but then thought the better of it and set it down. The Rangers picked up their beer mugs and moved them away from the congressman. He could be looking for a chaser.

"Six-shooter Junction?" repeated Black.

"Well," said Regan, "This is the place where the trunk line connects with the railroad main line. Cowboys comin' in town to wait for the train took potshots at the signboards beside the track. With their six-shooters. See? Six-shooter Junction."

"I got one myself."

Black pulled his coat aside and drew a revolver from a tooled leather holster hanging from his belt. He waved the pistol in the air. Whitey and Regan both jumped with alarm. Whitey knocked his chair over and stood erect. Regan scooted his chair backwards and, before he realized it, drew his own pistol, cross-handed. Damn, he thought, that's twice today I've been spooked into pulling iron.

The roar of conversation in the barroom quieted down to a murmur, as the crowd waited to see what would happen. Most of the men were armed; several put their hands on their pistols.

"Dammit, boys, I was just gonna show it to you." Black laid his revolver on the tabletop.

"Mister, you don't do that kind of a thing all of a sudden like that," said Regan. "Not around here, you don't. People might get the wrong idea and act a little bit hasty." Regan holstered his pistol and flexed his sore right hand.

Whitey, who had leaned his carbine against a chair, retrieved it and sat down again with the Winchester in his lap. He looked around the barroom, frowning at anyone who looked at him. Gradually, conversation resumed.

Regan picked up the congressman's little pistol and examined it. He passed it along to Whitey.

"They told me it's the latest thing here in Texas. A Smith and Wesson, thirty-eight caliber." Black looked back and forth between the two Rangers.

Whitey opened the pistol's action and removed a shell from the cylinder.

"Congressman, always keep your hammer leanin' on an empty chamber." He closed the pistol and handed it back to Black, holding the gun by its barrel. "That way, you won't accidentally shoot yourself in a place you hold sacred."

"But what do you think? Is it a good gun?"

"Well, Congressman," said Whitey, "it's a pretty little thing alright. A thirty-eight is a little light for general work here in South Texas. Probably about right for folks back East."

"It's a modern pistol," added Regan. "It's a double action, the latest thing in revolvers. Smith and Wessons are okay. Only thing is, it ain't a hundred percent reliable."

"Reliable?"

"Yeah," said Whitey, "it's apt to jam on you, just at the wrong time. Now, you take that Colt Peacemaker of Red's there. Single action, simple, and you don't go sprayin' lead all around. You fire thoughtful-like."

Regan slipped his pistol from its holster, using his left hand, and passed it carefully to the congressman.

"It's heavy." Black hefted the weapon. The Rangers watched carefully to see that he kept his thumb off the hammer.

"And hey!—it's got no front sight on it."

Regan and Whitey grinned at each other. This was a little modification they had learned from Nacho Ybarra. Regan had filed away the sighting flange from the end of the barrel.

"If you gotta draw, you don't want your pistol to get stuck in your holster," Regan said. "It slips out easy without that front sight catching on somethin'."

"How do you aim it?"

Whitey laughed. "If you gotta aim, you're too far away for a pistol." He hefted his Winchester. "This is the one you aim with."

Black shifted his weight in his chair and leaned forward.

"Listen, boys, I gotta make a report to the Congress and to President Wilson about these bandit troubles. What should I tell them? I'm getting several different viewpoints."

"Tell 'em the durn Mexicans are tryin' to take back Texas." Whitey spat on the floor. "Tell 'em we got our hands full here. We need to go across and settle things down some. Tell 'em to beef up those garrisons at Ringgold Barracks and Fort Brown. And up at Laredo, too."

Regan frowned at Whitey. This was not the message that Longhorn Maddox had been giving to the congressman. Maddox had made it plain that he thought a large federal garrison would provoke more trouble with the Mexicans. He had argued for a diplomatic solution.

But maybe Whitey was right. More troops would make it easier on the Rangers. If they didn't get out of control.

Regan shifted in his chair and leaned forward.

"Congressman," he said, "all of Mexico is in turmoil." He tapped his palms on the table, warming to his subject. "Nobody's in charge over there. We're feelin' the effects here. Bandits come across—well, it's like a rusty bucket. Where's the next leak gonna be? They cross the river to rob, or rustle, or just raise hell. Then they scoot back across. We ain't supposed to chase them into Mexico. They're safe there."

"And you Texas Rangers can't stop it?"

"Could if they'd let us," said Whitey. "Turn us loose to go across the river. We'd clean 'em out."

"You see, that's the problem," added Regan. "They can skedaddle back across the river. They're safe there. We can't follow 'em."

The sound of a chair scraping across the barroom floor interrupted them. A heavy-set giant of a man pulled a chair up to the table and sat down with a thump and a grunt.

"Hello, Lonnie," said Regan.

"What're you boys doing in my town?" asked the newcomer. His face held a serious expression, but his eyes twinkled.

"Lonnie Sterling here is a deputy sheriff of Cameron County," Whitey said to Black. "Lonnie, this gent is a congressman."

"I know who he is." The deputy eyed the congressman, frowning across at him. "You leaving town?" he asked.

"On the next train out." Congressman Black reached for the bottle of bourbon but the deputy beat him to it and poured a shot in a glass that he had suddenly produced.

"Well, sir, you're gonna have a lot of company." Lonnie downed the liquor and studied the empty glass. "That weren't bad." He reached for the bottle again.

Three mugs of beer suddenly clumped down onto the table. Harmon, grinning from ear to ear, slapped the deputy on the back.

"Keep an eye on 'em, Lonnie," he said, and turned back towards the bar.

"What do you mean, plenty of company?" asked Black.

Lonnie lifted a mug of beer and drained it with a series of large gulps. He wiped his mouth with his sleeve, stared across the table for a moment, and gave a hearty belch.

"Woulda been better if it was cold," he said.

"What company?" persisted Black.

"Well, Congressman, lotsa these farmers are givin' up. They're packin' up and headin' back north. To Iowa or Ohio or wherever they came from."

"Because of the bandits?" Black looked at the Rangers.

"That's part of it," said Lonnie. "But you know, these folks didn't know much about farmin' when they came here. They thought they could just throw seed in the ground and step back. Didn't quite work out that way. Look at that family over there." The deputy pointed across the room. A door was open into the hotel lobby, and through it a little group of people huddled, sitting on boxes and suitcases. A man and a woman sat side by side, surrounded by several children.

"They're waitin' for the train. Now papa will tell you that mama couldn't stand it, the heat, the bugs, the drought, and all that stuff. But you notice that papa is grinnin' his face off. He's happier to leave than she is."

"Now," he continued, "look over that way." He pointed to a table where four neatly-dressed men sat, their heads together in an animated conversation.

"That's a covey of land speculators," he continued. "They are the sonsa bitches that sold them the land in the first place. Now they've bought it back cheap. So's they can sell it again. All legal. I don't like it."

"What would you like the government to do about that?"

"Not a damn thing," said the deputy. He eyed the other two mugs of beer, which the Rangers had corralled on their end of the table.

Lonnie pushed back from the table. "Congressman, send us some more soldier boys," he said.

"Yeah, that's the ticket," said Whitey. "And get 'em permission to go down into Mexico and clean up." He beat his beer mug on the table. Regan looked at Whitey; he hoped Whitey wasn't gonna get his temper up. Was he feeling the beer?

"Oh, I think I can safely say that Congress will recommend that the army reinforce its efforts here on the Border," said Black. "Anything else?"

In the silence that followed, Regan spoke softly. "Captain Maddox says that diplomacy ain't workin'. Whatsisname? William Jennings Bryan? Secretary of State? We heard that he keeps sendin' those messages of protest to Mexico City. The Mexicans just tear 'em up. They think it's a sign of weakness. I guess we need a better diplomat to deal with the Mexicans."

"I'll point that out to President Wilson. From what I hear, there isn't much of a central government in Mexico today. I don't know who the diplomats can talk with. Do you?"

"Damn right." Whitey downed the rest of his mug of beer. "Mexicans don't know crap about government. Never did."

With a final look at the bottle of bourbon, Lonnie abandoned his chair. "Gotta go down to the station, try to keep order there. You gents better shake a leg if you're gonna try to get on that train."

Regan looked around. The barroom was emptying fast.

"C'mon, Whitey. Grab your carbine."

"Good luck to you men," said Black. "You'll be hearing from me, once I get back to Washington." The congressman struggled to his feet.

In turn, the two Rangers shook hands with Black. Regan doubted anything would result from the congressman's visit to the Valley. The problem must seem small to people in Washington.

The Rangers were hurrying down the sidewalk when Whitey suddenly stopped Regan by grasping his arm.

"Looky there." Whitey pointed with his Winchester. "Ain't that Doc Gaither talkin' with that old Mex? The one with the water cart?"

Across the street, the man Whitey had identified was in close conversation with the old Mexican. The Doc was waving his arms about his head and talking loudly. The Mexican stood with his head down, looking at his feet, answering softly. He reached out and stroked the shoulder of his mule.

"Reckon Doc don't have runnin' water at his place?" Regan pulled his arm free from Whitey's grip. "We better get goin'."

"Hang on a minute. Doc's crossin' the street."

Doc Gaither was working his way among the deep ruts in the street. He had seen the Rangers and held up an arm. He wanted to talk. At last he stepped up onto the sidewalk, dusting off his britches.

"Glad I ran into you boys. Where are you headed?"

"Gonna catch the train to Lyford, Doc. We gotta hurry." Regan took a step down the sidewalk. Lonnie's comments about the train worried him. There might not be enough room on that train, and they needed to get to Lyford or they'd face the wrath of Longhorn Maddox.

"Wait up there, Red. How about going with me?"

"How's that?" asked Whitey.

"Listen. Old Faustino just told me about a bandit gang headed up country."

"Is Faustino that old Mex with the water cart?" Regan interrupted. He nodded toward the old man across the street, who was now prodding his mule into high gear.

"That's right. Faustino knows just about everything that goes on around here. He says that a bunch crossed the Rio today about noon and already made it across the Arroyo Colorado just east of here. They're half drunk and spoiling for a fight."

The Rangers looked at each other.

"Well, well," said Regan.

"Might not be such a dull trip after all," added Whitey.

Doc Gaither grasped Regan's arm.

"How about it? Ride up to Lyford with me. I got my new Model T touring sedan parked down by the station. I gotta go home to Raymondville tonight. I'll take you as far as Lyford, if that's where you wanna go. I'd feel a lot better if you men would ride with me. Please?" Doc's voice took on a wheedling tone. He gestured down the street towards the railroad station. Regan realized that he was truly frightened.

"Guess we can do that." Regan looked at his partner. "Okay by you, Whitey?"

"Yeah, let's go. I didn't cotton to no train packed with farmers anyhow."

Doc Gaither tugged again at Regan's arm. Regan shook the doctor's grasp loose. The Rangers gathered their saddlebags and hurried off down the sidewalk towards the station, Regan in front, Whitey trailing behind. There was an unspoken thought between them. Mabel Steuben's favorite farm was on this route.

"You sure you wouldn't rather wait 'til morning, Doc? We ain't got a lotta firepower if we run up against a big gang of bandits," said Regan, frowning towards the doctor.

"No, I gotta get up to Raymondville tonight. Woman's gonna domino any minute and she might need me. Delivering babies has got to be my specialty these days. Replacing my former job of repairing broken bones and gunshot wounds. But there's a ten-gauge shotgun in my T Model, if you think you need more firepower."

"That and my Winchester oughta be enough," said Whitey. "Them bandits will be lookin' for easy pickin's. Likely they won't go up against flyin' lead."

"Like you said, Whitey. It oughta be interesting." But Regan continued to frown.

CHAPTER TWELVE

Nacho had taken over the large table at the back of the *Taberna calle Amistad*, where he sat alone. He was expecting Tomás, who should have been released from the *calabozo* early that afternoon. Paulo had also promised to join him at the *Taberna*. Nacho had been waiting, more or less patiently, for over four hours. Now he found himself increasingly uncomfortable. He caught Hector's eye and raised his eyebrows. Nacho watched the tavern owner grow increasingly nervous.

At first, Hector seemed comfortable with Nacho's presence in the *Taberna*. Nacho's new appearance reassured Hector. With his dyed and trimmed moustache and hair and the pressed woolen suit, Nacho no longer looked like a *vagabundo* or a desperado. But Nacho had been sitting for a long time at the back table, and Hector was acting nervous. Perhaps, thought Nacho, he is considering the reward offered for my capture. He stirred uneasily in his chair.

As the early evening hours approached, the time of the afternoon *siesta* ended. A crowd began to gather for drinks and light snacks, a specialty of the *Taberna*. The younger patrons liked to take advantage of the open-air patio facing the plaza. They gathered beside the sidewalk. Their conversations became happier and louder as Hector served them beer, tequila and other liquors. Older, quieter customers preferred the atmosphere inside. As more and more of the regular patrons entered the *Taberna*, Nacho realized that he was becoming a topic of interest to them. He was conspicuous, a stranger sitting alone, which made him the object of their curiosity. Nacho watched as Hector fussed over his regular customers. Perhaps he ought to absent himself for the rest of the evening.

Nacho was relieved when he saw Tomás peeking in through the door, looking over the room. Hector pointed towards the table at the back of the room. A smile split the youngster's face when he finally saw Nacho gesturing to him. He hurried across the room, weaving his way between tables. Heads turned and eyes followed him as he pulled out a chair and sat down abruptly.

"Nacho, at last I have found you! Let us leave this town and return to the camp of Don Francisco. I have had enough of this Matamoros."

"Patience, Tomás, my friend. We must wait for my cousin, who wishes to speak with us." Nacho saw that the clientele in the taproom was openly examining the two of them. He leaned his head closer to Tomás.

"And remember Chulo Valdez?" he continued in a soft voice. "Our task is to contact him. Pancho would not be pleased if we failed to do so. Let us wait and see if my cousin can bring us some news about this bandit. Then we will make plans."

"Paugh! I have met him already. *Es pura mierda*, that one. A fat pig, a braggart. He is no fighter. Don Francisco would not want him."

Nacho's jaw dropped. "How did you find him, Tomás? Where did you meet him?" He had not expected this development.

"At this place, the Yellow House, that Hector told me about."

Nacho turned his gaze towards Hector, who was busy serving a tray of margaritas to a table of laughing customers.

"So, Hector directed you to a—well, a bordello?" he asked.

"But a very classy place. Important people were there. The girls were beautiful, well dressed in the style of *china poblana*. Such lovely dresses, all those colors. You should see them, Nacho. They served me food. All with much decorum. It was very pleasant."

Nacho smiled. "And in this very classy place, you found Chulo Valdez, the man you say is a *puerco*."

"A *puerco, sí*." Tomás rubbed his chin. "He was rude to the girls. And to me. He would not believe that I came to him with a request from Don Francisco. He called me a *mentiroso*. No man calls me a liar. I struck him. One of his *compadres* decided to protect him. I struck him also. Then someone hit me from behind. As you saw, I landed in the *calabozo*." He shifted his weight in the chair, squirming.

"Well, you were fortunate that there was no gunplay."

"They were the fortunate ones. But guns are not allowed in the Yellow House. They are collected at the door, when you enter." Tomás clasped his hands in front of him.

Nacho gazed out across the room and fingered his beard. Customers at the other tables no longer seemed to be watching them. He shifted his attention back to Tomás and studied the young man.

"You look very different, Nacho," said Tomás.

Tomás continued to speak but Nacho waved him to silence. He needed a moment to consider Tomás's revelations. Tomás had alerted the bandit that Pancho Villa was in the area. Well, that would not remain a secret for very long in any case. Villa's army was a conspicuous presence in the countryside. Information about Villa's whereabouts had doubtless filtered into Matamoros by this time. Nacho decided that Tomás had done no real harm by telling the bandit about it.

Nacho shifted again in his chair, aware that Tomás was watching him closely, waiting for a reaction.

"You, too, look different, Tomás. Your clothes are—well, stylish."

"You like them?" Tomás straightened up in his chair. He tugged at the lapels of the dark blue woolen coat that covered his new white shirt. "The police commissioner, your cousin, gave me a hundred pesos and told me I should clothe myself. My other clothes were badly torn." Nacho could see that Tomás was wearing his two pistols again. They were barely covered by his coattails.

"I remember how you looked in the *calabozo*. You were wearing rags. I see you have recovered your *pistolas* also." He smiled at the youngster to reassure him. It would be unfortunate if Tomás decided to take some kind of independent action. He beckoned towards Hector, calling him to the table. Some food and drink might be a good idea.

The vague plan lurking in the back of Nacho's mind was beginning to take form. He could think of several arguments to help him convince Pancho Villa to attack Matamoros. For one thing, *general* Blanco's army of occupation appeared to be weakening day by day and was without the leadership of the *general*. And the bandit Chulo Valdez might assist the Villa army. If *villistas* won the city, then Nacho was confident he could secure the release of Marco Luís. The best strategy would be to lead Villa into a decision while letting him think that he had thought of it himself. Not an easy trick. Villa was smart and had a devious turn of mind, but he also had an enormous ego. If properly presented, the plan would be Pancho Villa's own.

What were the consequences, he wondered? Surely, Villa would not remain long in Matamoros. His ambitions were much larger than occupation of a simple border town. Possibly he would move south with a reinvigorated army and attempt to take charge of the federal government. Perhaps Villa would retreat towards the west, and return to his native area of Chihuahua, before launching an attack on Mexico City. The *americanos*, the soldiers, the Texas Rangers? Well, it was unlikely that they would interfere with Pancho Villa as long as he stayed on the Mexican side of the Rio Grande. *General* Blanco had welcomed *norteamericanos* as visitors to Matamoros. Nacho thought it unlikely that they would want to take part in any fighting. And the Texas Rangers? Nacho frowned to himself. He did not like the idea of associating with the Mexican bandits, even on a temporary basis. What would his Ranger friends, Regan and Wilson, the Red and the White, think of this? Those men had grown into leaders in the Ranger troop, but they still looked to him for advice. Nacho shook his head. He was playing a dangerous game. How could he avoid it?

Nacho was jarred out of his reverie when he realized Paulo was standing at his elbow.

"I have brought your saddlebags, Nacho, as you asked. And I have some information." Paulo pulled out a chair and sat down beside Nacho, opposite Tomás. He placed the saddlebags at Nacho's feet.

Had Paulo already discovered that Villa was in the area? That would be an unwelcome complication. Paulo and his friends might view Villa's presence as an opportunity to pursue their foolish plan of conquering the American side of the *río Bravo*.

"Chulo Valdez," continued Paulo, "can be found at a camp south of the city, where he waits for you."

"My friend Tomás has already contacted him," Nacho interrupted. "I will talk with him also." He reached down and began to unbuckle his saddlebags. He felt the need for his big Colt pistol.

"He has? *Bueno*, my friend. And señor Ortíz wishes to talk with you. I will take you to him. And Nacho, one thing more—."

Nacho had retrieved his gun belt and was checking his *pistola*.

"Yes, Paulo, what is it?" he said, spinning the cylinder carefully.

"Nacho. I have made some progress in the affair of your son-in-law," said Paulo.

This was unexpected. He put his *pistola* down on the table and turned to face his cousin. What had Paulo discovered?

Paulo spoke softly, his eyes fixed on Nacho's forty-five. Tomás leaned across the table, straining to hear Paulo's low whisper.

"I was too late to examine the murdered *teniente's* body, of course, but I interviewed the army doctor who performed a post mortem." He lifted his eyes and smiled at Nacho, who nodded for him to continue.

"The *teniente* was shot in the back, below his left rib cage and just above his kidney. He bled profusely, and was unconscious when the doctor first saw him. He died shortly thereafter."

Paulo reached into his vest pocket and retrieved a small packet wrapped in paper.

"Here, Nacho, is the bullet that the doctor took from the *teniente's* body. Do you recognize it? I have not seen one like it, but you are more experienced in these matters."

Nacho unwrapped the package and held a small bullet up to the light. He turned it over and over, studying it closely.

"It is not a forty-five, too small, and too big for a twenty-two or thirty-two slug. It may be a thirty-eight, but it is longer than the thirty-eight bullet I am familiar with."

Tomás extended his hand, palm up, and Nacho placed the bullet in it. Tomás tossed it in his hand, weighing it, turning it over between thumb and forefinger.

"There is a great variety of guns in Don Francisco's army. Perhaps it came from one of those old rifles," offered Tomás. He handed it back to Nacho.

Nacho thought about the odd looking little *pistola* that the man Steiner had given him. What did he call it, a Luger? This might have come from such a weapon. He decided to take a bullet from the strange little *pistola* later, when he was alone, and see if it matched. He wrapped the bullet in the paper and stuck it into his jacket pocket.

"So you see, Nacho, your son-in-law did not commit the murder. His *pistola* is a forty-five caliber." Paulo was now smiling broadly.

"We knew that already. The *pistola* of Marco Luís had not been fired. *Capitán* Arredondo told us. Remember?"

Paulo nodded soberly. "Yes, that is true. This is further proof. Perhaps the *capitán* will release him now."

Nacho smiled grimly. "No, not yet. We will have to provide the *capitán* with an alternative suspect. Paulo, you have more work to do."

"*Sí*, that is so. Well, I will see what I can do. Now, let us go and meet *señor* Ortíz."

Paulo started to rise. Nacho grasped his sleeve and coaxed him back into his chair.

"A moment, Paulito. Did you ask the *médico*—were there any gunpowder burns on the *teniente's* jacket or shirt?"

Wide-eyed, Paulo stared at Nacho for a moment.

"No," he said finally, "I did not ask. I will do so."

"And Paulo, please interview the others who were at the table when the shooting occurred. And talk with the bartender." That should keep him busy, Nacho thought.

"*Sí, sí*, of course." Paulo rose slowly, mentally arranging his agenda.

"And now," said Nacho, "let us see what *señor* Ortíz has to say to us. Will we meet with him at his *banco?*" He rose to his feet, fastening his gun belt around his waist. It might be a good idea to visit with the banker. Nacho's funds were running low. He smiled to himself. Pancho Villa might wish to make a withdrawal from Ortíz's bank, all for the *Revolución* of course.

"Come, Tomás. We go to the *banco*."

The horse was fresh; it maintained a steady gallop towards the setting sun. A good horse, the best the stable had to offer. Nacho flipped the reins across the horse's rump, urging it onward. He sat lightly in the saddle, leaning forward, boot tips in the stirrups. The physical activity offered a release from the tension that had accumulated in his body during the past two days. Tomás Aguilar had fallen behind him, and was now dropping further back to avoid the dust that Nacho's horse was kicking up. Nacho had the better of the two horses they had hired from the stables near the *banco*. The road they followed ended eventually in Monterrey, but it would pass close to the camp of Pancho Villa, south of the old village of Reynosa. Nacho intended to reach that camp during the evening hours. He was determined to press Villa to attack Matamoros. The occupying army was weakening. *General* Blanco was gone and the *capitán* Arredondo—well, Nacho thought he was arrogant and irritating. He did not seem to be a leader of men.

Nacho believed that Villa could easily capture Matamoros and take control of the city. Even if he did not succeed, an attack would throw Blanco's army into confusion. He felt confident that he could find an opportunity to rescue Marco Luís from the *calabozo* and spirit him away. I will collect my daughter and her husband, he thought, and take them back across the *río* into Texas. Away from the turmoil of the *Revolución*.

The late afternoon in Matamoros had not gone well. The banker, *señor* Ortíz, had lectured Nacho about the importance of their revolutionary plans, but he had not offered much in the way of details, only flowery language. As a banker, Ortíz was naturally more concerned with the outlay of money and how he might benefit from it. He had asked for a list of materiel that Nacho would require and for some kind of collateral. Nacho could provide neither. Ortíz had shown Nacho a list of armaments that the *señor* Steiner had prepared for him, together with the costs of the weapons. How did Nacho plan to pay for them? After considerable discussion, Nacho had managed to arrange a personal loan of a thousand pesos. Ortíz could hardly refuse him, not after he and his colleagues had argued so forcefully to involve Nacho in their plans. But Ortíz was not happy with the arrangement and showed his displeasure. Nacho had stomped out the door, angry with Ortíz. Now, as the tension eased from his body, he began to understand how Ortíz was feeling. If—when—their silly scheme failed, Ortíz was the one who stood to lose the most. A thousand pesos, at least.

Nacho shifted in his saddle, and his horse took the movement as a signal to slow its pace. Not yet, thought Nacho, and applied a light spur and a flick of the reins. He knew the horse would soon need to stop its rapid gallop, but he needed more time to think, free from Tomás and his persistent questions.

Chulo Valdez had proved to be an egotistical peasant, even more conceited than Nacho had expected him to be. Nacho and Tomás had located him easily by following the road out of

Matamoros to the south. Valdez had made a camp on the bank of a small creek. He was fat and greasy, dressed in dirty, torn clothes. He wore twin bandoleers across his chest, but they were no more than half filled with bullets. His two pistols protruded from crude, homemade holsters. His drooping belly obscured his belt buckle.

Valdez had paraded back and forth in front of Nacho and Tomás, strutting to the amusement of his little group of bandits. No, he did not think that Nacho brought a message from Pancho Villa. If Villa was indeed somewhere along the lower *río*, he would certainly know about it. And *cierto*, if Pancho Villa were to appear, he should join with Valdez, not the other way around. Valdez bragged about the fear the *norteamericanos* felt of him, about the way he raided their *rancherías* with impunity.

During this display, Nacho had kept the palm of his hand pressed against his *pistola*, his hip turned forward so that the bandits could see that he was prepared to draw his weapon. He kept Tomás slightly behind him, on his left side. He was prepared for a gunfight to erupt, but he felt sure that Chulo Valdez was putting on a mere display. Nacho soon realized that he could accomplish nothing with this visit to the bandit's camp. He had gestured to Tomás and they had backed away from the group of bandits, who continued to laugh at them as they withdrew.

This is not over, thought Nacho. He was sure to meet Chulo Valdez again, on one side of the river or the other.

One observation puzzled him. As Valdez paraded in front of him, Nacho could see the handle of a small *pistola* protruding from the top of his boot. It looked similar to the strange little gun that Steiner had given him. The one he called a Luger.

Nacho tugged on the reins to slow his horse. Tomás pulled up beside him, his horse blowing heavily. Well, it was a good time to rest the horses. So far, they had made good time, but darkness was descending upon them. They would have to proceed more cautiously. Nacho was determined to reach Villa's encampment if it required riding through the night.

CHAPTER THIRTEEN

The setting sun cast long shadows across the platform of the Harlingen railroad depot, illuminating the crush of waiting passengers with an eerie orange light. Some of them were sitting on their luggage; most were simply standing or milling about. Tired, discouraged, the mixed throng waited for salvation in some form or another. A few people managed to force their way inside the station house while others exited. The sea of humanity overflowed down the sidewalk along Commerce Street. Men shuffled their feet uneasily. Women attempted to comfort their exhausted children.

"Lookit that mess," said Whitey. He and Red had stopped to gape at the packed platform. "Think it's a riot buildin' up? It's awful quiet for that many people."

"Ain't gonna get all of them onto a train tonight," offered Red. "Could get nasty." He stopped beside a forlorn looking woman sitting on the edge of the platform and holding two young children, one on each knee.

"You all right, Ma'am?" Red removed his Stetson.

"I guess I'll make it." The woman did not look up.

"Your husband around here?"

"No, he ain't!" The woman shifted the children on her knees and looked up at Red. "He got stopped in Mexico, down near Victoria where he was workin'. He done sent me a message to skedaddle back to the States. I been ridin' a flat car all day on that damn Meskin railroad. Eatin' bugs and beggin' for water. It was the only way I could get here. I'm lucky to make it this far, I guess."

"We're Texas Rangers, Ma'am. Can we help?" Red looked at Whitey, who had come up to stand beside him.

The woman smiled. "I knowed it. I figgered you was. We're gonna make it. I got family in Houston. And I got money hemmed up in this dress. We'll be all right."

"C'mon, c'mon. Here's the Model T," said Doc Gaither, who had taken Regan's elbow.

The Rangers inspected the big black sedan sitting at the curb beside the train station. Its top was down, revealing leather seats. Chrome headlights sat on the fenders. Red stepped forward to examine them.

"Them's electric ones," said Gaither. "They operate off the magneto. No more climbin' out and lightin' them damn carbide lamps. This is the modern way. I got this Model T off the train just last week. Ain't she somethin'?"

Suddenly, a side door in the terminal building burst open. A pudgy man in a black suit emerged, pushing a tow-headed boy in front of him.

"Git! Git!" said the man. The lad ran down to the corner of the building, unhitched a large black horse from a post, vaulted into the saddle and galloped rapidly away.

"What the hell?" asked Whitey.

"Calkins, come here a minute," said Doc Gaither. "Boys, this is Chet Calkins, the Station Master for Harlingen. Chet, these hombres are gen-u-wine Texas Rangers."

The Station Master stopped and half turned to face Gaither. "Gotta hurry, Doc. This is a mess here tonight. Don't know how we're gonna work it out. A whole bunch of the train crew just decided they got sick. I think they're scared of bandits."

"Who's the boy?" asked Red.

"Oh, him. He's the call boy. He's the one we send out to round up train crew members in a hurry."

"He sure can ride." Whitey was watching the black horse disappear down the street.

"I hope he can find us a crew. He knows where to go." Shaking his head, Calkins disappeared back into the station.

Congressman Black hurried up the sidewalk towards them. His large black valise swung from one hand; the other held a sweat-dampened handkerchief.

"You boys see this mob?" he asked, gesturing back towards the railroad platform. "They say now that the train's gonna be late, and there's not enough room for everybody anyway. What are we gonna do?"

"Whitey and me are gonna ride up to Lyford with Doc Gaither here. He's drivin' this brand new Model T." Regan patted the car's fender. "Mebbe you oughta hustle back to the hotel and get a room for the night, Congressman. You wanna get there ahead of the rush."

"It's too late for that," said Black. "I already tried; there's no rooms left." He peered into the cabin of the Model T. "Say, could I get a ride with you men? If you're driving north? Maybe I can get a hotel down the line someplace and catch a train tomorrow." He looked back and forth at Red and Whitey.

Red looked down at his feet. Whitey shrugged his shoulders. "Up to the Doc," he said.

"If you want," said Doc Gaither over his shoulder. He had climbed into the Model T, behind the steering wheel. "Get in and let's go. I wanna get as far as we can before daylight runs out."

Whitey vaulted into the back seat, following his saddlebags and his carbine. Red put his hand on Black's shoulder. "Could be dangerous," he said. "We might run into some bandits."

Black shook him off and climbed into the seat beside Doc Gaither. "Well, I might get to see some of these problems first hand," he said.

"Gimmie a crank, Red," said Doc.

Regan stepped to the front of the car and gave the crank an expert flip. The four-cylinder motor responded with a metallic cough and then fired into life. Red hurried along beside the car and vaulted into the back seat, next to Whitey.

"All set, Doc, let's go," he said.

Doc Gaither opened the throttle lever and depressed the reverse pedal. The car backed away from the curb, settling into a large rut in the road.

"Dammit!" Doc shifted into first gear, gave the steering wheel a mighty yank, and managed to steer the car down the street. As the street surface improved, he worked the car through its gears, advanced the spark lever and eased the throttle further open.

"I figure, if the road ain't too bad, we can make about fifteen miles an hour. So, we oughta be there in about two hours. If we don't run into no trouble." Doc Gaither gripped the steering wheel with both hands.

"I don't think we gotta worry about those bandits," said Whitey. "They've had a long day. Likely they'll bed down someplace over in the desert for the night. Drink a little, eat some beans. Then attack somebody in the mornin'. Whattya think, Red?"

"Whitey's probably right. What did that old Mex say, Doc? They crossed the Arroyo Colorado downstream? I bet they're gonna bed down at El Saez. Think so, Whitey?"

"Yeah, that's about right."

"El Saez?" asked the Congressman. "What's El Saez?"

"A windmill. In the desert, the trails lead from windmill to windmill. And each one has a name. See?" said Red.

"I guess it's like oases in the desert, then," said Black.

"Wouldn't know about that. But El Saez is a good one, with a big tank. If anybody else is staying there tonight, there'll be trouble."

"You got that right." Whitey sighted along his carbine at passing trees. "I could get used to this car ridin'. Whatcha think, Red? Better than horses?"

Doc Gaither laughed loudly. "One flat tire, Ranger, and you'll call for your horse again." He pulled the throttle lever down another notch. "I'll be glad when this trip is done."

Red had dozed off, lulled by the gentle rolling motion of the Model T. As darkness enveloped them, Doc had switched on his headlights. Because they got their power from the car's magneto, the headlights shone more intensely when the motor ran at higher revolutions. Doc had adjusted the throttle lever to a speed of about twenty miles per hour, a pace that provided good light production.

Red was jarred awake when the car made a sudden stop. He sat forward, straining his eyes to see into the distance ahead. They had entered a small grove of mesquite brush. Both sides of the road were lined with it, a dense thicket of thorny branches and twigs. Their lacy spring foliage was sparse. Red could see a short man further down the road, standing in the light of the headlights, facing them in the road and waving a hat.

"Ayudame!" called the figure, waving his arms above his head. *"Socorro!*

"What?" asked Black.

"He's callin' for help," said Doc. "Wonder what he really wants." Doc sat still, peering forward into the light, both hands gripping the wheel tightly.

"Whatcha think?" asked Red.

"Turn off them lights," said Whitey. Doc reached forward and switched off the headlights. After a second, he turned off the motor also. In the sudden silence they could hear the man call again, more softly this time. Then, the only sound was that of the crickets in the trees.

"Could be either side," Red whispered.

"Take that side. I'll take this one over here. Let's go." Whitey vaulted out of the car towards the right.

"Doc, gimmie that ten gauge Greener." Regan was still unsure of his sore hand. For this type of trouble a shotgun was better anyway.

Regan clambered out of his side of the back seat, moving towards the left of the car. He slipped away into the darkness, the shotgun cradled under his arm.

"One thing, Red," called Whitey. "Be careful you don't tear that pretty suit of clothes." Chuckling, he disappeared into the brush on the right side of the road.

"What're they doing?" asked Black.

"Shh. They're gonna sneak through the mesquite brush, one on each side of the road. Looks like it could be an ambush. They're gonna check it out." Doc looked at Black. In the dim light he could see that the congressman had drawn his Smith and Wesson Pistol. Doc reached across and shoved Black's hand away. "Point it out of the car," he whispered.

The two men sat quietly in the front seat, listening for footsteps in the road. Only the songs of crickets drifted through the evening.

"Maybe it was somebody who really needs help," whispered Black.

"If so, he woulda walked up to the car. We'll know pretty soon. One way or the other. Be quiet and just listen," said Doc.

Both men jerked when a sudden flash of light burst forth in the brush ahead on the left. The loud thump of a shotgun blast followed immediately.

Black stood up in his seat, peering across the windshield. "What was that?" he exclaimed.

"Sounds like Red flushed somebody. Hey, don't shoot!" Doc grabbed Black's elbow, pulling him down into his seat. Whitey had materialized beside the Model T.

"Guess they were all over on Red's side," said Whitey.

The shotgun spoke again.

"Listen to that," laughed Whitey. "Red's scatterin' those folks pretty good. You can hear 'em tearin' through the mesquite. Sounds like four or five of 'em."

But after a moment, all became silent again. The men waited, hardly breathing, listening, until Red suddenly appeared beside the car. "Fire it up, Doc," he said. "We oughta get outa here now." He stepped to the front of the car and grasped the crank handle.

"Spin 'er." Doc retarded the spark and shifted into neutral. The motor caught on the first spin. Doc immediately switched on the headlights and revved up the motor. The lights revealed an empty road ahead of them.

Whitey had gained the back seat and offered a helping hand to Red. "You hit any of 'em?" he asked.

"Nope. Don't think so. I just scattered 'em some. Musta been four or five waitin' over there. It was an ambush, all right. You have this problem before, Doc?"

Doc Gaither engaged the gears, and the car lurched forward. "That's why I don't like to go out of town at night. No respect for the medical profession."

Black found his voice. "Was that the big group of bandits? The ones you were talking about earlier?"

"Naw," said Red, "Just a small bunch. Probably field hands by day. Mebbe just tryin' their hands as bandits come nighttime."

"Most likely," said Doc, "those were men who had been let off when some farmer or another sold out. So they were out of a job. Lookin' to pick up a little loot, then head for the Border."

"Could be, but they're just a buncha damn bandits any way you look at it." Whitey checked his carbine again. "Keep it movin', Doc. We might attract some more company."

"Say, Doc, what kinda loads you got in those shells? Like to took my arm off." Red had broken the shotgun open and was looking in a pouch for more shells.

"You like those shells?" laughed Doc Gaither. "Load them myself. Buckshot and plenty of black powder."

The road emerged from the grove of trees and curved over toward the railroad tracks.

"Looks like clear sailin' now, boys," said Doc. He moved the gas and spark levers down another notch. "Should be in Lyford in about a half hour."

The two Rangers looked at each other. "Hope they're ready for us," said Whitey.

Doc looked towards Congressman Black. "You can put that pistol away now, Congressman. The excitement's over."

Black looked down at his hand. "I didn't realize I was still holding it." He leaned back and tucked the revolver into the holster beneath his coat. "Tell me, does this kind of thing happen often? I mean, do you have to live with this uncertainty all the time? Bandit attacks and things like that?"

Whitey leaned forward. "This is South Texas, Congressman. This is all that's left of the western frontier. We kinda like the excitement down here."

"Whitey's layin' it on a little heavy," said Doc. "Things have just gotten bad the past few years. All that political upset down in Mexico spills over here. We're copin' with it."

"Well, it's been a revelation," said Black. "I can surely see that you people need some help. Those of us in Washington, well, we just haven't been aware of the events taking place on our southern border. I can assure you that I will get the attention of my colleagues in the House. We will alert the War Department as to your requirements for defense and protection."

"Sounds like some of that government speechifyin'," laughed Whitey. "The excitement musta got you worked up."

"Congressman," said Regan, "we would sincerely appreciate anything you can do." He nudged Whitey with his elbow.

"Yeah," said Whitey, after a moment's pause. "We'd appreciate it." He scowled at Regan for a second, and then grinned and winked at him. "We surely would."

Regan nodded and patted his partner on the arm. After all, they'd made a strong impression on the congressman. Shouldn't let it go to waste.

They began to see the reddish glow in the sky when they were a half-mile away from the little village of Lyford. As they drew near the village, the source of the glow soon revealed itself. There was a large bonfire blazing away in the center of town.

"What the hell," exclaimed Doc Gaither. He shoved the gas and sparker levers upwards, slowing the automobile's progress. The two Rangers leaned forward, squinting into the night. The congressman muttered something under his breath.

"Whatcha think?" asked Red Regan.

"Don't know," answered Whitey. He lifted his carbine from the seat beside him and laid it across his lap.

For the past half-dozen miles, the road had run parallel to the railroad tracks. The roadbed was firm, running straight beneath an open sky, and Doc had kept the Model T hustling along. But when they reached the outskirts of the village, the road swung away from the railroad tracks. It passed through a small clump of mesquite trees and entered the main street of the little town. Doc shifted the Model T down into low gear when they approached the edge of the plaza in the middle of the village. The car rolled slowly past the plaza where the bonfire blazed. Flames reached upwards and sparks were carried into the darkness. The light from the bonfire was the only illumination in the town. Buildings across the street from the plaza were revealed in patterns of shadows.

Doc and his passengers stared intently at the scene on the plaza. Outlined against the big blaze, figures of men could be seen, most of them standing still. Some were holding rifles. One man was heaving more of the twisted mesquite logs onto the bonfire.

Doc started to ease the car to a stop at the edge of the square.

"Keep moving, Doc," urged Red Regan. "Don't stop right here. Drive on over there by that buildin'."

"The drugstore?" asked Doc.

"Yeah, that'll do."

As soon as the car stopped, the two Rangers vaulted out of the back seat. They stood side by side, peering across the street at the images of men outlined against the bonfire.

"Red, I don't like this," said Whitey.

"Don't look good, does it?" Red answered. In fact, the group gathered at the bonfire could well be a mob about to get out of control. And mob behavior was an activity the Rangers both hated and feared. An armed mob would resort to gunfire sooner or later. Men who were peaceful, law-abiding citizens could become transformed into killers as a consequence of a frantic, unreasoned group activity. Later, after the damage was done and was beyond all remedy, they regretted their actions. But only after it was over.

Doc joined the men beside the car. He shaded his eyes against the glare and peered into the group silhouetted by the bonfire.

"Recognize anybody?" asked Red. "We gotta pick out the leaders."

"Nope. Too dark to see much. You think it means trouble?"

"Doc," said Red, "I think you oughta pack up that congressman and haul your butts oughta here. This situation might get nasty. You oughta scoot on up to Raymondville. Leave this mess to us."

"Good point. I'm goin'." Doc turned and climbed back into his car.

"One thing, Doc. I'd be grateful for the loan of that ten gauge. I'll get it back to you."

"Take it," said Doc. He reached into the car and retrieved the shotgun and the bag of shot. "Grab some shells. I'll find you later." Doc climbed into the Model T and eased it away, down the road. Congressman Black waved over his shoulder as the car disappeared into the darkness.

The two Rangers stood quietly, side by side, looking across at the bonfire, squinting into the glare. The group of men visible in front of the fire now stood unmoving, studying the two Rangers.

Both Rangers jumped when a tall figure suddenly appeared out of the darkness to stand beside them, and a voice broke the silence.

"About time you yahoos got here."

Red had elevated the shotgun barrel, but he immediately lowered it. "George Denham, by God!" he exclaimed.

"Where'd you come from?" asked Whitey.

"I been sittin' outside this goldurn drugstore all day and all night. Standin' guard. Thought I was gonna have to fight off that durn bunch of roosters over there. Glad you boys finally showed up."

George Denham was an ex-Ranger, a former member of McNelly's troop, the ones who had cleaned the bandits out of the Nueces Strip a decade earlier. McNelly's troop had been a hard-riding, shoot-first group of Rangers who interpreted the law of the land very liberally. Their actions were effective, and the rule of law was established in the Strip, but the cost in lives and race relations was high. When McNelly's troop was disbanded, many of them left the Valley. Not George Denham. Now a gray-headed, portly man with a full beard, he had settled into cattle ranching in the upper Valley. Denham had kept his reputation as a no-nonsense fighting man. He still kept in contact with the Rangers. He had developed a passion for local politics, and his forceful approach had made him unpopular with some of the newcomers in the area.

The light from the bonfire illuminated Denham's frown. He held a carbine in his hand, barrel tip down. Two pistols were stuck in his belt. Denham scowled towards the men gathered on the square. He spit deliberately into the dirt at his feet.

"George, what the hell are you tryin' to do here?" asked Whitey. "How'd you get them boys so stirred up?"

"I'm tryin' to protect my goldurn foreman. Those goldurn *pendejos* think he's a bandit. They were gonna try to lynch him." He spit again.

"Say, you got any other bandits here in Lyford?" asked Regan.

"What the hell you mean?"

"Longhorn Maddox sent us up here to get a bandit and take him down to Brownsville for trial."

"Yeah, that's Mercurio, all right. My foreman. I tried sending a wire to Maddox. Guess he musta got it, huh? Mercurio ain't no bandit, but those carpetbaggers think he is. Let's get him down to Brownsville where we can get him a trial. Before a real judge. Not in front of Judge Lynch here in this part of the County."

Whitey was peering up and down the street, looking into the shadows. "Where is your man?" he asked.

George laughed, and his expression relaxed for a moment. "On the roof. I put him up on the roof of the drugstore here. He's crouched down where they can't see him. And they can't get to the roof without goin' through me."

Red looked at the building, and then across the street. "I guess we oughta get your foreman and get outa here," he said. "Longhorn told us to take him by train, but I guess we need to get movin'. I don't wanna wait for no train. George, we're gonna need horses."

"I can get them. What about those yahoos over there?"

"George, what exactly is goin' on here?" asked Red. "Why do they wanna lynch your foreman?"

Denham looked down and dragged the toe of his boot through the dirt. "Aw, he did somethin' stupid. Some of them Mex bandits hoo-rawed a few folks night afore last. Didn't hurt 'em none, more's the wonder, but robbed 'em. A bit of that is goin' on around here. Seems like the bandits dropped part of the loot when they were riding back towards the border. A big quilt. Well, Mercurio done found it. He picked it up, and was headed to the ranch when them settlers caught up with him. I told 'em he was my foreman and he just found it, but they thought they'd caught themselves a bandit. Wanted to hang him on the spot. Might have, too, except there weren't no tree tall enough." Denham laughed again.

"So you caught up to 'em?" asked Whitey.

"Yeah, I did. Had to wave my iron around, but I got Mercurio away. Scared 'em pretty good." He laughed again. "Hell, I scared myself some. I was in the mood to perforate somebody."

"And you stuck him up on the roof of the drugstore," said Red.

"Yep. Ran him up a ladder and then took it down. I sent a wire, hopin' to reach old Maddox and get some help. Just before they cut the wires."

The Rangers looked at each other for a moment.

"They cut the wires?" asked Whitey.

"That's kinda serious," said Red. "They start cuttin' the wires, they're askin' for legal trouble. The railroad don't take kindly to that kinda action."

"It warn't too bright. I figger somebody's gonna come investigatin' by mornin'." Denham spat again. "If we can hold them off that long. They been gatherin' strength all evenin'."

Red looked towards Whitey. "How you wanna play this?"

"Lemme go over and talk with them." Whitey strode deliberately across the street.

"Goldurn," said Denham, under his breath.

Whitey stopped at the edge of the square. He held his carbine across his chest, pointed upwards. He squinted at the group of men, shadowy images visible against the light of the bonfire. They watched him silently, unmoving.

Finally, somebody in the group said, "Whatcha want?"

"Texas Rangers," said Whitey. "We come to get a bandit, take him to Brownsville to jail. You boys oughta get on home now. We're gonna handle it."

A big, heavy-set man swaggered up to stand in front of Whitey. "Ranger, huh? Don't matter none to us." He gestured back towards the bonfire, pointing to the crowd of men assembled there. "We're gonna take care of him ourselves, soon as that old fool over there gets outa the way."

Others walked over to gather behind the heavy-set man. Whitey inspected him carefully. A rancher, he decided, judging from his clothing and boots. As others stepped forward to join the man, Whitey looked each of them in the face. He then returned his attention to the big rancher.

"Naw, you don't wanna do that," he said. "Let us Rangers take care of him. You boys are gonna get in a whole lot of trouble here. Go on home, now. Git along with you."

"Mister Ranger," said the big man, "we got you outgunned." He looked around at the men gathered beside him, and then turned to face Whitey, grinning broadly. He took a deep breath. "We'll just..."

He got no further. Whitey swung the barrel of his Winchester across in a short, economical arc, and rapped the big man sharply in his right temple. He fell backwards, hitting the ground with an audible thump. Whitey stared intently at the other men, one at a time, frowning severely. He held his carbine at the ready.

"You heard the Ranger!" Red Regan had walked to the middle of the street, where he stopped. He held the ten-gauge shotgun leveled towards the group. George Denham stepped forward out of the darkness to stand beside Regan.

"Look at 'em step back," muttered Denham. "Starin' at the business end of a shotgun just tends to take the fight right out of a man."

The crowd was, indeed, beginning to step away from Whitey, back towards the bonfire. Regan stepped forward, walking slowly, to stand beside Whitey. "Make a nice target, don't they," he muttered.

"There's more of us than there is of you." The speaker was a tall cowboy standing to the side of the group, dressed in jeans. A black leather vest covered his shirt. He had not yielded any ground. The cowboy jutted out his chin. His right hand came to rest on the handle of a pistol in a low-slung holster tied down to his leg.

"Oh-oh," said Red softly. "Thinks he's a gun slinger."

Whitey swung his carbine across to point directly at the cowboy. "When the shootin' starts, you're the first to get it," he said loudly. "Keep your hand away from that hog leg."

The cowboy stood motionless, staring at Whitey. His muscles started to tense. Whitey's finger tightened on the trigger of the carbine. At this distance he could not miss, darkness or no.

"Give 'im one more chance," said Red suddenly. "Mister, you are askin' for a wooden suit of clothes." The ten-gauge shotgun slowly turned to bear on the tall man.

Abruptly the cowboy turned and walked rapidly away, waving his arm back at the Rangers in a gesture of disgust.

"Ain't worth it," he said over his shoulder. Others began to follow him away, slowly at first, but moving more rapidly as the crowd thinned.

Whitey lowered his carbine. "That wasn't too bad," he said to Regan.

"Gawdalmighty," said Red, exhaling loudly. He flexed his sore hand.

George Denham joined the two Rangers. He squatted down to examine the big man Whitey had poleaxed. The rancher was lying face down in the dirt, his arms stretched above his head. Carefully, Denham turned the man's head to the side.

"Seems to be breathin' all right. I know him. He owns a little ranch east of here. How hard did you hit him?"

"I gave him a right sharp rap. He won't cause you no trouble for a day or two."

"You think he's gonna be all right?" Denham felt of the man's temple. "Got a big goose egg comin' on here. You coulda put him under, hittin' him like that."

A shadow fell across Denham and he rose to his feet. Two young men had walked up to them. They stood, hands in pockets, looking at the unconscious form on the ground.

"Your pa?" asked Red.

"Our brother," said one. "Can we take him home now?"

Whitey laid his carbine aside and helped hoist the limp figure up. The two brothers struggled away into the darkness, sharing the burden between them.

"George," said Red, "how about them horses."

"I'll get 'em now."

"Tell George about those bandits down on the Arroyo," Whitey said to Regan.

Red turned and took hold of Denham's arm. "George, there's a bunch a bandits headed your way. We heard about 'em down in Harlingen tonight. You oughta get back to your ranch afore daylight. They were supposed to be headed north, mebbe over near the Laguna. Somebody saw 'em near the Arroyo this evenin'. Supposed to be lookin' for trouble."

"I'll give it to 'em if they show at my place."

"What about Mabel?" asked Whitey.

"There's another question, George," said Regan. "Are the Steubens stayin' up here right now? Somebody needs to warn 'em about those bandits."

"Old Man Steuben done took his whole outfit back to Harlingen," said George. "I was over there day before yesterday. Old Steuben don't like bein' too far away from his store."

The two Rangers looked at each other. "Well, I guess we don't gotta worry about Mabel just yet," said Red, smiling sheepishly.

"Yeah, I guess you gotta put your courtin' on the back burner, Red. Give you time to give it some thought."

"Courting?" asked George Denham with a grin. "Well, I thought Mabel seemed a little anxious to get back to Harlingen herself. Wonder why?"

"We better ride," said Red, "before your friends get itchy again."

CHAPTER FOURTEEN

C ome, Nacho, walk with me."

Nacho rose from his squatting position by the campfire and emptied the contents of his tin coffee cup into the dirt. Pancho Villa slapped him in the small of the back and propelled him forward into the night. Out across the prairie, as far as the eye could see, the cooking fires of the *villista* army twinkled in the darkness. With his arm across Nacho's shoulder, Villa steered him across the encampment. The large number of campfires meant that the army had grown in the past two days. Nacho wondered about the logistics of feeding this revolutionary horde. How long could Villa afford to keep these *hombres* in camp, waiting, without a target to raid?

Nacho was aware that he and Villa were accompanied by a half dozen of the *dorados*, Villa's special troops, who walked a few paces behind them. They made Nacho uncomfortable. He looked back over his shoulder, and made eye contact with a large *dorado* whose assignment seemed to be to watch only him. Others of the guards looked carefully from side to side as they moved through the encampment. Campfires cast shadows across the unsmiling faces of the *dorados*. Nacho was careful to keep his hand away from his *pistola*.

Villa was dressed in chinos, with the pants legs tucked into knee-high boots. He wore a felt hat pushed back on his head to reveal his black curly hair. He had attached a big *pistola* in a scabbard to his belt. Probably for show, thought

Nacho. With the *dorados* protecting him, he had little need for a personal firearm.

As they walked through the encampment, Villa kept looking at Nacho with sidewise glances. He realized that Villa was appraising his new appearance—the trimmed and dyed mustache, the new haircut. Suddenly, he wondered if the changes had somehow altered Villa's opinion of him. Was he in trouble? Where was Villa taking him?

They moved quietly through the smoky night, passing from one little group of soldiers to another. Men were squatting on their heels or sitting on bedrolls, gathered close to their small cooking fires. They wore shabby clothes, garments that could hardly be called uniforms. Their weapons, always close at hand, were a strange mixture of the old and the new. What they did share, every one, was a complete devotion to Pancho Villa and his vision of the *Revolución*. Each man greeted Villa as though he were a personal friend.

As soon as he had arrived at the camp, Nacho had realized that the army had grown. He shielded his eyes from the glare and tried to stare into the distance. He could see no end to the number of campfires. Pancho Villa's army of the *Revolución* now seemed to be up to full strength. What would the bandit do now?

Villa released Nacho's shoulder and increased his stride, moving ahead. Nacho hurried along, hustling to keep pace with him.

"Don Francisco," he began, "you have many more *soldados* in your *campamento* this evening."

"*Ay*, call me Pancho, my friend. We will talk of these matters later. Let us greet our *soldados*. And enjoy our *cena*. Let us dine." Villa stopped to pat a soldier on the back. While doing so, he took a taco from the man's hand, took a healthy bite from it, and then returned it. As they walked on, he said, "You see, Nacho, my *muchachos* share with each other and with me. None is above another in the army of the *Revolución*." Villa stopped beside another group of soldiers, called one of them by name, and helped himself to a tortilla from a frying plan. He gestured towards the pan, encouraging Nacho to help himself.

Nacho nodded to the soldiers, who were smiling up at him, and took a tortilla. He found that he was hungry. And, he realized, this action established him as a confidante of Villa's. Clearly, this could be important under the present circumstances, but it might be troublesome later. Who could tell?

He realized, with a start, why Villa was doing what he did. Pancho was afraid of being poisoned. That was the reason he was eating a bite here, a bite there. Now he recalled that Villa had, at times in the past, had a fear of poison, to the extent that he would eat only under the most careful circumstances. Had someone that Villa distrusted appeared with these new troops? Or was it simply one of Villa's occasional lapses in confidence?

Pancho Villa took a bottle of beer from a smiling soldier, and walked into the darkness. They had finally come to the edge of the encampment. His *dorados* clustered around him, their backs to Villa while they carefully surveyed the darkness. Finally, Villa waved them back. He beckoned towards Nacho. Stepping carefully, Nacho walked over to stand in front of Villa.

"Tell me of Matamoros," said Villa. The glow from the campfires cast a shadow across half of Villa's face. His black eyes bored into Nacho's. So Nacho gave his report, just the bare outlines. He said nothing about his cousin's attempt to involve him in their plans for empire. But he did tell Villa that his son-in-law was being held in prison, charged with murder.

"*Es nada.*" Villa waved his arm. "We will free him. I intend to capture the city."

Nacho could not keep himself from breaking into a broad grin. He had wondered how he might convince Villa to attack Matamoros. But no argument was going to be necessary. Villa was already making plans.

"I am grateful, Don Francisco. I have been worried about young Marco Luís. I am glad that you have assembled such a large army here. When will you attack, Don Francisco?"

"Call me Pancho. As you can see, Nacho, my *teniente* Ernesto has joined me here, bringing the rest of the army of Chihuahua." Villa chuckled. "Ernesto was hesitant. He thought he might keep part of my army for himself. I asked Rodolfo to talk with him. Ernesto decided to join me here." Villa chuckled again. Nacho did not laugh. He had no desire to fall into the bad graces of Rodolfo Fierro, Villa's designated executioner. He would not like to be standing in Ernesto's boots this evening.

"Tell me, Nacho, how did you find the army in Matamoros? Are they spirited? Will they fight?"

"You may know, Don Francisco, that *general* Blanco has left the army, perhaps to go to Veracruz," Nacho began.

"*Sí, sí, ya lo sé.* I hear that the *general* is now in Mexico City." Villa waved away the comment. "Is the army prepared to defend Matamoros?" he asked. Villa's stare had become intense.

Nacho hesitated, rubbing his chin with the back of his hand. This was an important point. He was aware that Villa was watching him closely, ready to gauge his reply.

"The army," Nacho said, "the army is now commanded by a Captain Arredondo. He is unwilling to take action in the absence of *general* Blanco. And—I observed that the army has poor discipline."

This latter comment was not strictly true. The army appeared to Nacho to be a poor military unit, somewhat lax in its behavior, but maintaining effective patrols. He did not want to give Villa the impression that the army was helpless, but at the same time he certainly did not want to suggest that the army in Matamoros was a strong one.

"Would that army fight? Or would they, perhaps, join us? Join the *Revolución?*" asked Villa.

Nacho considered carefully. Finally, he answered. "Don Francisco, I believe that they would fight you. At least, they would fight at first. After that, who knows?"

Villa nodded. "That is my belief also. You have confirmed the conclusion I had reached after talking with Tomás Aguilar."

So, thought Nacho, he has already talked with Tomás. He seeks to test me, perhaps. He looked past Villa at the group of *dorados*, watching from the darkness. A sudden chill ran down his spine. He looked into Villa's face and saw a wry smile. Well, I must have passed the test, he thought. At least, Tomás and I seem to have given him the same report. Nacho shuffled his feet. This could have become very unpleasant.

"Now," said Villa, "tell me about your meeting with the man Chulo Valdez."

"Tomás must have reported that, also," said Nacho. "The man is a *bandido*, not a revolutionary. I was not impressed with him, or with his little group of *rufiános*."

"Tomás was even less impressed than you." Villa chuckled again. "He used his most colorful language to describe the man. But, Nacho, you see, he is a problem for me." Villa took a deep breath and looked up at the sky. "Think of this," he said. "For my campaign to be successful, I will need the support of the people of Matamoros. If they choose to resist my soldiers, I will become a conqueror. I want to be a liberator. It is very important that I appear to be a liberator, especially to the *norteamericanos*."

Nacho nodded; this was logical. Villa still needed the support of the Americans to ensure his eventual success in the revolution.

"And," continued Villa, "Chulo Valdez is the local hero to many of the people of Matamoros. He has avoided the occupying army of *general* Blanco. He laughs at them. The people approve of him because of this. I know," he continued, raising his hand, "I know he is, as Tomás says, a *puerco*. But Nacho, I need him."

Nacho frowned. Was Villa telling him everything? Somehow this explanation did not ring entirely true. *Aquí hay un gato encerrado*, he thought. A small puzzlement.

Villa had fallen silent and stared into the darkness. Nacho bit his lip; he thought he could see what was coming.

Finally, Villa put his hand on Nacho's shoulder. "I need you, too, Nacho. I need you to return to this man and persuade him to join us."

"Don Francisco, he does not even believe that you are here in the lower *río* country. Did not Tomás tell you? He laughed at us."

"I know, I know." Villa patted Nacho's shoulder. "This time, he will believe. Look around you." He waved his arm towards his army camped on the prairie. "An army of this size cannot be kept secret. They must know of it by now in Matamoros. Valdez must know, unless he is a complete fool."

"That is a possibility," Nacho muttered under his breath. But Villa laughed. He slapped Nacho's shoulder and stepped back.

"I want you to leave in the morning. I will send a present to Valdez. A horse. I have a fine white gelding you can take to him. Bring Valdez back, Nacho. Bring him right away. I cannot keep this army camped here for very long. Do you understand?"

"*Sí*, Don Francisco, I understand. I will leave early in the morning."

"Good. See Ernesto about the horse. And call me Pancho." Villa strode back towards the campfires. The *dorados* emerged from the shadows and walked with him. Nacho stared after him, watching until Villa had disappeared among the soldiers of his army. This could work out after all, he thought. He had no intention of becoming so familiar as to address Villa as other than "Don Francisco." Villa was still a rattlesnake.

Nacho sat outside the *Taberna Calle Amistad*, leaning forward, his arms resting on a table he had turned upright. A light coating of dew covered the chairs and tables. Fidgeting, Nacho absently rubbed the tabletop with his forearms, clearing a dry spot on the table. It was too early in the morning for Hector to open the *Taberna*, but he had no place else to go. He stared across the street at the plaza, frowning at the pigeons and doves searching through the grass for their morning meal. Behind him, the white stallion gave vent to a loud whinny.

"*Cállate!* exclaimed Nacho. "Be quiet, horse!" He shifted in his chair and looked back over his shoulder at the gelding, which bobbed its head up and down and neighed again. He had tied the horse's bridle to a hitching post near a water trough. It was the only horse on the street, conspicuous enough without its snickering.

Nacho turned back to the table. He stared at the palms of his hands. Well, it was not the horse's fault. He turned his hands over, spread his fingers and examined his nails. Dirty now, not clean as they had been when he was at Paulo's house. He stroked his small mustache. Was the dye beginning to fade? He examined his fingers. No black stain there, at least not yet. What would his Ranger friends, *Colorado y Blanco*, the

Red and the White, think of his new appearance? He smiled as he considered what he might tell them. And how they would laugh. He sighed deeply and stared out across the plaza. Suddenly he felt a deep yearning to return to the Ranger camp, to free himself from the tangle he found himself in. *Must I always, ever, live between two worlds? To which do I belong? Perhaps, after all, I am doomed to live forever between them.*

Nacho's thoughts gradually returned to his present condition, and his countenance slipped into a frown. Events were moving rapidly, beyond his control, and here he was, able only to sit and wait. Behind his back, the white horse neighed again.

Earlier, in the darkness, he had ridden directly to the campsite where he had found Chulo Valdez on the previous day. All during the nighttime trip from Villa's camp to the city of Matamoros, Nacho had rehearsed what he might say to Valdez. How would Valdez act towards the gift of this fine horse? The scenarios Nacho played out in his mind, most of them anyway, had unpleasant endings. He would have preferred to refuse the assignment Villa had given him, but there was no help for it. He must get Marco Luís out of prison before he could free himself from Villa's plotting and escape back across the Border. Nacho had been at first surprised, then worried, and finally disgusted when he arrived at the bandit's campsite. He found the place abandoned. He had dismounted and poked at one of the campfires. The ashes were cold, the camp long abandoned. Nacho searched the ground, looking for horse droppings. He kicked a few of them and found that they were drying out. A few black beetles ran from beneath the ones he had disturbed. The horses had left a plain trail along the creek bank, and Nacho followed it until he lost it among other tracks on a major road leading towards Matamoros. He recalled that one of the bandit's horses was a distinctively patterned paint. Nacho rode the white horse slowly along the road, hoping to see the paint tethered someplace. Finally, he had to admit that the bandit chief had eluded him.

Nacho was disgusted with himself. Somehow, he had to locate Valdez, deliver the white horse to him, and then recruit the bandit for Villa. Then he could encourage Villa's cooperation, urge the bandit to attack Matamoros and see to the release of Marco Luís. But how to proceed? Who knows where Chulo Valdez might be? Nacho's head hurt from lack of sleep. He stared out across the plaza and sighed deeply. In his exhaustion, he was having difficulties deciding on his next step. Perhaps he should locate his cousin or the other conspirators, one of whom might be able to lead him to Chulo Valdez. Nacho did not want to have to talk with Paulo or his friends. The white horse would have to be explained. He could think of no way to do that without speaking of Pancho Villa. He considered going to the bank to talk with *señor* Ortíz, but of course it was not open at this hour of the morning. He might attempt to locate *señor* Steiner. Or *señor* Riviera. None of these options appealed to him. He stared at his hands again. Where was Hector? If the *Taberna* was open, he could get some coffee. Perhaps his head would clear.

He sighed deeply once again. The morning was cool and pleasant; the sun was climbing above the buildings and burning the dew from the grass. A summer morning to enjoy, but he could only fidget, sitting alone, waiting for Hector to open the tavern. Well, perhaps Hector would have some idea of where he might locate the bandit. Hector had many contacts.

Nacho glanced over his shoulder, towards the white horse, and was startled to see two soldiers standing there on the sidewalk. They had approached from behind; he was unaware of them until they appeared beside the white horse.

The horse shied away and whinnied when one of the soldiers attempted to rub its cheek.

"*Un caballo blanco, el diablo monte,*" laughed the other soldier. The two turned and looked at Nacho, who smiled and waved at them over his shoulder. They waved back, smiling, and proceeded down the sidewalk, their rifles slung over their shoulders. Nacho realized that he had placed his hand on the handle of his *pistola*, under the table where the soldiers could not see it. He shook his head, wondering at his state of mind. Did he really intend to get into a shooting scrape with two soldiers? Indeed, the devil does ride a white horse.

Nacho turned his chair around so that he had a clear field of view up and down the sidewalk. He searched the plaza across the street, studying the early morning scene. No one else was near the *Taberna*, but that situation would soon change as the morning progressed. He ought to get out of sight, he said to himself. If he stayed visible there on the sidewalk, sooner or later someone was sure to ask who he was and what he was doing, and perhaps raise the interest of the *soldados*. He rose and stretched his arms above his head, suppressing a yawn. Across the plaza, the rising sun had slipped into the space between the twin steeples of the cathedral. He squinted at the orb. Soon the morning worshipers would begin to climb the cathedral steps. Nacho looked at the white horse. It was certain to attract attention, tied at the edge of the street. Perhaps there was a stable nearby. Nacho walked over to stand beside the horse. He patted its flank and looked up and down the street.

A sudden movement further down the street attracted his attention. He shielded his eyes with his hand and saw the figure of a young man who crossed the plaza, head down, and walked rapidly towards the side street. There was something about the youth that seemed familiar. Suddenly, recognition flooded his mind. Mauro! His cousin Paulo's son. My nephew, he thought. Returning from a night's adventure, perhaps. Well, this was fortunate.

"Mauro," he called towards the boy. Again, louder, "Mauro!" The lad quickened his steps, head down, and hurried along towards the side street.

Nacho raised his voice in as authoritive tone as he could manage. "Mauro! *Ven aquí!*"

The boy stopped in his tracks and turned to face Nacho. After a moment he replied, *"Muy bien, mi tío."* Mauro walked slowly over to stand in front of Nacho, who reached out and put his hand on Mauro's shoulder. Wide-eyed, the boy looked into Nacho's face. Nacho smiled, hoping to reassure the lad.

"So, Mauro, it has been a long evening, eh? *Una aventura de amor, quizás?"*

Mauro looked down and shuffled his feet. Nacho decided that he had guessed correctly. The boy had slipped out for the night, possibly on an innocent excursion, but possibly something more intense, and certainly involving a young lady. Mauro was fourteen, after all, and his masculinity must be ready to assert itself.

"Pues, another evening *secreto,* just between us. *No?"*

The boy smiled up at Nacho and nodded. A secret between the two of them, not the first they had shared.

"Mauro, I need your help." Nacho looked at the white horse and then back at the boy. "Is there a stable nearby?"

The boy nodded quickly. *"Sí, mi tío.* Only two blocks away."

"Mauro, *mi sobrino,* I ask you to deliver this horse to that stable for safekeeping. Will you do that for your old uncle?"

Mauro looked doubtfully at the horse. "It is not—stolen, *mi tío?"*

"No," laughed Nacho. "The horse is mine. For now, anyway. Can you ride?"

Mauro gave a joyous laugh. He reached to the post and unhitched the reins. He grasped the saddle horn and swung himself onto the horse in a smooth, practiced motion, his feet slipping easily into the stirrups. Tugging the reins and digging in his heels, he backed the animal away into the street.

"*Sí, mi tío*, I can ride."

Nacho stepped into the street and took hold of the reins to stop the boy. "And Mauro. When you arrive home, please ask your father to come and meet me here at the *Taberna*. If you can manage to do so, this early in the morning. Can you do this thing?"

Mauro nodded and laughed again. He turned the horse away and galloped easily down the street, his back held straight, knees flexed, sitting easily in the saddle. Somehow, thought Nacho, that lad has learned to ride well. He doubted that Mauro had learned from his father. Paulo was not the type to ride boldly, even as a youth. Well, Nacho himself had learned many things after slipping over the wall. *Claro*, Mauro was growing up. Nacho watched until the boy turned a corner and vanished from sight.

He started back towards his table but stopped suddenly. He stared into the distance and tried to bring to mind the image of Mauro disappearing around the corner of the street. The boy's loose jacket had flared out just as he turned and disappeared. Had he seen a *pistola* in a holster, hanging from Mauro's belt? He rubbed his chin as he concentrated his thoughts, but the image would not come to him. Well, he wasn't sure; perhaps he was wrong.

He sat down heavily at the table he had cleared. Hector was going to be inconvenienced again.

The *río* was right in front of him, sunlight tracing wavelets on its racing waters, but Nacho couldn't reach it. He tried to lunge towards it, but his feet seemed to be stuck in sand. With a great effort, he picked up his right foot and moved it forward, setting it down, but his left foot would not follow it. Behind him, he heard Pancho Villa's laugh. The *río* shone brightly, and there was Texas on the other side, and safety. He began to struggle forward, ever so slowly, straining to shuffle each foot, thrusting with all the power in his legs.

"Nachito! Nachito!" Behind his back, Villa was calling him and laughing loudly. He twisted his body and flexed his legs, trying to draw them up so he could run. He looked into the distance. The *río* seemed to be farther away, retreating from him.

Now Villa was grabbing his shoulder. Nacho tried to shake him off. He struggled to turn around, but he could not. He tried to draw his *pistola*, but his arm was leaden. He shouted out in terror.

And awoke and opened his eyes wide, to see Paulo's face above his, staring down at him.

"Nachito! You are having a *pesadilla*! A bad dream." Paulo was leaning over him, holding his arms, pinning him down to the bed.

Slowly, awareness returned. He was in Hector's bed, where he had decided to nap until Paulo arrived. Hector had sent him along to the house where he would be out of sight. Lack of sleep had caught up with him, the bed was tempting, and he had drifted off.

He shook himself free from Paulo's grasp and sat up. With an effort, he swung his legs off the bed. He rubbed his thighs, a little sore from two days of riding. A servant appeared in the doorway, bearing two china cups of coffee. Nacho took one and smiled his gratitude. He sipped the coffee while Paulo talked to him.

"I am very glad to see you, my cousin. We thought—we were afraid you had left us. *Señor* Ortíz was worried that he had discouraged you. Nacho, we are very much committed to this *Revolución*. We need you to organize our army. Did you find Chulo Valdez? Have you enlisted his aid?"

Nacho reached his arm across to the washstand and carefully set his coffee cup down on it. Sitting on the edge of the bed, he curled his arms across his stomach and leaned forward. His pulse was still racing, tense from his dream. Gradually, he shifted his attention to Paulo's monologue.

"Paulito. Give me a moment, *favor*. Reach me that towel, if you would."

"Ah. Here it is. Yes, you are perspiring, aren't you? Perhaps I should leave you alone for now."

Paulo turned to go. Nacho reached out and grasped his sleeve.

"No, stay here, Paulito. I am all right. Talk to me. How goes your investigation into the shooting of the *teniente*?"

"The investigation goes very well. The *teniente's* name was Victorio Balderas. He was once a favorite of *general* Blanco's. His family is very well placed in Saltillo. His grandfather and his father both have been regional governors. He was an important young man, one with a future."

Paulo paused for Nacho's approval. Nacho grunted in reply and felt in his pocket for his tobacco pouch. He motioned for Paulo to continue.

"They called him *El lobo*. He pushed his troops very hard with frequent and unusual punishments. He was not a popular officer with his men. And," he continued, "the other officers disliked him, also. He was too ambitious."

"Ambitious," repeated Nacho. He made a little *cigarillo* and felt in his pockets for a match.

"Yes. He was *general* Blanco's adjutant at first, but the *general* dismissed him. He was too forward."

Nacho lit his *cigarillo* and drew deeply on it. The smoke had a calming effect. He could tell that his pulse was slowing. He looked intently at Paulo.

"And…"

"And Blanco put him in charge of a troop of foot soldiers. When Blanco left Matamoros, the *teniente* refused to recognize the authority of *capitán* Arredondo."

Nacho immediately thought of the *indio*, the swamper in the Laureles Bar who had signed that the shooter wore captain's bars on his collar. He frowned up at Paulo. "So what was the *teniente* doing in that bar, drinking with the other officers, if they disliked him so intensely?"

"Ah. The same question I asked of *teniente* Verde. One of the officers who had been sitting at the table, you know? He said that *teniente* Balderas had walked up and seated himself at their table, uninvited. He was laughing loudly. And at that moment your son-in-law approached them. And the shooting occurred."

Nacho reached across and recovered his cup of coffee.

"And this *teniente* Balderas was laughing loudly. Why was the man laughing?"

"Ah. The same question I asked of *teniente* Verde."

"And he said?"

"Well," frowned Paulo, "he said he didn't really know. *Teniente* Balderas was just beginning to tell them. Something about—something about an offer he had received, a scheme that had been revealed to him, something very stupid that amused him. He did not get to finish his story. He was interrupted by the arrival of Marco Luís. And then the shot was fired."

"And nobody saw who fired the shot?"

"No. They thought it must have been Marco Luís. There was nobody else there. But they had been drinking, Nacho. And there were no witnesses."

But there was a witness, Nacho reminded himself. The *indio*. But no need to involve Paulo at this juncture.

"You have done very well," he said. Indeed, Paulo had made a competent job of the investigation. Not that it mattered. When Villa took the city, he would free Marco Luís anyway. The important thing, he decided, would be to keep his cousin distracted and out of the way.

How would Paulito respond to an attack on the city? Would he join in the fighting? Nacho frowned at his cousin. Paulo and his revolutionary friends might find themselves in the thick of a battle. Nacho did not think they looked the part of gunfighters, much less revolutionaries. How could he protect his cousin if fighting broke out?

Paulo was leaning forward, studying Nacho intently. "I have more news, Nacho. Important news." He straightened his spine, nearly coming to attention. "I have information—Pancho Villa is nearby! Near Reynosa."

So, thought Nacho; as his friend *Rojo* would say, the cat is out of the bag.

"I have heard of this," he said cautiously.

"*Bueno, bueno*. Does the *general* Villa bring his whole army? We must contact him. Perhaps he will join us. Chulo Valdez could talk with him, one warrior to another. Surely we desire the same objectives."

"Paulo," interrupted Nacho. "Paulo. Indeed, Villa must be contacted." He was beginning to see his pathway, how he might proceed. This whole thing might work to his advantage. "To contact Pancho Villa—I think you are right, we will need

Chulo Valdez. I have lost contact with that *hombre*. Can you help me to find him?"

"Well, I do not know where he is. But—yes, I know who can help. *Señor* Steiner would know. He seems to be aware of Valdez and his troop of warriors, wherever they might be."

Nacho puffed on his *cigarillo* to give himself a moment to think. Steiner, that cold fish, what was his interest in this? Not a Mexican, but friend to Mexico? Here was a puzzle.

At last, he dropped the little cigarette into his coffee cup. "Well then, let us ask the *señor* Steiner to aid us in this matter."

Paulo leaped to his feet. "I will send to him immediately. Will you stay here, in Hector's house?" At Nacho's nod, he continued. "I will send a message to you." And he hurried out the door.

"*Vaya con Dios*," Nacho said, softly. Paulo was acting as impulsively as a teenager. But this was no *baile de sabado*, no weekend frolic. This dance was a deadly one.

CHAPTER FIFTEEN

W hitey Wilson leaned against the door of the hotel's coffee shop, a steaming mug in his hand. He watched Red Regan argue with the desk clerk at the Miller Hotel. Their prisoner, Mercurio, huddled close to Whitey. His eyes darted from side to side.

The two Rangers had managed a few hours of sleep in the hotel in downtown Brownsville. They'd had an anxious nighttime ride, a forty-mile trip, guarding their prisoner. Mercurio rode between the two, frightened, grateful for the presence of the two Rangers. At Brownsville's Miller Hotel, an irritated night clerk had given them one room. Red and Whitey had shared the bed; Mercurio had made do on a blanket on the floor. Whitey had slipped a rope around Mercurio's ankle. The Rangers did not think that Mercurio would try to escape; the man was grateful for the protection he had received. Still, that close to the Border, there would be a temptation to make a dash for the river.

"*Qué pasa?*" Mercurio was watching Red's exchange with the desk clerk.

"Well, it's like this, Mercurio. That bozo wants Red to pony up another two dollars 'cause you stayed in our room. Red is tellin' him you're a prisoner, and Rangers don't pay no room rent for no prisoners."

"*Señor*, I have the money. I will pay for myself."

"Forget it. Here, hold this." Whitey carefully handed his coffee mug to Mercurio. Hefting his Winchester, he lunged away from the doorjamb and stalked rapidly to the hotel desk. He leaned forward, laid the carbine on the desk and pointed his finger at the desk clerk. He began to speak in a low voice. Mercurio could not hear what was being said. Regan put out his arm to hold Whitey back. The desk clerk suddenly stepped back, waving his arms, and turned and hurried away. The Rangers walked back to where Mercurio waited for them. They exchanged grins.

"I keep tellin' you, Red, you gotta be firm with these little pipsqueaks."

"Well, that was firm enough. You wouldn't really climb over that desk, would you?"

"I might." Whitey took Mercurio by the arm and turned him towards the hotel door. "C'mon, let's go find that judge old George was tellin' us about. And gimmie my coffee back."

It was only a one-block walk to the courthouse. Mercurio squeezed himself in between the two Rangers as they walked. He kept glancing over his shoulder.

"Take it easy," laughed Red. "We gotcha. You're okay."

The Rangers made eye contact with each person they met on the sidewalk. Their fixed glances, and Whitey's carbine, were an unspoken language that marked them as lawmen on a mission. In return they received stares, some of them hostile.

The judge was already at the courthouse. This was a day when court was in session, and he had arrived early that morning. After brief introductions, a clerk admitted the three of them into the judge's chambers.

The judge was sitting behind his desk, holding a coffee cup of his own. He was attired in a dark business suit. His judicial robes were hanging on a nearby coat rack, ready for the morning court session.

"Been expectin' you boys. You must be the prisoner," he said indicating Whitey with his chin. "Just jokin'," he added, grinning at Whitey's scowl. "I got a telegram here from George Denham." He fumbled on his desk. "Here it is. From the looks of the wad of messages I have this mornin', bandits been busy up country."

"Where at?" asked Whitey.

"A bunch jumped George's ranch, among others. He gave 'em what for. I imagine they're headed back for the river by now. Now son," he pointed at Mercurio. "I'm gonna put you in a cell until George gets here. For your own protection. I think that's the best way. Then George can vouch for you. Louise!" he yelled towards his clerk. "Get that durned Willie in here. Willie's my jailor," he said to the Rangers.

A tall, uniformed Mexican man appeared in the judge's doorway.

"Willie, take this here prisoner and tuck him in his own room."

Willie nodded his head and took Mercurio by the elbow to lead him away. Mercurio shook himself free. He extended his hand towards Whitey.

"*Señor, mil gracias.*"

Whitey set down his coffee cup and shook the hand, slowly, three times up and down.

"You're gonna be all right, Mercurio." Regan solemnly shook his hand also. "George is gonna explain everything. Likely he'll take you back to his ranch. Better stay close for a while, hear?" Mercurio bobbed his head as Willie led him away.

The judge rubbed his chin and chuckled. "I coulda just turned him loose. A half hour later, he woulda been across in Matamoros. Now, old George wouldn't like that a bit, would he?"

"Reckon not. You just gonna turn him over to George Denham?"

"There's nobody here accusin' him of anything. Unless you Rangers wanna file a charge."

"Heck, no," said Whitey. "We gotta get back to the troop."

"You got that right!" came a voice from the hallway. The speaker wore dirty trail clothes. He swaggered into the judge's office, scowling at the Rangers. His slightly bowed legs were crammed into scuffed knee-high boots. A battered, torn felt hat was pulled down on his head. No badge was in sight, but a bright silver revolver was plainly displayed in a worn holster dangling from his belt.

"You Rangers oughta get your butts back up the Valley. There's a bad mix of people runnin' around there right now. Longhorn is gonna need you jaybirds."

"Good to see you, too, Sheriff." Red smiled at him. J. L. Wright had ruled the county with a firm hand and was quick to keep order.

"What's going on, J. L.?" asked Whitey.

"I'll tell you what's goin' on. Look out that window. Whatta you see out there on the street?"

The Rangers stepped across the room and studied the street below through the dirty window. Morning activity was picking up. Several dozen men gathered in small groups on the sidewalk. Others strode rapidly along the street. A mule-drawn wagon moved slowly, blocking the progress of a black automobile.

"Looks normal to me," said Red. "Just a buncha people down there." Whitey downed the last of his coffee.

"Normal, huh? Now you tell me which are just ordinary folks, which ones are the Mexican citizens, and which are bandits. I sure can't tell just by lookin', but I promise you that all of 'em are down there. I don't know who to protect and who to arrest."

"What're you sayin', J. L.?" Red turned back to face the sheriff.

"I'm sayin' that there's a buncha Mexicans in town that got run outa Matamoros. They're plottin' how to get back. Others are wantin' to extend their revolution, mebbe to this side of the Rio. Some are just plain tryin' to decide where's a good target for their bandit activities. And the citizens down there are confused about what to do."

"You got some help on the way, J. L." The judge waved a telegram at him. "Army troops supposed to start arrivin' later today. Some durn congressman has been rattlin' the cages up in Houston."

Red and Whitey looked at each other.

"Didn't take him long," muttered Red.

The sheriff snorted loudly. "Soldier boys! More trouble, unless I miss my guess. Them snot-nosed little kids ain't never seen a bandit."

"Now J. L.," said the Judge, "mebbe just havin' 'em around here will give those bandits somethin' to think about."

Red turned to Whitey. "We better get movin'. Mornin's gettin' along."

"Yeah, let's go." Whitey picked up his carbine. And glanced out the window. "Well, looky there." He put the carbine down. "Gawdalmighty."

Striding briskly down the sidewalk was an energetic young lady clothed in buckskin, blond hair slipping out from under a flat-crowned black hat. Her skirt, which barely reached her knees, was tasseled on the hem to match her sleeves. White riding gloves with long shanks and black cowboy boots sporting large white lone stars completed her outfit.

"Now ain't that a sight," laughed Whitey. Red stepped up to the window beside him.

"Mabel!" he exclaimed.

"Sure is," said Whitey. "There goes your intended." Regan stood, open-mouthed, watching as Mabel shoved her way among the men on the sidewalk. Her skirt swished around her thighs as she paced forward with a rapid gait, arms swinging and elbows out. Mabel left a wake of men who turned to stare after her.

"What's this intended business?" asked J. L., joining the Rangers at the window. Red grabbed Whitey's arm, a warning that was hard to miss.

"C'mon," he said, "Let's go."

"Right behind you."

The two bounded down the stairs and out onto the street, but not in time to catch Mabel, who was out of sight. "She musta gone to the market," said Whitey, looking down towards Market Square.

"Never mind. We gotta get moving." Red Regan was in no mood to contend with Whitey and Mabel together. Whitey was sure to rag on him about his stated intentions of yesterday. Red wanted a chance to talk with Mabel by himself, when they were alone together. How did Mabel really feel about him? He was still uncertain of himself, his own feelings. Was he going to propose marriage? He really didn't know. Anyway, this was not the time to delve into that possible future.

Whitey was looking up and down the street. "There sure are lots of things goin' on here. I'd feel better back in camp." He leaned his carbine against his leg and began to roll a cigarette.

"Yeah. I think J. L. got it right. That hotel was plumb full of people, wasn't it? You think mebbe they were Mexicans from over the Rio? Mebbe bandits themselves?" Red was glad to steer the conversation away from Mabel.

"I think we oughta get a train back up to Harlingen," he continued. "Right away. I don't feel like ridin' a damn horse, not after last night. And this town is making me downright nervous."

Whitey picked up his carbine and followed Red down the sidewalk. Regan hurried to stay in front of his partner. His thoughts were still swirling. Perhaps he could manage to spend another day in Brownsville. Maybe the opportunity would present itself to talk with her seriously. Did they have a future together? He felt a sudden need to take action, to settle his own mind and hers as well.

He realized that Whitey had caught up and was watching him with sideways glances. Did Whitey know what he was thinking? Maybe so. It was hard to keep secrets from your partner. Red shook his head; he could not seem to resolve the conflicted feelings, his long friendship with Whitey and his growing affection for Mabel.

Mabel of the long blond hair and dark eyes. Mabel whom he hadn't seen for several weeks, until today, and then only from afar. Mabel who might refuse him, who might prefer Whitey. After all, Mabel had not given him much encouragement. Not any more than she had given Whitey.

Red stopped suddenly on the sidewalk. Whitey slowed his stride, then stopped and turned around.

"What is it, Red?"

After a moment's hesitation, Regan answered him.

"Nothin'. You're right. We'd best be gettin' back to the troop. Some of these hombres do look downright unfriendly. Our guns may be needed back up the Rio, maybe before the day's out. Let's find that train."

Whitey urged the big stallion into a fast walk, then a gallop, when he and Red Regan were in sight of the Ranger camp by the river. Regan let him go ahead; he was saddle weary and in no mood for a race. His mustang loped along at a steady pace, ears up; the little horse had caught the scent of the camp and was ready for the journey to end. Regan caught up with Whitey and found him standing in his stirrups and surveying the campsite.

"You lookin' for somebody?"

"Thought Nacho might be back by now, but I don't see the old greaser no place." Whitey settled back in his saddle and urged the stallion forward.

Captain Maddox stepped forward and grabbed the reins of Red's mustang. "Glad to see you boys got back okay. Step down."

Maddox was speaking in his command voice, loud and abrupt. Both Rangers dismounted and stood by their horses. Regan reached forward and recovered the reins from the captain.

"Well, did you boys get that bandit to Brownsville okay? Any trouble?"

"Yes, Cap'n, we done it," said Regan.

Whitey's laugh interrupted him. "Weren't no bandit. It was George Denham's Mex foreman, gotten himself into trouble."

Maddox looked to Regan. "That right?"

Regan frowned towards Whitey and pushed back his Stetson. "Well, yeah, Captain, that's about it. A gang of citizens wanted to lynch that foreman. They thought he was a train robber. Or one of them durn bandits. George was tryin' to hold 'em off all by himself. It was a near riot. Whitey pretty much shut it down."

Maddox frowned and looked away into the distance. "George shoulda handled that hisself," he said quietly. "That telegram didn't explain much. Glad to have you boys back." He gestured towards the far edge of the camp. "C'mon, Red, I got somethin' to show you. You too, Whitey."

The two Rangers followed the captain as he strode deliberately along, his steps slow and careful. Whitey elbowed Regan and grinned at him. They knew that Maddox was troubled with digestive upsets, which sometimes left him with a sore posterior. He was stepping carefully, his knee high boots planted gingerly with each stride. Regan frowned back at Whitey. Maddox could be real trouble when his mood turned sour, and it was none too sweet under most circumstances.

The barricade of palm logs had been completed while the two Rangers were away. The captain stopped and placed his hand on it.

"Red, I'm expecting trouble. I can smell it. I want this fort manned day and night, with lookouts on the alert. I gotta get back to town right away. I plan to have somebody patrolling along the river, so mebbe we can bunch up our troopers if a fight starts."

"We can handle it, Captain," said Whitey.

"I figger this is the most likely crossing." Maddox continued to address Regan, his blue eyes fastened on Red's face. "You boys done scouted it out the other night. I'll try to get some intelligence in Edinburgh. I don't expect an attack in force. But you oughta keep some mounts saddled in case you gotta pull out quick."

"Yessir. Anything else?"

"That oughta be enough. I'll be back." Maddox grimaced and readjusted his pants as he started the long trek back across the camp towards his one-horse buggy. The two Rangers watched him go and then looked at each other for a moment.

"Whitey, our mounts need to be unsaddled," said Regan. "We need to throw leather on another pair, like Maddox said."

"I'm doing it." Whitey recognized his subordinate status. Maddox had clearly put Regan in charge.

Red paced slowly along the length of the palm log barricade. He studied the construction thoughtfully. Harold Johns, the elder Ranger in camp, kept pace with him, walking to the side and slightly behind Regan. He offered no comment but watched closely whenever Regan tested the sturdiness of the barricade. In Regan's absence, Johns had overseen the completion of the construction. It formed a bulwark thirty feet long, between three and four feet high, in the shape of a shallow arc facing the meadow that curved down towards the Rio Grande.

Regan stopped and shoved against the logs. Like Maddox, he felt a vague tension. He and Whitey had ridden hard from Harlingen. The atmosphere in Brownsville had been strained and had left the two men with a sense of foreboding. Regan rested his hands against the barricade and looked thoughtfully around the camp. The scene was quiet and orderly, but the uneasiness he had felt earlier in the day remained with him.

"Ought to do the job," Regan finally observed when his walk of inspection reached the end of the barricade. He grasped the last section of logs and gave them a good shake.

"Seems sturdy enough," he added. Johns made no reply; he simply nodded his head. Regan stood, hands on hips, surveying the arrangement of the camp. He noted the *remuda* of horses well to the rear, the tumble of the Rangers' war bags and other personal gear beside the barricade, and the carbines ready and propped up against it. The members of the little squad were standing some distance away, watching to see Regan's reactions to their construction.

Finally, Regan turned to Harvey Johns.

"Old Longhorn put you in charge whilst I was gone?"

"No," mumbled Johns, "not exactly. He just looked at me, pointed to them logs and drove off. You know how he is."

"Yeah, I know Cap'n Maddox pretty good. He done the same thing to me once. I think you been promoted."

Johns looked down and shuffled his feet.

"Guess so. Didn't ask for it. You know. I ain't meanin' to climb into your boots or nothin'."

"Ain't no hard feelings," said Regan. "You done earned it. This here is a good job of work. Could be you're better than I am in gettin' these jaybird Rangers to do hard labor."

"Aw, it weren't that hard. And I had some new help." Johns beckoned to a young Mexican hovering nearby. "Come over here, Angel. This here is Sergeant Regan." Johns pronounced the name as "An-*hel*." Regan looked at him curiously.

The youngster hurried up to stand in front of them. "I have heard much about you, *señor*. I am honored to make your acquaintance."

"Don't know about that," said Red. He smiled at the youngster. "Mebbe the honor's mine. Glad to have you here. Lord knows we can sure use help. You plannin' to join up? As a Ranger?"

Regan gave the young man a quick once-over. His cotton shirt and pants were dusty and barely broken in. His black leather vest also looked new. A pair of blond leather holsters hung from a broad leather belt. Each carried a Colt pistol, also new from the appearance of them. This man was no saddle bum. But what was he?

"I would like to join the Rangers," said Angel, "and *capitán* Maddox has offered me the chance to work with your *esquadrón*." He shifted his weight from one foot to the other, grinning excitedly.

"Angel is from Edinburgh," said Johns. "His father is a well-known medical doctor. He and Captain Maddox are friendly. Doctor de la Cruz thought his son could benefit from the experience. And I found out he don't mind working hard, building barricades."

Regan pointed towards Angel's right-hand holster and pistol.

"Can you use that hog leg?" he asked.

"*Seguro*," cried the boy and started to draw the weapon. Johns quickly reached out and grabbed his arm before the pistol cleared leather.

"I done told you, An-*hel*, be careful about waving that thing around."

"That's all right," said Regan. "Likely you'll have a chance before long." Angel nodded and started away, but Regan called after him. "Hold on there, Angel. Lemme ask you. You got any relatives across the border? In Mexico?"

Angel stopped and turned back to face Regan and Johns. He looked from one to the other.

"Excuse me, *señor*?"

"I wondered if you got relatives or friends across the river. What do you hear from them? About bandit activity, I mean."

"Oh. Well, *sí*, my mother has *mucha familia* in Reynosa."

"And..."

"We have heard—well, we heard that Pancho Villa is nearby."

"Villa!" Johns gave a snort. Regan silenced him with a wave of his hand.

"Could that be true, Angel?"

"Truly, *sargento*, I do not know. This is what my cousin was telling us. But who knows?" Angel was fidgeting, anxious to get away from this line of questions.

"Let me know if you hear anything more." Regan dismissed the boy with a nod and a wave. Angel hurried away towards the other end of the barricade.

"Do you really think," began Johns. "Really think that Pancho Villa is in the lower Valley? It's way outa his territory, ain't it?"

Regan was staring after Angel. "Not likely," he said. "Villa'd have to be ten men to show up in as many places as he's been seen. Wouldn't hurt to think on it, though."

He stared off across the barricade and studied the meadow and the wall of brushland across from it.

"Can't see the river from here. Mebbe you oughta send somebody down around that point of brush, take a look and see if anything's happenin' down there at the crossin'."

Johns smiled at Regan. He had asked Johns to give an order. Evidently Regan intended to leave him in command here, at least for a while.

"That's what Longhorn said for me to do. Send somebody down there to look around, about once an hour. I'll send Dolph Krieger. He's been actin' pretty salty. Give him something to do. We need to get them canteens filled anyway."

"One other thing. Harold, if I was you, I'd move that *remuda* of horses back aways and over to one side."

Johns studied Regan for a moment. He suddenly snapped his fingers and smiled.

"Line of fire! Where they're at, they're in the line of fire."

Regan smiled as Johns turned and hurried away, beckoning towards the other Rangers.

Whitey Wilson suddenly appeared beside Regan. He sat down atop the palm log barricade and stretched his legs out in front of him.

"Durn it, Red, I must be gettin' soft. I wouldn't want to sit in a saddle again for several days."

Red Regan grunted in response. He reached out and accepted the cloth Bull Durham tobacco bag that Whitey offered. He extracted a paper and tobacco but kept his gaze fixed on the grassy slope beyond the barricade. On his tiptoes, he tried to see into the distance.

"You think these palm logs would stop a rifle bullet?" Whitey asked. He patted the top log and looked up at Regan.

"Ought to. That Mex gunpowder ain't much. I think they make it up themselves." Red carefully rolled a small cigarette and wet it with his lips.

Whitey patted the log again. "I guess ole Longhorn Maddox knows what he's doin'. You think we're gonna have a fight here?"

"Maddox thinks so. Sooner or later."

"I'd just as soon get it over with," said Whitey. "Hi, Dolph," he added.

Dolph Krieger had walked up quickly to stand in front of Regan. Hands on hips, he looked back and forth between the two men. Regan noted that his black shirt and fitted black jeans were brushed clean. Any traces of dirt from work on the barricades had been eradicated. His gun belt was decorated with silver conchos. He pushed his black hat back on his forehead.

"You old guys are pretty tight with Maddox, ain't you?" he asked.

"Might say so," said Whitey. Red nodded.

"Then explain this. Now here's the river." He drew a line in the dirt with the toe of his boot. "And here's this grass strip leading up from the river." He drew a broader mark with his boot sole. "With brush on both sides of it. And at the top there's this meadow. And here we are, over on one side of the meadow, where we can't see the river. Now then. Why didn't

Maddox put the barricade here"—he drew another line—"where we could see the river from the barricade? Wouldn't that make sense?"

Whitey looked at Regan, a smile on his lips. Regan avoided looking at Whitey.

"Well, you see," said Regan, "If we could see the Rio, then any bandits startin' across could see us, too, couldn't they? Mebbe they'd just go someplace else to cross."

Dolph frowned for a moment.

"Well, I guess that does make sense. But it means that somebody's gotta saddle up every hour and go down and take a look."

"Be sure and take yore pistol along." Regan reached out and patted the boy on the shoulder.

"'Course I will." Dolph walked off to find his horse.

Regan looked at Whitey, who was smothering a laugh.

"You didn't tell him he's bait."

"Now Whitey, like everybody else, he's gotta learn by experience." Regan struck a match on the top of the barricade and applied the flame to the tip of the cigarette he had been holding. Last night he had slept in a bed, in a genuine hotel room. Tonight—well, it promised to be a long one.

CHAPTER SIXTEEN

Chulo Valdez was pleased by the gift of the white horse. He swung his considerable girth into the dark leather saddle and paraded the horse back and forth in front of his troop of bandits. He laughed aloud like a child as he put the gelding through its paces. Nacho thought he looked absurd. Chulo's stomach protruded so far that it rubbed against the saddle horn. His clothes were those of a bandit, frayed and tattered. His toes protruded through the end of one boot. The rowels of one of his spurs were broken. Nacho tried to catch a glimpse of Chulo's pistol; it sat too far down in an oversized holster. At least he is happy now, thought Nacho. On the occasion of their previous meeting, Chulo had been in a nasty mood.

Nacho had dozed off again in Hector's bed, only to be awakened by the servant. She had received a message from *señor* Steiner, giving directions to Chulo's new campsite. It was almost thirty miles west of Matamoros, a two-hour ride. Nacho had presented the horse, compliments of Pancho Villa, and watched as Chulo Valdez received it with joy. Probably, thought Nacho, this was the best horse Valdez had ever seen, much less owned.

Now, Nacho had another problem. He had no horse himself. The bandits' camp had a small *remuda* of horses, a scraggly looking string, and possibly not enough mounts for them all. Valdez's camp was not far from Reynosa and was reasonably close to Pancho Villa's army. What I must do, thought Nacho, is to lead Chulo down to meet Pancho. He wondered what kind of subterfuge he might use. Valdez would have to furnish him a mount of some kind. Doubtless he would want to take his ragged band of outlaws along. Again, Nacho wondered why Pancho Villa had placed so much importance on his scheme to pamper these ruffians.

The white horse came to a stop in front of Nacho. With a loud grunt, Chulo swung heavily out of the saddle. The effort of dismounting pulled the saddle sideways. The white horse stomped its hooves and snorted. That horse is going to suffer, Nacho thought. Chulo stepped forward and stroked the horse's neck and nose.

"A fine animal," he said to Nacho. "Pancho Villa is generous indeed."

"Indeed. He admires you and wishes to meet with you." No point in holding back, thought Nacho; this is the time to lay it on thick. "Let me escort you and your brave men to the camp of Pancho Villa. *Seguro*, he will be pleased to see you."

That will fulfill my obligation to Villa, Nacho decided. He is certain to attack Matamoros, and during the battle I will be able to secure the release of Marco Luís. And, finally, this nightmare will be over. Perhaps I will take Marco Luís back to the Ranger camp. Working there would be beneficial for that young *hombre*.

But Chulo Valdez was looking at Nacho quizzically. Have I gone too far, he wondered? Valdez was becoming suspicious again. A small frown flitted across his forehead and his eyes darted from side to side.

Abruptly Valdez turned around.

"*Muchachos*! Let us ride!"

As the bandits scurried to locate their horses, Valdez turned back to Nacho, who was watching him open-mouthed.

"*Señor* Nacho, you will ride with us. We must secure a gift for Pancho Villa, something of value. Then we will visit him. When I can repay his generosity."

Valdez thrust a boot into the stirrup and laboriously swung back into the saddle, astride the white horse. Nacho stepped forward and grasped the horse's reins.

"That is unnecessary, *señor* Valdez. Don Francisco is waiting for you. I can take you to him now."

Valdez walked the horse backwards, jerking the reins free of Nacho's grasp. He wheeled the horse away. Over his shoulder, he shouted a command.

"Saddle my old pony for the *señor* Nacho. He will accompany us. *Hola, muchachos! Arriba!*"

Nacho stood helpless as the little band of men mounted and turned their horses to follow Chulo Valdez, who rode away towards the north. He jumped and turned when a hand from behind grasped his shoulder.

"Here, *señor*." A young boy handed Nacho a set of reins attached to a wild-eyed paint.

Well, there is no help for it, thought Nacho. I cannot lose Chulo Valdez now; I must follow him wherever he is going. He grasped the worn saddle horn and heaved himself up. The pony bolted off after Chulo Valdez. Nacho braced his boots in the stirrups and hauled back on the reins but the pony simply hunched its neck and continued running.

Soon the pony's frantic stride brought it up to the rear of the bandit pack. Nacho squinted his eyes against the dust raised by their drumming hooves. He attempted to wipe his face with his forearm, but the effort nearly cost him his balance.

Off to one side, through the cloud of dust, a familiar young figure appeared momentarily. Nacho groaned aloud when he recognized the rider as his nephew Mauro. Suddenly Mauro's secretive behavior was explained. This was why he had been so evasive when Nacho had questioned him the other day. Mauro must have been riding with these bandits for some months. Well, thought Nacho, this will have to stop. I will break Mauro free from this group of *bandidos*. But at that moment, Nacho's full attention was needed to keep him in the saddle. The pony's gait was a frantic one; it rolled from side to side.

In spite of Nacho's efforts to control it, the pony continued its headlong dash, and soon Nacho saw the rump of the white horse immediately ahead of him. That horse suddenly slowed its pace to a brisk walk, and Nacho's pony came abreast of it, blowing and shaking its neck. Nacho realized that Valdez's old pony was trying to keep up with its master.

Valdez drew his pistol and waved it in a circle above his head. He rose slightly, attempting to stand in his stirrups.

"Muchachos, vámonos!"

With a war whoop, Chulo Valdez galloped forward at the head of his troop of bandits. Nacho and his pony were left in the pack again, and the pony began to strive forward, trying to reach Chulo Valdez. Enveloped in the cloud of dust that arose, Nacho was carried along with the pack. He could not make out his surroundings. He was surprised and then alarmed when the horses' hooves began to splash through shallow water. The dust cleared, and Nacho realized they were crossing a gravel bed in the *río Bravo*. Valdez was leading his bandits across the river into Texas!

Nacho had no intention of riding across the Border with these bandits. He pulled at the reins with all the strength he could muster, but the pony had the bit in its teeth and surged forward. He tried to turn the pony aside, sawing at the right rein; he could turn the pony's head, but the pack of horses simply gave it no place else to turn to.

Abruptly, Valdez halted the white horse. Nacho and the rest of the bandits pulled even with him and stopped. Nacho blinked his eyes to clear them and stared ahead, up a grassy slope. Suddenly, he realized how close they were to the Ranger camp. He must go back! Valdez leaned across and grasped the mane of Nacho's pony.

"Now you will see, *señor* Nacho, how brave are the revolutionary warriors of Chulo Valdez. And you must report our valor to Pancho Villa."

Waving his arm above his head, Chulo Valdez gave a loud *grito*, "*Ay Ay Ay...,*" and spurred forward.

Nacho did his best to stop the pony. The animal simply did not respond to any commands. It seemed determined to keep as close as possible to Chulo Valdez. Nacho could not think of any plan of action. He was caught up in a bandit raid. His mind went blank. Staying atop the straining pony required all of his attention.

He was not prepared for another sudden stop. Chulo Valdez had halted, his arm held high above his head to stop his band. Nacho's horse lunged forward and poked its head against Chulo's leg. Chulo did not notice. He was staring straight ahead. Nacho followed his gaze and saw a horseman facing them some fifty yards up the slope.

It was Dolph Krieger of the Ranger Troop D. That slim figure in black was easily recognized. Nacho yanked again on the pony's reins with all his strength, but it was useless. The pony kept poking its head against Chulo's leg.

Krieger wheeled his horse and galloped back up the slope at full flight. He snatched off his black hat and beat the horse's flanks.

"*Hijo de puta!*" Chulo cursed and drew his *pistola*. He leveled it and fired at Dolph before urging his horse forward.

Several of the bandits began firing as well, as they gave chase. With Chulo in the lead and Nacho's horse at his flank, the bandits raced up the grassy slope. Nacho continued to saw on the reins, but the effort was futile. The pony was going to follow Chulo wherever he went. Nacho crouched low on the horse's neck, hanging on with both hands.

He could see that Dolph Krieger had a good lead on the bandits and that the lead was increasing. Krieger had lost his hat. He was now flicking the horse's flanks with the ends of the reins. The bandit pursuers kept their pistols blazing. Nacho did not think they posed much of a danger to Krieger. Firing a pistol from horseback was mostly a waste of powder. Only an exceptional marksman could hit a moving target from horseback. Nacho didn't think these bandits could.

He reached a conclusion. He could stop this raid by shooting Chulo. Never mind about Villa's wish to meet the bandit. This attack on the Rangers took priority. His right hand released the reins and drew his *pistola* from its holster. The pony, sensing slackness in the reins, gave a lurch. And Nacho dropped the weapon before he could level it.

At the barricades, the sound of gunfire had energized the Rangers.

"What the hell?" asked Whitey. Nobody answered him. He and Regan grabbed their Winchesters and gazed out over the log barricade. The sounds of gunfire continued to float across the meadow.

"Pistol fire," said Whitey.

"What's happening?" said young Tommy Mabry, who had rushed up to the barricade.

"We're gonna find out. Get ready to fire." Regan levered a shell into the chamber of his Winchester.

Harold Johns and Angel de la Cruz settled in at the right end of the barricade. Johns loaded shells into his carbine. Angel slowly drew his two pistols, his eyes large, a wide grin on his face. They all stared out across the stretch of meadow. Nothing moved.

Suddenly, Dolph burst into view, around the corner, racing towards them at top speed. He did not slow down for the barricade. He urged his pony into a jump, easily clearing the top log. Before the horse could stop, Dolph had swung out of the saddle and grabbed for a carbine.

"Bandits," he shouted, unnecessarily.

Regan looked over at him. "How many?"

Whitey spoke before Dolph could answer. "Count 'em for yourself. There they are."

"Well, let's slow 'em down some." A blast from Regan's Winchester was the signal for the other Rangers to open fire. Crouching behind the barricade, they sent a fusillade of bullets towards the bandits.

Chulo Valdez slowed his horse. What was this they were facing? He only wanted to find a *rancho*, maybe a few houses, for his bandits to raid. He had not planned to face organized gunfire. On his left, a bandit tumbled from his horse. Then another one fell. This was not good.

But Chulo's blood was running hot. His *muchachos* had slowed their charge to a near standstill, firing their *pistolas*. Chulo looked to one side, then the other. The roar of the gunfire began to spook the white horse. He neck-reined it back and forth, side to side, to offer a more difficult target. He tried to count the puffs of smoke coming from the barricade. No more than five or six guns faced him. If this was an ambush it was a poor one; there were too few of them. He outnumbered those *pendejos* four to one. He stood in his stirrups and scanned the little log fortress in front of him. He could see no other defenders. Surely those men realized that they were outnumbered. Would they not take flight when they saw what they were facing?

This was the place for a cavalry charge. That is what Pancho Villa would do. Charge directly ahead, and carry the fight to those Texans. Chulo gave a loud *grito*, waved his *pistola* above his head, and urged his troop forward. With a burst of gunfire his men followed him, shouting through the noise and the hail of bullets. Once again Nacho was carried along on the unmanageable horse, entirely out of his control.

"Hold it. Hold your fire!" Regan waved his arm toward the other Rangers. "Let's try and get them in closer."

"They're close enough for me," muttered Whitey. The bandits' fire was tearing chunks out of the palm logs.

"Here they come!" shouted Dolph. "They're charging. They ain't stopping for nothing." Dolph's carbine suddenly clicked on empty. Uncertain what to do next, he drew his pistol and began to fire it. He looked towards Regan. Were they going to be overrun?

"Aw, shit!" Whitey suddenly stood erect behind the barricade. Ignoring the bullets whizzing by him, he leaned into his Winchester and began firing slowly, deliberately, choosing his targets carefully. Whitey was in his element, standing and taking careful aim, regardless of the danger.

Tommy Mabry, following Whitey's lead, steadied his carbine on top of the barricade. He picked his targets carefully. Johns squatted down to insert shells into his Winchester. Angel the new recruit stood tall beside him, pistols in each hand, firing away and laughing loudly.

Regan started to rise also, but suddenly stumbled and sat down. He rolled onto his knees and tried to stand, but he fell down again. Regan sat still for a moment. What was wrong? He looked up to see that Whitey had emptied his Winchester. Regan reached for it and passed his own carbine up to Whitey, who took it and continued firing. Regan slipped cartridges from his belt and reloaded Whitey's gun for him. He was beginning to feel sick.

Dolph stood beside Whitey, reloading his pistol and staring at the charging herd of bandits. "Hey, that fat one is the leader," he shouted over the roar of the gunfire.

"Let's get him." Whitey and Dolph both focused on Chulo Valdez, one with a rifle and the other with his pistol. They fired rapidly. Suddenly Chulo's white horse reared backwards and collapsed. The bandit charge slowed and then stopped. The riders milled around, leaderless, and were easy targets for the Rangers. Harold Johns got to his feet and began levering shots out of his carbine.

Nacho was still beside Chulo when the white horse was struck by gunfire. Chulo had attempted a flying dismount from the horse as it fell backwards. He landed on his hands and knees. His foot was caught beneath the horse's neck but he was able to pull it free, and he scrambled quickly to his feet. Nacho's pony stumbled forward and nuzzled Chulo. The bandit leader reached up and grabbed Nacho's arm with both of his hands and yanked it hard. Taken by surprise, Nacho lost his grip on the saddle horn. He was pulled out of the saddle and fell to the ground on his back. Chulo grasped the pony's reins, got a foot into a stirrup and mounted. Circling the pony, he waved to those bandits still riding and galloped away, leading them on a mad retreat back towards the river and the safety of Mexico. The fusillade followed them until they rode around the corner of the brushland, out of sight.

Nacho lay on his back, the breath knocked out of him. The Rangers were sure to find him, unhorsed, on this battleground. And they would know that he had been riding with the bandits. A Mexican riding with Mexicans. There was no explanation that would excuse him. He had to get away somehow. He pulled himself to a sitting position. He saw another bandit on foot, running across the swale and diving headfirst into the chaparral. Bullets kicked up dirt at the bandit's heels, but the man made his escape into the thicket of thorns. Maybe I can, also, thought Nacho. Rolling, crawling, gasping for breath, he made his way across the grassy prairie towards the brush. A bullet smacked the ground beside his head, harmlessly. Another smacked into his calf, knocking his leg out from under him. Then he was into the thorn bushes.

Keeping low to the ground, crawling along on his elbows, Nacho worked his way forward. He ducked under the thorns as best he could. The long spines of the chaparral raked across his face, one narrowly missing his eye. He tasted blood. Suddenly the ground gave way beneath him, and he tumbled into a small arroyo. It was dry, about six feet deep, and ran down towards the river. Nacho staggered to his feet, but fell again. Peering down the arroyo, he could see two bandits making their way south, stumbling away from the battleground, towards the *río* and Mexico. Clumps of thorn bushes were slowing them. Would they make it to the river? Would the Rangers be waiting for them?

Nacho couldn't rise. He sat up, shaking, out of breath, nauseated. Sweat covered him. His arms were trembling, and he wrapped them around his body to steady himself. I'm too old for this, he thought. Too old by far. He forced himself to examine his wounded leg. Still dazed, he managed to wrap it tightly with his kerchief.

Suddenly, he heard the scraping sound of leather being pushed through the thorns in the chaparral. One of the Rangers must be forcing his way through the brush to look for escaping bandits. What to do? Fleeing down the arroyo would be inviting a bullet. Nacho heaved himself up. With a half-crawl, half-stagger, he made his way up the arroyo, away from the river. The Ranger was sure to search down towards the river.

The arroyo soon narrowed. Nacho discovered a small hollow beneath an overhang in the bank, probably a coyote's den. He squeezed his body into it. He considered cutting some brush to hide the entrance, but he was simply too tired. He licked his lips; he craved a sip of water. First, though, he needed rest. He lay on his side, cradling his head in an arm. Unexpectedly, he fell asleep almost instantly.

CHAPTER SEVENTEEN

Whitey Wilson watched the last of the bandit gang disappear around the bend, headed towards the Rio Grande at a gallop, the pounding of their horses' hooves fading away into the distance. He slumped forward and leaned his forearms on the log barricade, looking out over the meadow. Just a thin haze of gun smoke hung in the air, but the acrid smell of cordite was strong. It burned his nose and made his eyes water. His ears rang in the sudden silence. The carbine slipped through his fingers; he let it fall. Dead Mexican bandits sprawled where they had fallen, a dozen twisted forms. One bandit, still alive, tried to prop himself up, yelling something in Spanish. The white horse cried loudly and tried to rise to its feet and then slumped down. Its side was smeared with its own blood.

Whitey gave a start when Dolph Krieger vaulted over the barricade, his pistol held out to the side. He strode deliberately towards the white horse. Whitey looked away and bit his lip when the gunshot echoed back across the field. He had a fleeting thought. Would Krieger execute the wounded bandit also?

Down behind the barricade, Harold Johns stood trembling, his hands twitching and jerking. Johns was trying to reload his revolver, slowly and deliberately, but the bullets only slipped from his fingers and fell to the ground. Further back, the youngster Angel lay sprawled on his back, arms outstretched, pistols still grasped in his lifeless fingers, a wide grimace on his tan face.

Whitey looked down at his own hands, surprised to see them trembling with palsy. He tucked them into his armpits to steady them. He watched Johns groping for his dropped bullets. Whitey had a sudden image of his younger brother, picking pebbles out of the creek bed. His eyes started to water. He squeezed them shut. He realized that his head was throbbing. That fight was a near thing, he thought, a very close thing. We got out of it lucky.

He was vaguely aware of Captain Maddox's carriage rattling up behind him. He straightened up and turned to see Maddox hop down and walk slowly up to the barricade.

"Good Lord!" muttered Maddox. "Good! God! Almighty!" He stared wide-eyed, automatically removing his fringed gloves and tucking them into his coat pockets. The captain slowly took in the scene at the barricade, noting the remains of the gunfight. Finally, he looked towards Whitey. "Report," he ordered.

"Cap'n, they come up from the river, about two dozen of them, yellin' and shootin'. We returned fire. They broke off." Whitey bit the words out, fighting to keep a tremor out of his voice. "It was pretty fierce. They got young Angel there, dead to rights. It was a near thing. They like to overrun us."

Maddox stared at Whitey for a moment, assessing his condition, noting the tremor in his voice and his shaking hands. He placed a hand on Whitey's shoulder. "I can see," he said slowly and deliberately, "that you boys done give a good account of yourselves. Only lost one man. But what's wrong with Red, layin' there?"

Whitey looked down to see Red Regan slumped limply at his feet. He gasped in sudden shock, and knelt down beside his partner.

"I don't know! Red! Red!"

"He's hurt," said Captain Maddox, his voice soft, concerned as much for Whitey as for Red.

"I done taken a hit, Whitey." Regan's voice was low and strained, coming between his clenched teeth. "Hurts some." He lifted his hand from where it was pressed against his hip. Blood was oozing between his fingers; his trousers were soaked with it. Maddox leaned over the men, looking at the ground beside Regan.

"Gawdammit, he's losin' a lot of blood." Maddox straightened up and looked around, left and right. "Don't know what we can do."

With a grunt, Whitey lifted Regan up from the ground, grasping him under the arms, and half-carried, half-dragged him to Maddox's carriage. Regan cried out before slumping unconscious against Whitey.

"Whitey, what you tryin' to do?" Maddox called. "We shouldn't move him around. He'll likely bleed to death."

"He'll die if I don't get him outa here." Whitey propped Regan on the carriage seat and leaped in beside him. "I'm takin' him to that hospital down the road in Edinburgh. *Hoah, yo, yo, yo!*" The horses sprang to life as Whitey yelled and yanked on the reins. He turned the carriage and forced the horses into a dead gallop.

The rig sped out of sight into the brush. "Fool's errand," Maddox muttered to Johns who was standing beside him. "Red's bled himself dry." He turned around to see Dolph Krieger pulling the body of one of the dead bandits up to the barricade. "Johns," Maddox ordered, "wrap Angel in his blankets. Too durn bad about that young man. Durn it! Then, help Kelly there; help him to get them bandits up here. See how bad that one yellin' is hurt. I wanna take some of these corpses into Brownsville. Show them what we're doin' here. I'll take young Angel's body back to his father," he added.

"Cap'n, look here." Dolph Krieger pulled a revolver out of his belt and handed it to Maddox. "This Colt look familiar to you? I found it out yonder."

Maddox turned the weapon over and over in his hand. "Yep, it does," he said slowly. With his forefinger he traced the big letter "Y" carved into the wooden handle of the old Colt. "Belongs to Nacho Ybarra, unless I miss my guess."

"That's his, all right." Johns looked over Maddox's shoulder. "He was showin' it to me a couple of days ago. Tellin' me the old Colts were better."

"Where'd you say it came from?" Maddox asked.

"Found it just layin' on the ground out there. Somebody musta dropped it."

Maddox straightened his spine and tucked the pistol into his belt. "Well," he said, "I guess Nacho musta run into some bandits he couldn't handle. Too durn bad. I liked that old greaser. Boys," he continued, "we're gettin' shot up pretty bad." Maddox stared off into the brush for a moment. "We'll pull back and regroup after we git this here mess cleared up."

Nacho awoke suddenly, disoriented. It was pitch black. His eyes were on fire. Maybe he was blind. But no, he rubbed his face and realized that it was badly swollen. Memories flitted in and out. The battle, Chulo Valdez, the escape crawling through the chaparral. He thought he could hear someone calling his name. Was he dreaming? He felt for his *pistola*, but found it missing. He fished deep in his boot for his backup revolver, the little short-barreled thirty-eight.

"Nacho! Nacho!" The whisper was soft but urgent; it sounded familiar. Nacho realized that it belonged to his young nephew, Mauro. A dream? He hefted the little pistol. The voice called again, urgently, louder. It wasn't a dream.

"*Aquí*!" Nacho struggled out of the coyote and fell into Mauro's arms.

"I have you, my uncle." Mauro held him until he was able to stand by himself. Nacho kept holding onto his nephew.

"I cannot see; my face has become swollen."

"It is the thorns of the chaparral, my uncle. Some are known to be poisonous. And your leg is wounded. Can you walk? Now that night has fallen, I believe we can reach the *río* safely. But we must move quietly. I heard the *rinches* go, but they might have left a sentry."

"How did you find me?" Nacho's memory was still shrouded in a fog of confusion. He raised a hand and rubbed his eyes, trying to clear his vision.

"I followed you through the brush and saw where you had concealed yourself. I crawled onwards for a few hundred meters more and then waited for night. From my hiding place, I could see the *rinches* break camp. They took the bodies away on a wagon. Come now, take my arm. We must reach the *río* before dawn."

"Mauro. My nephew. How long have you been riding with that filthy bunch of bandits, those...those..." Nacho's voice failed him.

"Shh, my uncle, we will talk later. Let us now return to Mexico."

Whitey squinted into the darkness, half-awake, in a semiconscious dream state. The battle with the bandits replayed itself in his mind. He thought he saw a big Mexican bandit approaching him slowly, winding a path through the chaparral, waving a long knife and laughing. No, thought Whitey, suddenly awake, that didn't happen. He shook his shoulders and drifted back into a light sleep. He tried to see what had happened to Red, how he got hit, but that image would not come to him. Again he saw the bandits, their horses circling in confusion, their pistols firing constantly. The image was clear. Too clear. Abruptly his body jerked and he was awake again. The image of the battle stayed with him. He closed his eyes to help visualize the attack. Where was the gun smoke? The Mexicans had been blazing away, but there was so little gun smoke. Just a thin haze. Mexican gunpowder was notoriously poor, often crafted locally from charcoal and sulfur, smoky and weak. But not this time. He felt in his pocket for his tobacco pouch, now considering the battle with clarity.

The palm logs had been chewed up by the Mexican bullets. Whatever shells they had used were much more powerful than their usual ammunition. That's what happened to Red. Shot right through the palm log barricade. Of their own volition, his fingers rolled a cigarette. He put it into his mouth, no matter that he had no matches. He closed his eyes and drifted off again.

He jumped with a start, suddenly awake, when a gentle hand tapped him on the shoulder.

"*Señor, señor,* wake up! You are having a dream. A bad dream." Whitey focused on the hand. It came from the sleeve of a white robe. He struggled up to a sitting position and turned to see one of the Sisters of Mercy standing beside him.

"No, I ain't. I'm awake now." He looked around, orienting himself in the early morning light. "Who are you, Sister?"

"I am Sister Angelica. A good morning to you, Sir. You have been here, in this chair, the whole night?"

"Good mornin'. Reckon I have." Whitey shrugged his shoulders to loosen them, and reached around to rub the back of his neck. He surveyed his surroundings. His cane chair sat on a porch, a screened porch, in the pink light of dawn. His memory came back with a crash. This was the hospital where he had brought Red Regan the evening before. He forced himself to his feet, nearly overturning his chair in the process. Sister Angelica held up a painted lamp, its oily light probing into the corners of the porch.

"How is he?" Whitey turned back to the Sister.

"How is who, *M'sieu'*?

"Red. Red Regan. Where...?" Whitey looked around, frantically, his voice rising.

"Hush, hush." Sister Angelica took him by the arm. "I have just come on duty for today. Our patients are still sleeping. Who is it you ask about?"

Whitey shook free. "Regan. The Texas Ranger, hip-shot. I carried him in here last night."

"Oh, that one. He lives, but he is badly hurt. Come with me."

Stumbling slightly, still half-awake, Whitey followed the sister along the screened porch towards the hospital wards. He remembered, now, finding his way here in the dark, collapsing into a chair to wait for the doctor's report on Red. Yesterday must have been too much for me, he thought. It's not like me to drop off like that.

Inside the cramped little wardroom he could see a row of five hospital beds, all occupied by men. Whitey located Red lying at the end of the row, on his stomach, face turned away. A large bandage swathed his hips, traces of bloodstains showing at the edges.

"He sleeps," said Angelica, in a whisper. "He is drugged. With morphia. He has had much pain. He needs the rest."

Whitey looked around. "Where's that doctor?" he demanded.

"Hush now. Do not make noise. I will find him." With a pat on Whitey's shoulder and a rustle of her white robes, Sister Angelica swept away through the room and out of the far end. Whitey stood at the foot of Red's cot, looking down at his friend. "Old pal," he muttered to himself, "I done the best I could. That doctor said I damn near killed you, bringin' you in that way. But you were bleedin' like Hector, and I had to get you to a hospital." Whitey closed his eyes tightly. "Don't leave me, Pard," he pleaded.

A rustle of robes approached him. He looked up to see Sister Angelica accompanied by an older woman, garbed in a gown robe with gold trimmings.

"I am Sister Gerda, Mother Superior in our Mission here. Is this your friend? Are you the person who brought him in?"

"Yes, I am," said Whitey. "Reverend Mother," he added, suddenly remembering his manners. "How is he?"

"Very ill, but better this morning. Your friend is fortunate. He had lost much blood. We found that Sister Ann had a suitable blood type, and we were able to give him a transfusion. Now, he rests."

"A—what?"

"A transfusion of blood. It is a procedure now practiced in Germany, where I studied nursing. Your friend here might have died, otherwise"

"Is he gonna make it?"

"The doctor can tell you more when he returns later this morning. But I believe he will recover."

Whitey squinted, trying to stop the sudden rush of tears springing from his eyes. He hung his head and wiped his forehead with his sleeve. Sister Gerda patted Whitey's sleeve. "Now, you must let him rest. You, also, could use some, I believe. Angelica?"

Sister Angelica took Whitey's arm. "Follow me, Sir. I will find you a place to rest. And a bite of breakfast?"

"Just coffee," mumbled Whitey, following Angelica unsteadily out of the wardroom.

"I'm Doctor de la Cruz." Whitey rose to shake the large hand offered to him. The doctor was equally as tall as Whitey but much bulkier, not a man to challenge in a fistfight. That thought sprang unbidden to Whitey's mind. The doctor radiated confidence.

"Your friend's a tough one."

"You said it," Whitey offered, his spirits rising a bit. He studied Dr. de la Cruz carefully, taking his measure.

"He's gonna make it," the doctor continued, "barring infection or something like that. He should pull through. He'll be here about thirty days, I'd say."

Whitey blew a breath, slumping down, momentarily overcome.

"There's more," said the doctor, after a moment's hesitation. "I couldn't get the bullet out. It's too close to the base of his spine." He held up his hand, palm out towards Whitey. "It won't kill him. But it will hurt him all his life. He will walk with pain." The doctor hesitated again. "Possibly he will be unable to walk."

Whitey stared at the doctor for a moment, then he shook his head. "No," he said loudly. "Red's a tough one. You said so yourself. He will walk. He's a Texas Ranger."

The doctor nodded. "Yes, he's hardy and in good physical shape. I would bet on him. But he won't be a Texas Ranger."

"You don't know the Rangers!" Whitey's voice soared. "I seen men hurt worse than Red jump up and fork a mustang and take out after a killer. You don't know!"

Doctor de la Cruz stepped backwards and held his hand up again. "Fine, fine. As you say, I don't know Rangers. But I know wounded men, and your friend needs a bunch of rest. We will take care of him, don't worry."

"The best care." Whitey's ire was up now, and he stepped closer to the doctor, following as he moved backwards. Finally, the two men stood face to face, staring into each other's eyes.

"I said we'll take care of him."

A white-robed sister inserted herself into the conversation. "Doctor, will the Ranger be all right?"

The doctor gestured towards the sister. "This," he said to Whitey, "this is Sister Ann. Your friend is in her debt."

Whitey calmed himself. "I done heard. Sister. I don't know what to say."

"I thank the blessed Jesus that my blood matched his." Sister Ann smiled up at the two men.

Suddenly Whitey jerked erect. "De la Cruz. Was it your son...?"

"Yes. Angel. His ambition, his only ambition, was to be a Texas Ranger."

"He died as a Ranger," said Whitey softly, but he was talking to de la Cruz's back. The doctor stalked away.

That evening, Whitey found himself on the screened porch again. They had arranged a cot for him, so that he might sleep better this night. And Sister Angelica had left her oil lamp; it sat on a table beside him, and its warm, friendly light oozed around him.

A dim figure entered the far end of the porch and approached rapidly. Whitey squinted. The shape was familiar. When she entered the pool of light, Whitey rose to greet Mabel Steuben.

CHAPTER EIGHTEEN

Nacho sat quietly at the little breakfast table, arms at his sides, staring down at the remnants of his meal. Paulo and his wife Consuela continued to eat, saying nothing, but watching Nacho closely. Across the table, Paulo was frowning. This day he must resume his full duties as Commissioner of Police. He would have to confront Captain Arredondo and establish a firm division of civil and military authority in police matters. He did not look forward to this meeting. Paulo was dressed in his best dark suit, white shirt and black tie. His face shaven and hair neatly combed, he was the image of a young, plump businessman of Matamoros.

Bright sunlight bursting in from the patio illuminated Consuela, dressed in a full yellow skirt and red blouse and covered by a white morning apron. Once again in charge of her household, assisted by a servant girl, she was the picture of confidence.

Nacho knew he offered a contrast. His appearance was shabby. His hair was unkempt and his clothing rumpled. He walked with the aid of a cane, his wounded leg slow to heal. *I am now truly a* viejo, *the old uncle who must be cared for. And who will sit by the fire and get in the way.* His thoughts whirled. A wave of depression swept over him. *What is my future? What can I do? My life has escaped from me.* He swallowed a small sob, coughed and cleared his throat.

"Nacho? *Estás bien?*" Paulo put down his knife and the piece of bread he had been buttering. He leaned forward, his brow wrinkled in concern. Nacho nodded his head, not trusting himself to speak aloud. With an effort, he picked up his coffee mug.

"*Más?*" said Consuela quickly, leaning across from Nacho's left side. When Nacho did not respond, she poured more coffee from the earthenware pitcher into Nacho's cup. He nodded his thanks and sipped slowly. I am disgusting, useless, he thought. *Desagradable.* What would his comrades in Texas think? Nacho Ybarra, a Texas Ranger? No longer, he realized; that part of his life was past. That Texas Ranger badge? I should get rid of it; the badge can bring me nothing but trouble now.

The little Indian servant girl suddenly scurried into the room to Consuela's side and spoke softly into her ear. The servant then stepped back against the wall, hands folded in front of her.

"It would seem that we have a visitor." Consuela rose from her chair. "Keep your place," she continued as Paulo started to rise to his feet. "I will see to it." She strode purposefully from the room.

"She worries," murmured Paulo. "Mauro has not been home these past three days."

Nacho sighed. What was the boy trying to do? Mauro had brought him here to Paulo's house, a tiring two-day trip because of Nacho's weakened state. The boy had helped him to bathe. Consuela had put a poultice on his face, a mixture of oatmeal and bacon grease, which seemed to help. His face was no longer swollen where the thorns had scratched him. His eyes had cleared and his vision was restored. Consuela had offered to trim his hair and would have applied more black dye, but Nacho demurred. He accepted the return of the gray hairs. However, when Consuela offered another suit of clothes, Nacho reluctantly accepted. His trail clothes were ruined, and his saddlebags, with all his belongings, were long gone. Now he wore a plain suit that had once belonged to his uncle. No embroidery or conchos on these clothes. They were dark blue, which suited his mood. He had no pride in his appearance. *Gracias a Dios*, he had kept his Stetson. The coins hidden in the hatband might prove essential to his survival. The Texas Ranger badge was there also, secure inside the hat. Well, it must go.

Consuela reappeared in the doorway, arms folded, worry spread across her face. "Paulo," she began, but stopped when she was abruptly but gently set aside. Captain Arredondo, commander of the occupying military force, stepped forward and stopped opposite Paulo.

"Commissioner DeLeón, *buenos días*. I have business with you." He stared closely at Nacho, who sat unmoving, still holding his coffee cup halfway to his lips.

"*Capitán*, please seat yourself," Paulo said with a gesture towards an empty chair. "I had intended to come to your office." He pushed himself back from the table and dropped his arms into his lap. Nacho wondered if his cousin had grasped a *pistola* hidden below the table. Arredondo carefully seated himself between Nacho and Paulo, one of them on each hand. He looked up thoughtfully when Consuela set a cup in front of him and carefully poured coffee into it.

"Not *capitán*. Not anymore, Commissioner. Address me as *general*. I have promoted myself. You see," Arredondo smiled sardonically, "The *general* Blanco will not be coming back to Matamoros to take charge of this little army. He has run afoul of rivals in Oaxaca. I now report to no one. So, I have become a *general*." He stared intently at Paulo.

"My congratulations," muttered Paulo, frowning slightly. He twitched in his chair. What would this mean for the city?

And himself as Police Commissioner. Nacho cleared his throat, thinking to divert attention from Paulo while his cousin digested this information and composed himself. Consuela had slipped back to her seat at the table, scraping her chair on the tile floor.

Arredondo glanced toward her and then turned a burning gaze to Nacho. "You," he said, "you we will discuss in a moment." He looked back at Paulo. "Be not concerned, my friend. Our business this morning will be most pleasant. A trade. And an exchange of information."

The self-appointed *general* leaned back in his chair, tipping onto the back legs, and clapped his hands together, twice. A sergeant appeared at the doorway, pushing in front of him a youngster. Nacho started to rise; the boy was Marco Luís, his son-in-law.

"Yes, yes, be calm." Arredondo motioned Nacho to resume his seat. He snapped his fingers twice and the sergeant unlocked the cuffs binding Marco Luís's wrists. "I release this boy. I parole him in your custody, *señor* DeLeón." Arredondo straightened himself up in his chair. "He is yours," he continued.

Fear was stamped across Marco Luís's dirty face. His hair was matted and dirty, his clothes ragged. Consuela rose from her chair and took him by the arm. "*Pobrecito!*" she exclaimed, leading him away towards the kitchen, the servant girl following. The boy stumbled slightly but followed her, head down, without a backwards glance. Nacho watched them disappear. Relief that the boy was freed was quickly replaced with a feeling of foreboding. What did Arredondo want? Why the sudden courtesy from this arrogant officer?

The *general* quickly answered that question. "I have another prisoner I believe will be of interest to you, *señor* DeLeón. And I seek information in trade, information that you and your—

guest—may have." Arredondo fixed his stern gaze on Nacho once more.

Paulo's apprehension was written on his face. "*Señor*! What prisoner? Who do you mean?" He pressed his hands on the table and started to rise.

Arredondo held up his hands, palms outward. "*Señor* DeLeón, relax yourself. All will be well." He extracted a thin black cigar from his jacket pocket, bit off the end and discarded it into a saucer. Finding a match in his other pocket, he struck it and applied it carefully to the end of the cigar. When the cigar began to burn, he took it between his teeth, shaking out the match. He blew a large cloud of smoke towards Paulo.

Nacho realized that he was rubbing his own right hand over his hip, unconsciously looking for a weapon that was not there. He glanced over at Paulo, who remained unmoving, half out of his chair, propping himself against the table, eyes wide. Nacho took note of the kitchen knife beside his own plate. Any weapon in dire need, he thought, and started his right hand moving slowly towards it.

"Now," said Arredondo, a satisfied smirk on his face, "Now let me tell you of my other prisoner. A nice lad, about so high, well-bred and well-mannered, dark hair, features similar to yours, *señor* DeLeón. I have him in my *cárcel*." He gestured at Paulo, waving his cigar. "Do not worry, my friend, he is unharmed. But—and here is the problem—he refuses to talk with me."

Nacho's forefinger and index finger had reached the handle of the knife. Slowly, a few millimeters at a time, he scooted it towards him.

"He seems a good lad," Arredondo continued, "but he was riding with *bandidos. Ahora bien*. I am quite willing to parole this lad, as well, into your custody. But first, I want some information. In exchange."

Nacho cleared his throat. "Of course, *general*, we will cooperate with you in any way we can." He reached across the little table and put his left hand on Paulo's, squeezing it. Paulo looked at Nacho and slowly sat back down. "I do not know what information we have that would be of interest to you," Nacho continued. Arredondo was staring fixedly at the knife, now safely clutched in Nacho's right hand. Meeting his stare, Nacho released Paulo's hand, picked up a hunk of bread and proceeded to smear butter on it.

"Of course, of course," exclaimed Paulo. "Whatever you wish." He waited for Arredondo to explain.

"Excellent." Arredondo leaned back, his eyes following Nacho's knife with the butter on it. "I have only a few questions, mostly to verify information I already have."

Nacho shifted his feet beneath him. From his sitting position he could lunge and strike out with the knife, and stick Arredondo in the throat before the officer could defend himself. He suddenly realized that he was feeling much better. His feelings of helplessness had left him. This potential action had sharpened his senses. He took a deep breath.

Still eyeing the knife, Arredondo set down his cigar. "*Señores*, tell me this. Is Pancho Villa here in Tamaulipas? Near to us here in Matamoros?"

Paulo gasped, but it was Nacho who spoke, quickly. "Yes," he said. "Pancho Villa is near here. South of Reynosa." He sent a warning glance towards Paulo; this was Nacho's game to play.

"You know this for a fact?"

"I do."

"You have seen him?"

"I have."

The two men, soldier and Ranger, stared eye to eye. Then Arredondo leaned back and relaxed somewhat. "*Bueno*. You have told me something valuable. Namely, that there is something you do NOT know. *Señores*, Pancho Villa has left the State of Tamaulipas. Presumably, to return to Chihuahua." He retrieved his cigar and tried to coax smoke from it, unsuccessfully. He carefully examined the tip.

"With this question I have tested your willingness to cooperate. You," he added, gesturing at Nacho with his chin. "I still do not know exactly who you are. Nor do I care, as long as you plan to leave Matamoros. Soon."

"He is my cousin," Paulo exclaimed. "Surely..."

"I think he is more than that," Arredondo interrupted. "But let me explain about Pancho Villa. He has left me with two problems. One, he has recruited nearly half of my army and marched them away. I am left with a much smaller squadron of *soldados*. It would be difficult for me to defend the city. Or to continue to police it. *Señor* DeLeón, I will need your help in that matter."

Paulo hastily nodded his agreement. Nacho smiled to himself. So, Don Francisco had managed to recruit some fighters after all. Without resorting to Chulo Valdez and his bandits. His brow wrinkled. Why would Villa even be concerned with that rag-tag clown Valdez?

The answer came immediately when Arredondo continued speaking. "Problem number two. Pancho Villa sent that *pendejo*, Chulo Valdez, to rob our *banco*."

Nacho sat up, eyes widened. Of course! He couldn't help but laugh. Villa would want the bank robbed but would not do it himself, not with the army in town. Such a robbery attempt would have provoked an outright battle. Villa would lose men in the process, not gain them. Get the local bandit, who knew the ins and outs of the city, to do the job for him. And he, Nacho, had been the monkey's paw used to bring Valdez into the fold. Nacho quit laughing. He cursed himself for a fool.

Arredondo was grinning at him. "I thought you would find that amusing, *señor.*"

"The bank was robbed? Money stolen?" Paulo's thoughts turned immediately towards Ortíz, the bank president. What would this mean for him? Paulo's own deposits were there, as well.

"No, no." Arredondo laughed loudly. "Nothing was taken. The whole robbery was a comedy." He sat forward, grinning. "If you can believe it, my friend. The big vault was locked. The head teller convinced Valdez that only the bank president could open it. So, Valdez held the teller hostage and sent an assistant out to fetch bank president Ortíz. Of course, that man came directly to me instead. We captured the entire group of bandits."

Abruptly, Arredondo lost his smile. "Your son was among them, *señor* DeLeón. He was outside, holding the horses."

Paulo propped his elbow on the table and leaned his forehead against the palm of his hand. Arredondo retrieved his cigar and struck another match, giving Paulo time to digest this information. Nacho watched his cousin. He wondered what thoughts Paulo must have coursing through his mind. This could mean serious trouble for the DeLeón family. His first thought was the usual one, a large bribe. Nacho sat back in his chair. I might be able to arrange help with such a solution.

"Your son is a brave boy," said Arredondo quietly. "He did not attempt to deny his guilt. He spoke of the *Revolución.* And he would not answer questions."

Paulo lifted his head. "He is not hurt?"

"No, no, the lad is fine. And we will have a trade. As I told you." Arredondo puffed smoke from his cigar.

Nacho glanced around the room. His gaze fell out through the doorway into the patio. He felt a sudden chill when he realized that a soldier, possibly that sergeant, was standing just outside the jamb. Nacho put down the knife he had been holding. And chided himself for his lack of attention to that little detail. An attack on the *general* would have been foolish indeed.

General Arredondo straightened up in his chair. "*Señores*, let us proceed to address a problem. The robbery attempt provided me with an opportunity I have been seeking. Questions, rumors, had circulated among my officers. I had a lengthy talk with *señor* Ortíz, our banker. He was reluctant at first, but then he told me of—a plot to invade Texas."

Nacho felt his muscles tense; he looked at Paulo who was carefully looking down at the table.

"Now, understand me," Arredondo continued. He carefully set down his cigar. "Plotting to invade a foreign country is not allowable, certainly not in *ciudad Mexico*, at least. Here in Matamoros, this would not be such a concern. Aside from the fact that it would be senseless. A revolution against a civil authority, or a military one in my case, would be a crime. Clearly. But hatching a plot to invade across the *río Bravo*—that is merely foolish. Especially at this time. Troops of the *Estados Unidos* army have begun to appear across the river in Texas. I wish only friendly relations with the *americanos*. I intend to meet with their officers and with the leaders in the city of Brownsville. I will tell them that I have captured and imprisoned the *bandido* Chulo Valdez." He slammed his hand down on the table. "*Señores*, I do not want anyone to start a war."

The *general* turned his attention to Nacho. "You, *señor*, do not strike me as a fool. Yet, Ortíz pointed you out as the leader of this planned invasion of Texas."

Nacho made no reply. Was Arredondo confident in his information? Where was this leading?

"He did not tell me your name, *señor*. You do not even appear to be the person he described. But I have seen you before, in different guises. I believe you are the one he meant."

Arredondo picked up his cigar. He took a long drag, filling his mouth, and expelled the smoke slowly. He studied the end of the cigar. "What is your name, *señor*?"

Paulo started to speak but Nacho stopped him. "I am Ygnacio Ybarra," he said quietly. And waited.

The *general* studied Nacho for a moment. "That name is familiar to me, although I do not remember the circumstances. I have told you, *señor*, to leave Matamoros. I think it is best."

He turned his attention back to Paulo. "Tell me, Commissioner DeLeón, who else was involved in your invasion scheme?"

Paulo shot Nacho a worried glance. "You already know about *señor* Ortíz. Yes. And my friend *señor* Riviera..."

"That one!" interjected the *general*. "A civic leader. But also a man who would wish to reclaim old family properties across the river. No? And who else?"

"The *señor* Steiner, the German." Paulo shrugged his shoulders. "That is all. No one else."

Arredondo leaned back in his chair. "That is the information I have from Ortíz. A sorry little group of conspirators." He was looking at Nacho, speculatively.

A sense of calm descended over Nacho. He was beginning to see the direction of this interrogation. He gathered himself together. No course of action suggested itself, but he felt sure that one would emerge, and shortly. He was surprised when Arredondo began to chuckle.

"*Señores*! We have all been duped. Myself as well. We have been used as chips in that German's little game of chance. I see it now—the banker, the money source. Riviera, the would-be conqueror. You, DeLeón, the patriot. And you, *señor* Ybarra, the military leader. And to what purpose?"

Nacho and Paulo exchanged quick glances, watching Arredondo.

"*Señor* Steiner often encouraged me to seize control of the army. Which, incidentally, I finally did, but not to his satisfaction. No. Steiner's charge from his government was to foment a war between Mexico and the *Estados Unidos del Norte.* To keep the *americanos* away from the European conflict. He offered me money. And ammunition. He also provided for Chulo Valdez and his little horde, guns and funds."

Nacho gasped. How had he overlooked this obvious connection? Chulo, not a successful raider, had been well supplied with excellent ammunition, much better than the black powder used by most bandits. Steiner had provisioned them. Of course!

Arredondo watched Nacho, eyes narrowed, waiting for him to put the information into perspective. Nacho rubbed his chin. The *general* was waiting. What more? What else did this mean?

It hit Nacho like a blow to the head. He could not help flinching. Pancho Villa! That was why Villa had come to the Valley. To see Steiner. Not just for recruits or to rob a bank or two. He needed ammunition. Villa's sources, across the river in El Paso, were no longer supplying him. He needed the German to provide for his revolutionary army.

And I? Villa used me for a diversion, he realized. The whole Chulo Valdez scheme was but a smoke screen, while he made an arrangement with the German. Villa wanted a lightening rod.

Arredondo was smiling at Nacho. "So, my friend, I see from your expression that you have reached a conclusion. You have been foolish."

Nacho nodded slowly. It occurred to him—Villa might have slipped away, virtually unnoticed, had he not gotten greedy and tried to use Chulo as a bank robber.

"We all make mistakes," Nacho stated softly. But he continued to puzzle over these things. If Steiner had indeed supplied Pancho Villa—what would Steiner want in return? It was obvious. He wanted Villa to attack the United States. Well, Steiner would be disappointed. Don Francisco was not so foolish at that. Did Steiner want something else?

CHAPTER NINETEEN

Herds of clouds scurried across the western sky, pink and blue tufts, catching light from the sun, which had slipped below the horizon. Whitey sat with Mabel Steuben on a low bench in the hospital garden, watching the cloudlets race into the darkness. She held his hand and gave it an occasional squeeze. Beside them, a statue of Our Lady of Guadalupe implored with concrete gestures.

"Whitey, listen to me." Mabel spoke softly but urgently, whispering in Whitey's left ear. "The doctor seems real sure about it. Red's not gonna walk. Never again."

Whitey withdrew his hand from hers. He bowed his head and covered his face with both hands.

"Even if he can walk, he won't be able to ride. His days as a Texas Ranger are over. You know it's true."

He uncovered his face and looked into hers. His cheeks glistened with teardrops. He tried to speak, but his voice turned into a sob. He stood erect and turned his back to Mabel.

She rose and tugged at his sleeve. "I think the Ranger days are over for you, too. Maybe it's time to move on. Army troops are arriving in the Valley. I saw some soldiers when I was on the road. The army will take over. Texas Rangers won't be needed." She pulled at his sleeve again. "That time is past."

Whitey jerked his sleeve free and stepped over in front of the Virgin's statue. The failing evening light caught the flaking paint on her blue robe, her outstretched arms. Flowers, wreaths, had been placed at her feet. He stooped and picked a red rose, held it in his fingers.

"I brought some flowers, too." Mabel put her arm around him.

When he turned, her face was at his shoulder, offered to him. He kissed her cheek and took her in his arms. His grasp tightened; he began to weep. His shoulders trembled; he convulsed as sobs shook his tall frame. Mabel tightened her arms around him and held him, feeling his sorrow wrack through his body.

Finally, the tremors spent, he eased his grasp and sighed deeply. They kept holding each other.

Whitey followed willingly, blindly, when Mabel took his hand and led him back into the darkness behind the statue of the Virgin. She eased herself down onto the grass, taking both of his hands and calling him to her. He followed, lying beside her and nuzzling her neck. A welcoming sense of belonging, a sudden rush of contentment, overwhelmed him. His thoughts surrendered to the moment.

He rolled onto his side, gathering his strength back, and felt in the darkness for his Stetson. Fixing it on his head, he climbed to his feet and began buttoning his clothes. He realized that Mabel was doing the same thing, arranging her garments, standing near him in the night.

He felt for words, choosing and discarding them, speaking none of them. Finally, he reached for her. "Mabel," he began. He placed her fingers on his lips.

"Don't say anything, Whitey. Don't spoil it. It was wonderful. That's all. It was wonderful."

They stood together, not moving, clinging, each lost in thought. Whitey's mind slipped between images, not settling on one or another, feelings blending in confusion.

"I love you, Whitey." Her voice was soft, intriguing. He tightened his grasp.

"I love you, too." His voice was a whisper.

Suddenly, she pushed him to arm's length. "Let's get married. It's time. We'll make a home. Why, we can care for Red together. You can resign from the Rangers, get a steady job."

Whitey's mind found its focus. He regained his resolve.

"I ain't quittin' the Rangers. That's what I am, a Texas Ranger." His voice rose. "I got a job to do. Killin' bandits. It's Red's job, too. He'll do it. You'll see."

She shivered, suddenly feeling the night chill. He shuffled his feet, his arms still holding hers. "I do love you, May," he said. "But Texas Rangers ain't for marryin'. They got no business with a wife and family."

"Whitey," she tried again.

"No, I can't have a wife. I'm real fond of you, May, you're pretty and you're fun. If it was time for marryin'...but it ain't."

She pushed him away and turned her back to him. She had hoped for better. Her parents encouraged her to seek the company of a young minister, newly arrived in Brownsville. The life of a preacher's wife did not appeal to her. Whitey was her choice. He had another love in his life—the Rangers. She could see that, now, perhaps too late. She'd gone too far.

"Red needs you," he said. She couldn't bring herself to turn and face him. She might break into tears at any moment. He must not see her cry.

"I think you should stay here and help Red. He told me he's gonna marry you." Whitey spoke softly again, just above a whisper.

"What? What?" Had she heard him right?

"Red said he wanted to marry you." He said it louder this time, real plain, just out there. He heard the rustle, the whisper of her footsteps across the grass. He stepped forward, straining to see into the darkness. She was gone.

He sat there in the hospital garden, on the bench, emotionally spent. Mabel. He hadn't lost Mabel; he'd never had her, really. He began to admit to himself that he *had* lost Red Regan, though. He must accept the doctor's verdict, that Red couldn't be a Ranger, not anymore. Whitey's vision blurred with tears; his throat constricted. He strained to swallow and rubbed his eyes. "Damn sand," he muttered to himself.

Whitey sat up when he heard the crunch of footsteps on the gravel path. Was Mabel coming back? The shape that emerged out of the evening gloom was that of Captain Maddox.

"Whitey?" Maddox stopped, feet apart, thumbs in his belt.

"Captain." Whitey acknowledged the old Ranger and climbed to his feet, his hands massaging the backs of his thighs.

"Doctor de la Cruz just told me that Red is gonna make it. He's still knocked out but is startin' to rally." Maddox chuckled. "That Steuben girl is hoverin' over old Red like a broodin' hen. He's gonna have his hands full when he wakes up."

"Guess so."

"I brought your big red horse and your war bag. The Troop is pullin' out. Going up to Kingsville tomorrow, then likely on to Austin. Ain't heard definite."

"Pullin' out?" Whitey's mind struggled to grasp the captain's statement.

"Pullin' out," Maddox repeated. "We're shot up pretty bad. The army is takin' over. Troops been movin' in to Fort

Brown, Fort McIntosh, all the way up to Fort Bliss in El Paso. Patrols beginnin' to work up and down the river. That old congressman was as good as his word, I guess." He shifted his weight and heaved a sigh. "I'm kinda glad to leave it to the Blue Boys, Whitey. It was gettin' to be too much for us."

"Pullin' out." Whitey said it again, staring away into the night.

"You need to hop that big horse and head for Harlingen. We're gonna ride the train out tomorrow night." Maddox moved in closer. "You know Red is in good hands here. I done mustered him outa the Rangers. He'll get some kinda pension from Austin. Whitey?"

"I'm stayin' here. Captain, I got work to do here in the Valley. Bandit work."

Maddox noticed the set of Whitey's jaw, his red-rimmed eyes, stubble of beard, clenched fists.

"You can't help here, Whitey. The Ranger Troop needs you. Think about it." Maddox put his hand on Whitey's shoulder. "I need you myself. I want you to be my sergeant. Take over Red's duties." His voice began to rise. "We'll be pickin' up some new hands and they'll need trainin'. It's important, Whitey."

"Ain't goin'. I'm stayin' here."

"You can't help Red none. It's over for him."

Whitey drew himself up to his full height. "I can do somethin' for Red. Them Mex bandits owes him. They put a slug in him. I figger the balance is ten to one. I'm gonna kill me ten bandits."

Whitey's gaze was intense and challenging. Maddox met it with his own. Neither man spoke for a moment. Then, slowly and deliberately, Whitey reached up and began to unpin his Texas Ranger badge.

Maddox shook his head. "No, keep the durn badge. I can see you're set on this. I'm gonna put you on extended duty down here. When you come to your senses, I expect you to show up in Austin." The captain's steely eyes bored into Whitey's. "You hear what I'm saying? Them's orders."

"Yessir, Captain."

Maddox turned on his heel and started away, then stopped and turned back. "If you're gonna go payin' back, you might wanna use this." He handed Nacho's Colt pistol to Whitey.

"Be damned," said Whitey. He inspected the gun carefully. "Where'd you get it?"

"One a them bandits was carryin' it. Krieger done found it, layin' on the ground."

"I guess we know what happened to old Nacho." Whitey stuck the pistol in his belt.

Without another word, Maddox stomped back towards the hospital ward. Whitey watched him go. Would he ever see his captain again?

CHAPTER TWENTY

A full moon rose over his shoulder, casting long shadows into the June night. Whitey slumped in the saddle, his body adjusted to the rhythms of the horse's plodding footsteps. Gaunt, tired, and hungry, he struggled to stay awake.

It hadn't worked out like he'd thought it would. For the past two months he'd ranged up and down the Border, near the river, searching, but hadn't found a single bandit. Not one. Army patrols, yes, and he'd avoided them. Maybe the army's presence was keeping the bandits across the river.

Whitey scratched his face, fingers digging into his scruffy beard. He needed a decent bath. His clothes were dirty. One of his boots had come up with a loose sole. The food supply was exhausted. He'd used the last of his funds to buy oats for Cimmie. He still had plenty of ammunition, just no targets for his guns.

Tomorrow would be better. Whitey had joined the army. Not as an enlisted soldier, however. He would be a civilian scout. Tomorrow's train would take him over to El Paso, and a new phase of his life. He still hoped for a chance to fight Mexican bandits.

Now, tonight, he intended to visit Red Regan at the hospital in Edinburgh. He hadn't seen his partner since that night, weeks ago, when Maddox dismissed him. He'd heard that Red might walk again, perhaps even recover more fully from his wound. Whitey intended to say goodbye, one last handshake.

He reined Cimmie to a halt at the edge of the hospital grounds. The full moon, now well up in the sky, gave a daylight clarity to the scene. He sat in the saddle, wondering how to proceed. Was this a good idea after all?

A couple emerged from the hospital ward and walked out into the moonlight. Squinting, Whitey recognized the form of his old partner. Red Regan was walking, leaning on a cane and moving slowly, but still walking. And at his elbow, holding tightly to his arm, was Mabel Steuben. Whitey backed his horse into the shadows and watched them. The pair circled through the grounds, slowly, and returned to the building.

Whitey sat, thinking, wondering, until the big horse nickered and shook its neck.

"Okay, Cimmie," he muttered softly. "I guess we've seen what we need to see. Old Red is doin' okay. Let's go find the army." To himself he said, "Goodbye, Pard."

The coffee was cold and bitter. Nacho made a wry face and pushed the cup away from himself, across the table. That's what I get, he thought, ordering coffee in a barroom. He looked around for the bartender; no one was in sight. Three o'clock in the afternoon and the Laureles Bar was deserted. Nacho pushed away from the table and eased back in his chair. It was peaceful here, a warm late June afternoon. He needed the rest.

So much had happened the past month. Here he was, Chief of Police in Matamoros, where he had been wanted as a criminal until recently. Chief of Police, indeed. It had its disadvantages. He brushed the legs of his trousers. This suit of clothes was not pleasing to him, the blue coat with brass buttons, the heavy blue trousers, the wide black Sam Browne belt. And the silly cap. He did not like the heavy black leather holster with its flap fastened down over a small thirty-eight revolver. He knew the uniform was necessary as the symbol of his newfound authority. Nonetheless, it made him uncomfortable. No, he decided, this will not last, not for long. Nacho Ybarra would move on.

Matamoros seemed peacefully quiet this early summer afternoon. The city was returning to normality. The *alcalde* had crossed the bridge from Brownsville and assumed command of the city, but not before *general* Arredondo had marched away with the remnants of his army. The *general* was bound for Monterrey, and doubtless his group of soldiers would be factored into the *federales*. Nacho smiled to himself. Arredondo would become a captain again. And he would find the ladies of Monterrey very friendly, according to rumor.

Most of the former city policemen had returned as well. Paulo had given Nacho the task of organizing them. They took charge of the city just as the military was leaving. Some problems remained to be solved, and there were constant requests for policemen in the *barrio des mujeres*.

He squirmed inside the blue suit; perspiration was beginning to form in his armpits. He had released most of the bandits from the *calabozo*, warning them to get out of Matamoros and stay away. Chulo Valdez remained in jail; Nacho was happy to let the *alcalde* deal with Chulo and the attempted bank robbery. *Señor* Ortíz was very insistent that someone should be punished for the attempt on his bank. Ortíz had been helpful when Nacho decided to transfer some money from the bank in El Paso to a Matamoros bank.

Nacho's thoughts ranged back to his days in El Paso, and memories of Villa and his brother Hipólito and the arms trades. Too bad that the United States government had finally banned the shipment of arms to Mexico. He now realized that

Villa's presence in the lower Valley was the bandit's attempt to acquire guns and ammunition. Doubtless the *señor* Steiner had been most helpful to Villa. The El Paso arms trade had been lucrative for Nacho. He still had a substantial bank account in El Paso. Now, comfortably settled in Matamoros, he could use it to good effect.

Leaving El Paso had given him the opportunity to join the Texas Rangers. Ah, the Texas Rangers. What would his friends *Colorado* and *Blanco*, the Red and the White, be doing now? Probably up in San Antonio, according to rumor. It was whispered in Matamoros that the Rangers had left the Valley. They had been replaced by U.S. Army troops. And some of the Texans who had fled the bandit attacks were returning to the Valley. Well, that is good. Nacho smiled. All in all, it was just as well that he could not return to the Rangers. He would rather remain here on the Border. How much longer as Chief of Police? *Bueno*, I will stay here as long as it suits me, he decided. And then—*Quién sabe?*

He stretched his arms over his head, relaxing his back muscles. Perhaps I will visit El Paso, he thought. A nice train ride, dressed as a gentleman, just enjoying myself. Perhaps I can do something about that bank account there. I might even go further, to California.

A shadow fell across his face, interrupting his thoughts. He looked up to see *señor* Steiner standing there, frowning down at him.

"So, your name is Ygnacio Ybarra."

Nacho stared up at the man. No longer impeccably dressed, Steiner wore a wrinkled suit. A stubble of beard covered his face, and his hair was in disarray. His shirt was open at the neck. Towering over Nacho, Steiner scowled at him.

"You have made things difficult for me, you and that coward Arredondo. I had to hide from that fool. Fortunately it was easy. And now he has left Matamoros."

"You should leave also," Nacho said quietly. "We thought you were gone. You have accomplished your purpose, no? You supported the local bandits. You have given arms and ammunition to Pancho Villa. He will begin to make trouble again, thanks to you. What more do you want with us?"

"Revenge. My efforts have come to nothing. I believe you are responsible for that."

Nacho thought for a moment. "I do not see how," he said.

Abruptly Steiner sat down at the table, opposite Nacho. "There is no war!" he exclaimed. "No one attacked the Americans. That is what I wanted. That was my mission. To see war break out between Mexico and the United States."

Nacho shifted his feet. "It may happen. Sooner or later, there will be an incident. The American troops are here on the Border. A fight will be provoked. It will happen, *señor.* What did you expect?"

"Arredondo! That weasel. I wanted him to lead his army across the border. And what of our little conspiracy to invade the Americans? You were supposed to be a leader, an organizer. You did nothing. And Villa! I wanted Pancho Villa to attack the Americans. I gave him guns. I gave him ammunition. And money, too."

Nacho laughed. "Don Francisco is too smart to attack the Americans. He has taken your supplies and your money and gone back to Chihuahua, to put down his enemies there. Perhaps he will unseat President Carranza and control all of Mexico. But I doubt it." The last he muttered to himself.

"You, Ybarra, whoever you are, I think you have frustrated all my plans. You stopped Chulo Valdez and broke up his band. I think you had the ear of Pancho Villa. You gave him council, convinced him to leave this region. I blame you!"

Steiner pushed back from the table and rose to his feet. "And the white horse," he continued. "That is the worst thing. You cost me the white horse."

Nacho straightened up in his chair. This was unexpected. "The white horse? The one Villa sent to Chulo? That horse?"

"Yes. Pancho Villa promised that horse to me, once he recovered it from that silly bandit. That horse was supposed to be mine. And you got it killed."

"It was just a horse, *señor.*"

But Nacho was frowning. Something had been stirring in the back of his mind. There was something nagging at him, something about Steiner. He could see that there were two scars on the side of Steiner's neck, visible beneath his open collar. Nacho searched his memory. Something about those scars.

"Saber cuts," exclaimed Nacho suddenly. "Those are saber cuts. Those scars there, on your neck."

Steiner stared back, not speaking.

"The *indio.* When I questioned him about the shooting here, he gestured like this." Nacho tapped the side of his neck with two fingers. "I thought he was mimicking captain's bars, an insignia. But he meant your scars.

"It was you!" Nacho continued, raising his voice. "You shot the young officer, the one my son-in-law was nearly executed for killing. It was right at this very table. The *indio* saw you. Yes. That brash young *teniente* was interfering with your plans. Wasn't he? Now I understand."

"Understand this." Steiner jerked a little pistol from his pocket. "I have had enough of you." He looked quickly about the bar; no one was in sight. Nacho, too, saw that they were alone.

Steiner extended his arm, pointing the Luger at Nacho, but before he could fire Nacho shoved the table forward and into Steiner, knocking him backwards. The gun discharged, but Nacho had crouched down, shielded from Steiner's view by the upended table. Steiner fired again. This time, the bullet knocked chips of wood into Nacho's face.

Nacho could not get the flap unbuttoned on his new black holster. How did that clasp work? He clawed at it, now desperately. After a moment Steiner rose and walked deliberately around the table. Nacho crouched there in plain view, still struggling with his holster, both hands working at the clasp. He looked up and met Steiner's eyes and his sardonic smile. Steiner aimed carefully at Nacho. *"Auf Wiedersehen,"* he sneered.

Nacho couldn't move. He stopped tugging at the holster. He met Steiner's stare and awaited his fate. He flinched and closed his eyes at the blast of the gunshot; his body went rigid and then limp. For a moment his mind was blank. Then he realized he had not felt the impact of a bullet. He carefully opened his eyes and saw Steiner lying prone on the floor. A hole had been blown in the back of his head. Blood splatters and bone chips were smeared across Nacho's blue uniform. He stared at the blood, not comprehending what had happened.

"My uncle?"

Nacho turned his head, to see Mauro standing in the doorway, gun leveled, a thin stream of white smoke trailing away from its muzzle.

"My uncle, I could not get a clear shot until he moved. It all happened so quickly. He nearly killed you."

"He very nearly did." Nacho rose unsteadily to his feet, rubbing at the smears on his uniform. "Mauro, what are you doing here?" He staggered momentarily and leaned against the upturned table, staring at the boy.

Mauro stepped carefully into the restaurant, one foot at a time, still holding the pistol in front of him. His eyes were wide, and his face was pale. "I was following the *señor* Steiner. I thought you would want to talk with him. I only wanted to see where he was hiding. Then I could come and tell you." Mauro's voice trailed away.

Nacho studied his nephew carefully. The lad looked as though he might be getting sick. Doubtless he had never shot anyone before.

"Give me the gun," Nacho said, quietly but forcefully. "Hand it to me."

Slowly Mauro extended the weapon, butt first, to Nacho who took it and stuck it under his belt. The gunfire had attracted some attention; men were gathering at the door, peering into the bar.

"Stand back." Nacho waved away the onlookers. Among the little group he noticed one of his city policemen. He pulled himself up to his full height, grateful now for the uniform and the authority it conveyed.

"Someone has shot this man, through that window. Someone out on the street. Begin a search." The policeman, wide-eyed, turned to look up and down the street.

Nacho took Mauro's elbow and led him up to a seat at the bar. He stepped behind the bar, where he picked up a bottle of tequila and two glasses. He poured two generous shots, immediately downing his and watching Mauro do the same. Mauro coughed but then began to breathe more regularly.

Nacho refilled the glasses and rounded the bar to take a seat beside his nephew.

"Mauro. That was a good shot, right in the back of the head. My nephew, you should always aim at the body. It is a bigger and easier target than the head."

Mauro turned to him, wide-eyed. "But—I was aiming at the body, my uncle."

Nacho could not help himself; he laughed out loud. He could feel the tension draining from his body. He downed his second shot of tequila. A hand holding a bar rag swept away the empty glass. He looked up to see a bartender frowning at him.

"So, you have returned," said Nacho.

"*Sí.* What has happened here, *Jefe?*"

"A shooting." Nacho gestured with a toss of his head. "A man has been killed."

The bartender peered across the room towards the body lying prone on the floor. He began to swipe at the bar again, with slow, even strokes. "*Sí,*" he sighed. "*Es México.*"